F

Death's Legacy

"A fascinating new world and a marvelous new voice. Dennis Crosby has come out of the gates with a high-powered, action-packed story. I loved the way the backstory was done, I liked how we were invested in the main character from the start. There is SOOOO much going on in this book, you won't want to stop reading it until everything is done. I am so excited to continue following this author and his writing."

—The Indie Express

"Death's Legacy is a strong debut from author Dennis K. Crosby, and I can't wait to see where the story goes next."

—Reader's Favorite

"This book delivers a good story with compelling characters and great fight scenes. The ending is both satisfying and intriguing. Looking forward to the next one!"

—Goodreads Reviewer

"Dennis Crosby has penned a wonderfully crafted fantasy world. Equal parts fantastical, thrilling, and even a bit dark at times. It came across as unique and imaginative. The author really gave us something different."

—Texas Book Nook

DEATH'S DEBT

A KASSIDY SIMMONS NOVEL

The Four Are Coming!

DENNIS K. CROSBY

ACORN PUBLISHING

FROM THE TINY ACORN . . .
GROWS THE MIGHTY OAK

This is a work of fiction. References to real people, events, establishments, organizations, or locales are intended only to provide a sense of authenticity and are used fictitiously. All other characters, and all incidents and dialogue are drawn from the author's imagination and are not to be construed as real.

Death's Debt

Printed in the United States of America. For information, address Acorn Publishing, LLC, 3943 Irvine Blvd. Ste. 218, Irvine, CA 92602

www.acornpublishingllc.com

Cover design by Damonza

Interior design and formatting by Debra Cranfield Kennedy

ISBN-13: 978-1-952112-62-1 (hardcover)
ISBN-13: 978-1-952112-61-4 (paperback)
Library of Congress Control Number: 2021911655

For Herb Jones, Jr.

Friend, roommate, and brother.
You brought a community of people together
and made us a family.
You are missed, good sir.
I'll see you on the other side.
Next round is on me.

◆ ◆ ◆

It had been well over a hundred years
since Jaxon Burke last died.
Today would mark the first time he'd die by fire.

CHAPTER ONE

THWACK!

The sting across Jaxon's face jolted him from unconsciousness. In a matter of seconds, he went from surprise to anger.

"What the fuck?" he asked absently.

He tried to stand, only to find himself bound. His ankles were tied to the legs of a chair, his hands strapped behind him. And there was a smell.

"You can stop struggling," said a voice in the background.

Jaxon was groggy and disoriented. His head felt heavy as he tried to hold it steady to take in his surroundings, but, like a newborn, he struggled. Throughout his life, ropes, handcuffs, binds of any type for that matter, had been of no consequence to him. His strength was always a secret ally. He wasn't on an invulnerable superhero level. He couldn't fly, but while he wasn't a speedster, his reflexes were remarkably fast. Not a superhero, but definitely superhuman.

Not now though.

Maybe he'd been drugged. That would account for the brain fog and blurred vision. Jaxon's arms were weak, limp, no better than al dente pasta. And damn . . . that smell.

Every time he inhaled, his skull throbbed. It was familiar, the smell, but his brain fog was so thick, he couldn't place it. He couldn't place much of anything. As his head lolled to the left, his body followed and fell to the ground with the momentum. Halfway through his fall he realized he wouldn't be able to brace himself. His shoulder and arm hit first, then his head bounced against the concrete.

"Motherfu—"

The shooting pain cut him off mid curse. Jaxon tried to roll but was met with a great resistance. As the brain fog lifted a bit, he realized he was not only tied to a chair, but toppled over in a pool of . . .

Gas? Oh, fuck me sideways with a diamond tipped drill, he thought to himself.

If this were a movie, he'd come up with some last-minute escape from the ropes that bound him. After all, that's what happens to the hero. He gets into a jam, some impossible situation, and at the last minute remembers the Swiss Army knife he put in his boot after finding it underneath an old box that held his father's belongings. Somehow, the sentimentality transforms into some cosmic understanding that it was his father who saved him as he uses the knife to cut the ropes, free himself, and go get the bad guys.

But Jaxon Burke was no hero.

Moreover, he had no idea who his father was.

Jaxon tried to turn his head to take in more of his surroundings.

"Nope, shouldn't have done that. Shouldn't have done that at all," he said to himself as sharp pain ran from the top of his skull to his back. His pain was only matched by confusion. Despite being immortal, at least up to this point, he felt pain. He bled like a human being, he cried like a human being, he felt everything like a human being. Including nausea, courtesy of the gasoline the side of his face was swimming in.

In the distance, he heard footsteps. Louder with each step.

They were coming closer . . . closer . . . then stopped. With blurred vision, he saw what seemed to be two expensive leather dress shoes before him. He strained to look up, but through the pain and dizziness, he could not make out the figure looming above.

"Looks like you fell over," said a rough masculine voice.

I know that voice. "LaVelle?" Jaxon asked.

"Oh well. Sucks for you," said the blurred figure.

Jaxon heard the snap-hiss of a lighter and caught sight of a blurred glow and tendrils of smoke.

Ohhhh fuck. Oh fuck oh fuck oh fuck oh fuuuuuuck.

The dark blurred figure began to move away. Jaxon heard the footsteps, wet now, as if walking through puddles of . . .

"No!" screamed Jaxon.

"The job is done," began LaVelle, "and we don't need any loose ends on this."

"Don't do this, LaVelle! Don't do this. Look, we can work something out. Whatever they're paying you, I can triple it," said Jaxon.

"You literally told me you were ready to check out," said LaVelle. "Just last week you were all 'woe is me' and ready to die. Well . . . here you go. Consider this a farewell gift for services rendered."

Jaxon watched the blurred glow arc through the air and fall to the ground. It seemed to happen over the course of a year, but once it hit the wet concrete, there was a flash of blue, then red orange.

Then it moved.

Jaxon felt the heat on his foot seconds before the flame attached itself to him. It was startling, like a thousand needles puncturing one spot at the same time. He cried out. The scream was loud and desperate but found no ear. If there had been hope before, for even a second, it was gone now.

There was a rush of hot air on his foot, quickly followed by icy cold as Jaxon's nerves cauterized. The scent in the air, no longer just gasoline, now rubber, clothing, hair, and flesh, filled his nostrils and his mind. It triggered a memory of a fire in Rome almost four hundred years ago. He'd watched people ignore one another's cries for help, one of the many times he'd truly been disappointed by humanity. It was as if compassion had been burned away with everything else.

The flames continued from his feet to his legs, then his thighs and groin, followed by his stomach and chest. He took a deep breath and held it, though he didn't know why. Jaxon's clothes offered no protection from the heat as the gasoline had burned sufficiently to set his entire body aflame. He felt them dance across his skin, and he screamed. A gut-wrenching, agonizing sound that could crack the coldest of hearts.

His mouth open, he could almost taste the heat and lick the flames upon his lips. He'd wanted to die. He'd longed for it. Hungered for it. After seven hundred years of life, he was done, a spent, tortured soul ready for the end.

But this was no way to die.

The pain was indescribable.

At some point he could no longer feel the flames, but he was still on fire. His nerve endings were gone and now he was simply a suit of burning flesh. The icy cold he felt when his nerves had burned away was matched in intensity only by the darkness he felt where his soul had been. It, too, had burned away as the tide of death rolled in.

Finally.

The ropes, the only things holding him in place, had burned off. He slumped over to the side, out of the chair to the flame riddled floor. Cold and numb, he felt one other thing. Despite the darkness that seemed to replace his soul, he felt fear. Fear of the unknown. There was no possible way he could regenerate from this. No way his charred carcass could come back.

Right?

As the flames—now inside him cooking his blood and organs—continued to dance, he saw only shades of red and orange.

Before long . . . he saw nothing.

Then . . . he heard nothing.

The darkness came . . . surrounded him . . . and pulled him into an embrace of death.

His end had come.

Finally.

CHAPTER TWO

"YOU SURE YOU WANNA BE HERE FOR THIS? IT COULD GET UGLY."

"Listen, Mr. Frost—"

"Alex, please," he said.

"Alex . . . whatever." Kassidy threw him a look of annoyance and impatience. "I'm not sure what London told you about me, but trust me when I say, there's nothing that's about to happen that's going to throw me off."

Kassidy wanted to get this thing done. She wanted to finish up in Chicago and get back to St. John. But duty called. Duty that required her skillset.

"All right." Alex knocked on the apartment door. "Here we go."

Kassidy stood off to the side, out of view, as the door opened. She caught a glimpse of the red-haired woman at the door through a reflection in the painting hanging on the wall across from the apartment. The smell of weed and incense escaped the tiny room that doubled as an apartment.

"Hey, honey," said the woman. "You can put it anywhere you want, and you can cum anywhere you want. I'm on the pill so it's okay. Just don't cum in my hair. It cost me a fortune to get it done, and that shit does not comb the fuck out."

Okay, consider me thrown off, thought Kassidy.

It was a rare thing to catch Kassidy Simmons off guard.

Considering the events of recent weeks, she figured she'd had the last of "strange" firsts. She was not typically at a loss for words, but this woman had her perplexed. A thousand responses jockeyed for position all at once, while at the same time, a voice in the back of her head wondered what this woman had been through in her life to make this the way she answered the door to a stranger. Strange in the supernatural world did not hold a candle to strange in the human world.

The redhead was pretty. A little worn in the face in a way that betrayed her true age. Alex said she was thirty, but the years had been tumultuous, as evidenced by the greeting at the door. Her scarlet locks were matted on the sides of her forehead. She'd clearly been sweating recently and had done little in the way of freshening up. Her hair was not too long, falling just past her shoulders, complete with split ends and evidence that she'd used an inferior dye. The crow's feet framing her green eyes were not the result of age, but stress. She had a twitch, one that she seemed to ignore. Or, more likely, had simply learned to live with after years of looking over her shoulder and wondering if her next date would be her last—her last anything.

Kassidy processed everything and gave an internal nod to herself, acknowledging that she was ready for whatever was to come next.

"So, I'm thinking you're expecting someone who is not me," Alex said. "Are you Jessi Trager?"

The woman stepped back, wary, no doubt suspecting Alex was police. Probably an autonomic response in her line of work.

"Who the fuck are you?" she asked.

"Normally, I'd ask you to relax and tell you that I'm a friend, but I'm certain you hear that far too often," Alex said.

"Spot on, buddy."

"Clearly, I'm not your friend. In fact, I don't particularly care about you one way or another."

Easy, Frost. Shit. She's the fucking victim. Kassidy immediately sensed pain in the woman. The words had hurt her. Strangely, though, she felt some guilt, too, and it wasn't hers. *Frost?*

This guy had come highly recommended. She'd been warned he could be a little rough around the edges. In fact, she'd been told they were a lot alike in many ways. "So, he's an asshole," she'd said. And she quickly found that, in many ways, he was. If for no other reason than the lustful impulses that radiated from him when he looked at her. These were the moments she hated being an empath. She'd dealt with it her entire life. Didn't mean she liked it.

Except when those impulses came from London.

Or Traci.

In any event, the guy *was* an asshole . . . on the outside. But that surge of guilt that just left him told her there were layers to this guy. Digging deeper, she found more. He was pained. This woman in front of him pained him. He cared, deeply. Seems he was adept at not showing it. Perhaps that's what London meant when she said he was a lot like Kassidy. She'd spent years building up walls and letting only a select few people in. She cared a great deal, about virtually everyone. She didn't necessarily want to, but that's the way she was built. She told people that she'd learned to compartmentalize her feelings, and she could, to some degree. Nevertheless, she felt it all, and not just because she was an empath. It sucked, because no matter what she did, no matter how hard she worked, she couldn't save everyone. Least of all those that weren't looking to be saved.

Jessi Trager was certainly not looking to be saved.

"At least you're honest," she said. "If you're not here for the cooch, then what do you want? How the fuck do you know my name?"

Jessi moved inside. Alex followed, and Kassidy stepped in behind him. Kassidy saw and felt no surprise when she caught Jessi's eye.

"The chick is gonna be extra," Jessi said. "Not much though. She's kinda hot."

Jessi backed up, walked to her dresser, and grabbed a cigarette. Correction—a joint. There was no chance that it was medicinal. She lit, puffed, inhaled, and blew it out like she was possessed by Willie Nelson and Snoop Dogg at the same time. Kassidy suspected that given the way Jessi's life had progressed, she likely needed whatever she could find to take the edge off. Looking back on her own proclivity to bourbon and Vicodin for pain relief, Kassidy could certainly find no fault and made no judgment.

Jessi was giving off some clouded arousal directed at Kassidy. She had the body of a runner. Lean, a little top heavy, but proportionate. Kassidy saw beauty underneath the shell of the woman before her. Maybe, after tonight, Jessi could find her way back to that.

"Jessi, my name is Alex. Alex Frost."

"Should that mean something to me?"

"No, not a damn thing," he said. "But it should mean something for the thing currently possessing you."

Kassidy gave him a side eye. Conceited? Convinced? She didn't know which he was, honestly. And with a proclamation like that, she expected some type of response from Jessi. She didn't know *what* she was expecting, but there should have been *something*. Anything. Laughter, denial, at least a "what the fuck are you talking about, weirdo" type of thing. But there was none of that. Instead, Jessi sat on the bed of her single room occupancy domicile and continued to puff away at her joint.

"My fucking parents sent you, didn't they?"

Kassidy's eyebrow cocked up.

"Those motherfuckers!"

Kassidy put her hands in her pockets. She noticed that Alex had done the same, taking a more casual stance. Jessi was smiling and shaking her head—the international reaction when thinking of people who have the audacity to do or say something to you that you loathe.

"Please go back and tell them to take their Christian judgment about my life and shove it up their asses. If they're so concerned, perhaps they could have shown some unconditional love instead of throwing me out on my ass after catching me in bed fucking my girlfriend when I was sixteen."

Kassidy didn't know who the girl's parents were, but she was disturbed by this. No, not disturbed, angry. Angry that the self-righteous roamed the streets with their limited knowledge of the universe and miniscule understanding of their place in it, yet, with a straight face, told people how they should live their lives. It was that type of treatment that made people susceptible to possession. Feeling abandoned, unloved, almost soulless—it was a playground for demons, or in this instance, the Wraith within Jessi using her for amusement. She had no idea it was even in her. She didn't know when it took over her body or when it compelled her physical form to do things that she wouldn't consciously do.

It wasn't responsible for her choosing the life of a prostitute. But it was responsible for the two men and the married couple killed last week.

"Your parents didn't send me, Jessi," said Kassidy. "Your body count did."

They say that when people stare at you for a long period of time, it's because they're lost in thought about all the things they want to do to you. Jessi's look was one of both possible flirtation and possible homicide. She stared, took a long drag from her joint, and held it with her eyes closed for what seemed like an eternity as if savoring the taste, smell, and feel of the flower. It was the exhale that told her intentions though. When she released the smoke, her eyes opened, and the pale green was replaced by coal black orbs. Smoke escaped from her mouth and nose in a proportion inconsistent with the small joint in her hand. Two horns burst through the skin of her forehead, blood dripping from the fresh wounds into her eyes, down the bridge of her nose, and onto her lips.

She lapped it up like a hungry, rabid dog.

Jessi flicked the remainder of the joint at Kassidy and Alex, then stood, her hands down at her sides. Claws ripped through the skin of her fingers. She threw her head back, and when she brought it down her skin was dry, cracked, and bloody. A low feral growl emanated from her throat. Kassidy felt bad, and she could sense Alex felt the same.

Bad for the life Jessi had endured as a kid.

Bad for the life she'd led as an adult.

Kassidy felt bad because one of the beings from her world was affecting this woman's life to the point where she and Alex would likely have to kill her to save her.

"I've been waiting for you, fledgling," said the Wraith.

"Well, here I am," said Kassidy.

"And you," the Wraith said, pointing to Alex, "I don't know who the fuck you are. But I'll take your soul once I'm done with this Reaper."

"Guess you haven't heard . . ." Kassidy let her words trail off.

She allowed power to fill her and felt her eyes change to blue. A glowing, striking, powerful blue. The mark of a god.

The look on the Wraith's face went slack. In that moment, Alex rushed the creature, pinning it to the bed with the weight of his body.

"This man is going to separate you from the human," Kassidy said. "Then, I'm going to dispatch you. You could make this easy and simply evacuate."

"Fuck you," the Wraith said through jagged teeth jutting through bloody gums.

Kassidy's right hand transformed to vapor, then coalesced into an onyx scythe. She nodded to Alex . . . then smiled at the Wraith.

The door behind her slammed shut.

CENTURIES AGO

Solomon always *felt* the tear in his skin before he heard the crack of the whip. The anticipation affected his mind more than the physical contact. At one point he considered that maybe it wasn't the sting of the whip and the molten hot sensation of broken skin that caused pain. Maybe it *was* the anticipation. Maybe *that* was the true reminder of who he was and what he meant to the person holding the instrument of his subjugation.

He was to receive ten lashes today for daring to shield a new woman on the plantation from the hand of the taskmaster. She'd done nothing more than spill a bucket of water, and it was Solomon's fault. He'd inadvertently moved in her way as he attempted to load a wagon. But she was new, and they always blamed the new slaves for mistakes to remind them that they were, in fact, property and less important than the material luxuries surrounding the plantation. Solomon knew their game, but on that day, he didn't want to play it. He felt protective of her. Not because she was new but also because, from the moment she arrived at the plantation, he loved her.

So, he took the punch meant for her.

Later, she got it anyway.

And now he was receiving his third lash.

This was usually where he became numb. He felt nothing in his body, but his mind worked. He subconsciously counted the cracks of the whip, so he'd know when it was done. In his conscious mind, though, he thought of a future where he was free. Where he was powerful. Where he could exact revenge on his masters.

In this future, he stayed in the south and avenged those who'd been hurt, maimed, or killed. He stayed in the south to serve as a beacon of hope, dispensing justice in the shadows for those who were unable to fight for themselves. In this future, *she* was with him. When the fourth lash came, he whispered her name.

"Dominique."

Her name felt light. He could almost see it carried on the winds as it escaped his bloodied and chapped lips. Her hazel eyes simultaneously strengthened and weakened him. She renewed his spirit. He dared to think of a life beyond the present. In his mind, her hand was in his, and they walked barefoot along cool green grass while their children played in the distance. As sure as he could taste the coppery cocktail in his mouth, he could envision this future. It's what made him smile.

Even when the fifth lash came.

The man he'd met in the woods had told him that a different future could be his. One with power. Solomon could live in a world where he could take vengeance, bring hope to the living and peace to the dying. Solomon had been skeptical. The mystery man was white, sort of. He had enough color to suggest he wasn't from around the area, or the colonies at all. His skin was more olive, like that man from Europe who had visited the plantation last month. Solomon's mystery man spoke with a slight, sophisticated accent, that was giving way to something else.

"You have great strength, my friend. I've been watching you."

"I was bred to be strong," he'd replied. "Bred to tend to the fields owned by others."

"No, I don't mean your physical strength, though that too is formidable. No, my friend, I speak of your strength of will. Your . . . determination. Your spirit."

"Not sure what you mean by that, sir," responded Solomon.

"What I mean by that is, no matter how hard they knock you

down, you get back up. For yourself, and for others like you," said the stranger.

Solomon remembered his chest swelling at that, with a rush of satisfaction. If this strange man in black could see what Solomon was doing for his people, then perhaps they could see it, too. Perhaps Dominique could see it. Maybe that was the pathway to her heart.

The sixth lash sparked another memory of his conversation.

"I can offer you a way out," said the stranger.

"They won't sell me. And even if they would, I wouldn't go without—"

"Her?"

He knew? Who was this man? How did he know? Where had he been watching? Solomon thought it best to be mindful of what he said. The man could be an agent of his master. Someone put in place to trick him into trying to run just so they could beat him more. He was strong, maybe the strongest of them all. If they beat him more, if they broke him, his people would be broken. He carried their spirit. He was their hidden champion. He could not fall prey to tricks.

"I don't know what you mean, sir," said Solomon.

"It's all right, my friend. I know. And I will not tell. What I will say, though, is that I can give you the power to protect them all. I can give you the power to free them and give them all the life that dreams are made of."

"I should not entertain such things, sir. I am meant to be here, and here I shall stay."

"Oh, but you are meant for so much more, Solomon Steele."

The realization that the stranger knew his name came at the seventh lash.

His flesh was torn. The only thing he felt was a cool sensation as a gust of wind offered its gentle kisses against the burning numbness. It took him back in time to the stranger again.

"Don't be surprised that I know your name, Mr. Steele."

He called him "mister." No white man had ever called him mister before. Solomon liked the way it made him feel.

"I . . . I . . ." stammered Solomon. He was at a loss for words. He didn't know what to feel, or how to feel, for that matter. He feared the man in some ways, yet he also dared to feel uplifted at the possibility of liberation.

And power.

Power would be nice.

"I am offering you salvation, Mr. Steele . . . Solomon. A place with me, to be a power in this world and the next."

"How?" asked Solomon.

"You need do nothing but say 'yes,'" said the stranger.

"They'll kill me if I try to leave," said Solomon.

"And that, my friend, is when you call my name and say . . . *yes*."

The stranger lingered on the word "yes," as if it filled him with satisfaction. When he said it, Solomon could have sworn his eyes had turned red, just for a moment. It must have been a trick of the light. A reflection of the sun off . . . something.

In both eyes.

At the same time.

Right?

The ninth lash made him forget about the stranger's eyes. It startled him, bringing him back fully to the present. Back to the realization that, once the final lash came, he'd be given no respite. He'd be forced to go right back to work. They'd force him to wear a shirt. A coarse, itchy, torn shirt. He'd bleed through it. It would stick to his back. Solomon already dreaded the moment he'd have to remove it. When that shirt came off, so too did skin, and the pain would be renewed. He wouldn't cry out, but he would be reminded of each lash that caused the evening pain. He'd sleep on his stomach after a salve was applied to his lacerations. He'd be up all night from the stinging sensation, holding back tears, trying not to move for fear of tearing his skin further.

He'd think of Dominique.

He'd think of the stranger.

When the tenth lash came, Solomon decided he would take the stranger's offer. What did he have to lose? At best, he'd have the promised power, and he could avenge the brutality. At worst, he'd be dead, and would no longer have to concern himself with it. When he heard the tenth crack, he decided he would say the stranger's name. He would say his name, and he would say yes.

"Azra-El," whispered Solomon, "yes."

In the distance, Solomon saw a small flash of red, and a dark figure.

On the winds, he heard laughter.

Then he smiled.

CHAPTER THREE

SOLOMON STEELE SAT BACK IN THE BEAT-UP, DUSTY, OVERSIZED LEATHER chair, his large frame taking up every bit of it. The air around him smelled of burned flesh, hair, and gasoline. It was horrific. He stared at the charred carcass across the warehouse floor, and thoughts ran through his mind. He wondered what it was that had called him to this place. Typically, when a Reaper felt the pull of imminent death, it was followed shortly by an instinctive call to transition to the Nexus, pull the soul, and guide it to the Beyond or the Void. He'd felt the pull with this one. Well, he felt *something* with this one. Whatever it was, it was strong. Strong enough to bring him straight here to watch the man take a final look at life and flicker out.

So, where was the rest?

Given what he had witnessed the night Azra-El died, Solomon decided to wait. So much had happened that night. Watching Senaya get ripped apart by that girl. Watching the Primus drain that damned girl of her life only for her to fight back and take his head. All of it continued to cause an anguish Solomon had not felt since he was human. He'd lost so much that night. Because of that damned girl.

"Fucking Kassidy Simmons," he said through gritted teeth.

Solomon shifted in his chair, pulled a cylindrical tube from his inside jacket pocket, and opened it. Inside was a Cohiba cigar.

He removed it, discarded the tube it came in, and reached for his lighter in another pocket. The small lighter, a torch, had a convenient pull-out feature along the body. Flipping this feature down allowed Solomon to punch a hole into the cigar instead of cutting it. He preferred this method as it provided a better draw, or intake of smoke, and it also kept him from cutting too much of the tip, a skill he'd still not mastered after several decades. Solomon activated the torch and allowed the tip of the flame to touch the end of the cigar. Once he saw the nice reddish-orange glow, he put the tip to his lips and pulled. Satisfied with the burn, Solomon put the torch away, sat back, and puffed . . . and waited.

And waited and puffed.

He thought back to nights when he'd shared a cigar and whiskey with Azra-El. It was something they'd begun during Prohibition. It was a way to acknowledge a friendship that had meant a great deal to them both. At least, he *thought* that's what it had meant. To this day, Solomon didn't know if Azra-El had been his friend. He'd felt as if he were. Even though he knew he'd never be equal to the Primus, there had been a certain shared camaraderie. Solomon cared for Azra-El in a way he could never express. There was nothing sexual or salacious about his feelings toward the Primus. If it could be summed up in one word, it was gratitude.

Azra-El took him away from a life of slavery and put him in a position of power. Solomon found that in some areas, though the world modernized, people's thoughts did not. He was grateful to have the power he did in a world that hated him simply for the color of his skin.

Over time, he cared less about those thoughts. Mostly because he knew he'd outlive them, and there would be a reckoning for those who held them. For that, he was forever grateful to Azra-El for making him a Reaper. He was honored when the Primus elected to give him a small portion of power to elevate him to Wraith. Solomon had been the first. He'd had no illusions that he'd succeed Azra-El because of it. In fact, if there was to be any succession plan in place, he assumed it would go to Senaya.

And, for so many reasons, Solomon was okay with that.

But any thoughts or plans to make that happen had been dashed by Kassidy Simmons.

What that girl did that night was unbelievable. Had the victims been anyone else, perhaps Solomon would be in awe. But it wasn't anyone else, and awe was the last thing he felt.

As his emotions took hold, Solomon put the Cohiba to his lips again, took a long draw, and held the smoke for several seconds before letting it out. He turned his attention back to the charred body on the ground.

"Why am I here?" he asked aloud.

Analyzing the events of his arrival further, he realized that he wasn't so much pulled to the location as he was directed. In many ways it was similar to the mental push he felt when summoned by Azra-El, only . . . stronger. He wondered if it was a trap set by Kassidy. She'd been working around the clock to dispatch Wraiths and do away with any link to Azra-El. The girl was now a god. She could have lured him here to ambush him.

Solomon rose from the chair immediately, careful not to drop his cigar. He closed his eyes and took in his surroundings. Nothing felt off or strange, save for the charred carcass on the ground.

Then he heard it.

Crumble.

The sound of . . . pebbles?

He wasn't certain, but it continued intermittently. Opening his eyes, Solomon looked around trying to determine the source of the sound. It reminded him of rock or marble chiseled away by sculptors. Not the loud violent sound of hammer meeting chisel meeting rock. But the subtle sound of a sculptor using expert skills to address the details of their art. The eyes of a statue. The fingers and toes. The nose and ears.

Crumble-crumble.

This time, the sound pulled Solomon's attention to a specific location. A dark, messy, ugly location. He slowly walked toward the source and simply stared and smiled.

The charred carcass was coming back to life.

Solomon had somehow stumbled across an immortal. He wasn't sure what it was, but he knew it might be something he could use to his advantage. An advantage against that damned girl, perhaps? Time would tell.

As the body slowly reanimated, Solomon returned to the old leather chair, sat, and took a long pull on the cigar as his eyes went black.

CENTURIES AGO

Staring at the crimson liquid as it slid down the blade, he smiled. Satisfaction filled him, and with it, desire. He rubbed the blade against his cheek. The warmth of the blood felt good against his skin. Turning the blade over, he stared, fascinated, reverential . . . hungry. When the blood touched his tongue, he heard their screams. Hundreds of warriors cried out in unison, just as they had when he took their lives. He relived each death, each thrust of his sword, each kill a declaration of victory over one foolish enough to think they could best him.

"You've been busy."

Looking around for the source of the voice, he saw nothing. Then, to his left, a man shimmered into view. He was tall, dark, imposing. A sight that, to anyone else, would create fear. But not in this instance. No, in this instance there was understanding. There was kinship. There was respect for their respective roles and duties.

Mostly.

"Thanatos. You're early. Some of these men aren't even dead yet."

"Oh, I'm not here for them. Not yet at least. I just thought I'd greet you."

"And perhaps thank me for keeping you busy?"

"Thank you? I certainly need no help staying busy. If anyone is going to thank you, it's likely Hades. He has as much love for death and destruction as you do," said Thanatos.

"You're the Death God. Are you telling me this doesn't please you?"

"Death, in and of itself, does not please me. It is not my place to like or dislike it. I am simply its vessel. This is something you've never understood. About me, and most certainly about yourself."

The warrior snickered, then wiped his blade on his tunic before returning it to its sheath. The sword was elegant, an indestructible silver, capable of cutting through the thickest marble. The bronze guard atop the hilt was in the shape of a venomous snake. The grip, custom made for his hand, was the color of the blood he shed in each battle. The pommel, also bronze, had the image of a dog on one side, and a vulture on the other. It was among the finest weapons ever created. And in his hands, among the deadliest.

"Are you here to lecture me, Thanatos? I'm not sure I'm in the mood to be educated on what I should and should not be doing. From the looks of things, I'm doing fine." The warrior gestured to a field of dirt and blood, littered with fallen soldiers.

"Indeed," began Thanatos, "you are doing fine. But this is not all that you are. This is—"

"Who I was born to be!"

The warrior, blood still on fire from the battle, struck the Death God, sending him to the ground. He prepared to unsheathe his sword again but was quickly caught in the grip of an invisible hand. Arms pinned at his sides, he was lifted off the ground where he kicked and writhed, and his bloodlust boiled. Below him, the Death God, hand outstretched, squeezed his fist, causing the warrior to cry out.

"You were not meant to simply be this, Ares!"

"Release me, Thanatos! Release me now, or I swear I'll—"

"You'll what? Kill me?" asked Thanatos.

The chuckle began light, then grew. Ares clenched his fist at the mockery. His eyes shone a bright blue as he felt his power grow. It was electric, an untamed horse rebelling against an attempt to break it. He wanted free of this invisible prison. He wanted to take Thanatos's head and bathe in his blood. His anger, not the pain of the grip, caused him to cry out again.

"There is only one weapon that can kill me, and it's not that shiny sword of yours, boy," said Thanatos.

"Then I'll kill you with your own Scythe."

"You cannot wield it. And you well know that."

"Release me, damn you!"

Ares squirmed further. But somewhere, deep down, in a place he rarely ventured, he knew his weakness was getting the best of him. His pride was the cause of many unnecessary battles and had incited many baseless wars among mortals. It was his pride that struck Thanatos. It was his pride that currently held him prisoner. Athena had long imparted to him the importance of balance. She had mastered it.

Ares had not.

He could hear his sister's words. In many respects, they angered him more. Not because she said them, but because he could not follow them. She was a fine warrior. Better, in many ways, than him. He was cunning, strong, skilled, and ruthless—but she beat him every time. Because of balance. Ares closed his eyes, breathed in, then out, practicing what he'd witnessed in Athena.

"Very good," said Thanatos.

Ares unclenched his fists, relaxed his shoulders, and breathed rhythmically. When he opened his eyes, he was once again on the ground. Now able to move his arms, he stretched. His eyes, still blue, were dulled, his power no longer at its apex.

"Why are you here, Thanatos?"

"My, my . . . so calm. Finally listening to your sister?"

Ignoring his instinct to strike, Ares simply inclined his head. It was a struggle, though. Still on the battlefield, he heard the moans of soldiers near death. It delighted his soul. He felt the heat in his face. Blood and carnage filled his nostrils, and his pulse picked up speed.

"Why. Are. You. Here."

"I can sense your struggle, so let me get to it and leave you to your . . . well . . . whatever it is you do," said Thanatos.

Ares placed his hand on the pommel of his sword, seeking calm. As much as the Glade was a weapon, it was also his totem, his center, the single thing that kept him grounded. It was an extension of him.

"Talk, Death God."

"I am in need of your . . . talents," said Thanatos.

"The same talents you've been mocking?"

"Not the talents of a warrior. Frankly, if I needed that, I'd go to Athena."

"Your flattery makes me disinclined to agree to anything you could possibly propose."

"Apologies," said Thanatos, inclining his head in satirical reverence. "As much as you are a War God, you are also skilled at locating prey. It is those skills I need."

"Surely, you'd want my sister, Artemis, for this task?"

"I don't think she'd be up for this particular mission. In fact, she'd likely help the quarry escape even further."

"Who do you seek?"

"My wife," said Thanatos.

"Allesandra?"

"Yes."

"I think you mean the woman you took against her will as further retaliation against the mortal who killed your son."

Ares sensed the tension and the rise of power within Thanatos. A portion of his pride returned. He'd struck the Death God's own hubris with nothing more than twenty-one words. Perhaps it was foolish, but he was needed. Ares knew no other god would help Thanatos with this. They all mocked the god for what he'd done. Ares could see Thanatos struggle to maintain calm as he continued.

"Call her what you will. She has something of mine. Once I get it back, I'll be more than happy to release her."

"And what does she have?"

"My child grows within her womb."

A pang of shock ran through Ares. He wondered the lengths Thanatos had gone through for that coupling. He'd taken Allesandra, who'd sought to destroy him for taking her love, Tyran, now known as Azra-El. As much as he was the Death God, Thanatos was right in what he'd said earlier. He was nothing but a vessel for a natural consequence of life. He did not seek to cause death. He simply existed as its manifestation. Why had the events surrounding this woman affected him so?

"And she's vanished?"

"Yes."

"If you cannot find her, what makes you think I can?"

"I believe that Allesandra's sister knows her location. I need you to go to her, extract the information in your own way, and bring it to me."

"Extract the information . . . in my way?" asked Ares.

His question was met with a smirk.

"And you're unable to do this because . . . ?"

"Because I'm clearly going to be busy cleaning up the mess you made on this battlefield," said Thanatos.

"And to save you from the potential of further embarrassment by the Twelve," said Ares.

His response was met with silence. Once again, he felt his pride growing. He didn't hate Thanatos. No god hated him. Some feared him, to be sure. He was, after all, the only being capable of killing them with that damned Scythe. Ares wanted that weapon. It had been his grandfather's, why shouldn't it be his?

"Will you help me?" asked Thanatos.

After short deliberation, he said, "I will."

"I am in your debt."

"Indeed, you are."

With mutual understanding, Ares watched as Thanatos shimmered out of view. Thoughts swirled in his head, but they were quickly belayed by the sound of soft steps behind him. With a grin, Ares unsheathed his sword, spun, and impaled his would-be attacker. Staring into the eyes of the mortal, Ares's bloodlust was reborn. The mortal's cheeks and lips were smeared with blood. He'd fought fiercely, no doubt, but pushed his luck in trying to take on a god. He wouldn't have known, though. On the battlefield, Ares looked like any other soldier.

The soldier softly moaned as his life slipped from him.

Delighted with his agony, Ares kissed the mortal's bloodied lips.

CHAPTER FOUR

CHARLES CARTWRIGHT STOOD IN FRONT OF THE WINDOW IN HIS OFFICE overlooking the city his family had built . . . or, at least, had a hand in building. Anyone in the Cartwright family would have the world believe they were Chicago's royalty, the city's salvation. Really, they were just a family with deep pockets and a lengthy history. They kept meticulous records to preserve their mythos. They were, as the saying goes, legends in their own minds.

It would be a mistake to discount their impact, though. Cartwright Industries was the largest company in the city and, subsequently, the largest single employer around. They consistently donated to schools at all levels as well as various charities. For a politician, an endorsement from Charles Cartwright made almost any election a formality. His family had been responsible for putting men into the White House, and that influence carried on through generations. Charles was a powerful man to be sure. He wanted for nothing.

At least from the outside looking in.

There was something that constantly eluded Charles, though, a thorn in his side that caused him equal parts anxiety and annoyance. Something had stuck with him since he was a boy, something he wanted so badly after seeing it happen to that soldier, the one who'd saved him and his mother in a bank robbery. Immortality was the stuff of legends. It was a plot found in books and movies and was reserved for stories of mythological gods and goddesses. But he'd seen it. At least, he thought he had. When that soldier was shot, shielding his mother from the gunman, he dropped to the ground. But when it was all over, just before the police had arrived, Charles saw the soldier awaken. And by the time the police entered, and the commotion had settled, the soldier was gone. No one had collected the body; it had simply vanished. Charles was certain the man had died and come back. He had power, the power of immortality, and Charles wanted it. He craved it. He was born to privilege, but it had taken him decades to finally ascend to power. He wasn't ready to give that up.

He would never be ready to give that up.

Charles wanted to live forever. He'd wanted that since he was a boy. But he eventually accepted that such dreams were childish. So, if he could not live through history, he would shape it and ensure his legacy lived on. Those politicians he'd elevated were at his beck and call. And so was classified information about the inner workings of governments, both foreign and domestic. Cartwright used that information to his advantage. He manipulated world events to benefit him and his company, and for special political favors, he manipulated events to benefit his country. He rarely hesitated when it came to making the difficult calls . . . the final calls. For him, they were all a means to an end.

"Mr. Cartwright?" said a voice through the intercom behind him.

Charles walked to his desk, sat down, and reached out to press a button on his phone.

"Yes, Samantha?"

"Mr. Cartwright, I have Mr. LaVelle on the line to speak with you. He says it's urgent."

Charles's heart skipped. Damien LaVelle was one of the deadliest men on the planet. He was lethal, pure and simple. Some might say he was pure evil. Where Charles was both devil and angel, depending on the circumstances, Damien LaVelle was a cold and heartless enforcer. LaVelle was intense and confident, as was Cartwright. But where Cartwright worked hard to keep his sinister side in the shadows, LaVelle did not. Damien LaVelle was not the type of man to wait until dark to meet his objective. He took opportunities as they came. At times he was spontaneous, which posed a threat to his employer. Thankfully, he wasn't reckless. Cartwright was a son of bitch, to be sure, but nobody needed to know that. LaVelle worked for Charles, and on the surface, there were no issues. The company was as legitimate as any other. From hiring practices, to the benefits offered, to taxes paid, everything was in order. If anyone did any serious digging, they wouldn't find anything they weren't supposed to. Underneath Cartwright's organization, though, Damien LaVelle was the man who made problems go away. Cartwright worked to change the course of governments, but it was LaVelle who cleaned up the aftermath and tied off loose ends.

"Thank you, Samantha," said Charles. He picked up his receiver and pressed the button for his private, encrypted phone line. "Yes?"

"It's done," said the gravelly voice on the other end.

"Did he talk?"

"He's not the type," said LaVelle.

"Did you ask him?"

"I didn't need to."

"So, no?" asked Charles.

A beat.

"No," said LaVelle.

That word flowed into Charles's brain and immediately went to his stomach, which in turn tightened and flipped. His hand gripped the phone tighter in an effort to control his body's automatic response to disappointment. To failure. LaVelle was prone to shoot first and ask no questions at any time. All Charles needed was to be certain that Jaxon Burke had spoken to no one about his contract. It was that simple.

There was a silence on the phone, and a part of Charles wondered if it was wise to yell at a man who simply did not care about anything except himself and money. Actually, that wasn't true. Charles had known Damien since they were pre-teens, and he knew full well that Damien didn't care about money. He cared about action and pain. More importantly, he cared about inflicting it.

"Look," began LaVelle, "you pay me to know about certain people and to understand how things work in the dark. Burke is, well, was . . . a pro. He does a job, he completes a job, he moves on. His reputation is, well . . . was, stellar. Frankly, I'm a little disappointed we just didn't try to bring him in. This is how you want things, though, and I'm your guy, so I do what I'm asked. I got the guy, I strapped him down, he went up in flames. Done deal. Though you'll probably never find another shooter as good as—"

"Flames?" Charles asked in a loud voice. "Who the hell told you to use flames?"

"He needed to be gone with no trace, so I made him gone with no trace. I don't understand what the problem is here, Charles," said LaVelle.

Charles squeezed the phone even harder as he caught the sarcastic tone from LaVelle.

"So, you naturally went to the most extreme form of death possible."

"Yep."

"And there is no indication that anyone knows what's happened?"

"Take a look for yourself. I took him to the warehouse. You can watch his demise to your heart's delight," said LaVelle.

Again, the sarcasm was there. Charles disliked when people underestimated him, and disrespect was a sure sign of underestimating him. He wasn't sure what had gotten into Damien. He was never this . . . cocky. It disturbed him. Led him to wonder what else LaVelle might do. Maybe a lifelong friendship wasn't worth anything anymore.

"Fine. Perhaps I'll take a look," said Charles.

"And let me know when I can expect—"

Charles hung up on him. Probably not the best idea, but he didn't care. He was angry. He needed to get refocused on the bright side of things. Burke had carried out a job that sent ripples through the Middle East. Further unrest meant destabilization. Destabilization meant war. War meant profits. For Charles Cartwright, profits secured his legacy.

"Maybe I should have kept Burke around after all," he said to himself as he watched the news unfold on his computer screen.

CHAPTER FIVE

"GOOD EVENING, I'M MARILYN SIMMS. AS AN UNPRECEDENTED LEVEL OF violence escalates in the Middle East, we are seeing tensions rise both here and in other countries. Tonight, we bring you an exclusive interview with General Marcus Kelly, former Chairman of the Joint Chiefs of Staff. He'll share with us his perspective on the catalyst for what we're seeing in the world, and possible solutions. General, welcome."

"Thank you, Marilyn. Pleasure to be here."

"General, since the assassination of Kareem Nasir, peace talks have all but ceased. In your opinion, was he the true lynchpin in maintaining diplomacy?"

"Marilyn, he was essential to successful diplomatic talks. What he brought to the table was order, stability, an understanding based on his own heritage of the needs of both peoples. They were resistant to speaking to each other without him. Reluctant but willing to negotiate with him involved. And now, with his death, each country is primed to blame the other for the assassination."

"General, there are reports that the assassination of Nasir was orchestrated by US intelligence. What do you say to that?"

"Hogwash. Pure, unadulterated, and unsubstantiated hogwash. Listen, the US has nothing to gain and everything to lose by peace talks breaking down. Without stability in that region, we'll see continued violence, uprisings, and attempts by outside forces to take advantage and control. If that happens, we will have a moral and political obligation to step in and assist."

"And what impact does that have on us?"

"It forces us to commit significant resources that could potentially leave us vulnerable in other areas. If our allies are not in support of our actions, our involvement has the potential to affect our international relationships."

"And by extension, that could give rise to other conflicts."

"Exactly. The General's assassination was the absolute worst-case scenario. The mastermind behind it did the one thing that could effectively cause a third world war."

"That truly is the worst possible outcome of all this. It just boggles the mind. We have to take a quick break here, General. Do you have time to sit with us for another segment?"

"Absolutely."

"Thank you so much. If you're just joining us, we're here with an exclusive interview with General Marcus Kelly. We're taking a quick commercial break, but we'll be right back."

◆ ◆ ◆

The Diva watched with sinister satisfaction as the news report shifted to commercials.

"All this unrest, and the world is still concerned with ad revenue? You all make it so easy, don't you?" she said to herself.

She rose from her chair and went to the mini bar, poured another brandy, then walked to the window and stared. When she'd been released from that accursed prison her brother had put her in, she'd marveled at how much the world had changed. Since her release, two decades of advancements had occurred. Human beings were truly remarkable creatures, capable of so much. So much growth, so much evolution . . . so much good. What had not changed in those twenty years, or in the millennia she had been locked away, was man's inability to see their own potential. What had not changed was their selfishness, cowardice, thirst for power, and refusal to see that they were part of a larger symbiotic unit. What had not changed was their ability to be easily manipulated.

And when it came to manipulation, she was an absolute master.

In the past, her proclivities toward deceit and deception had been frowned upon, at least in public. But behind closed doors, even the gods sought out her skills. Hera sought her out to exact revenge on a mortal lover of her brother, husband, and king, Zeus. Gods and mortals alike were caught up in their own vanity, their sense of what they assumed to be right and wrong. In that, they were alike, and because of that, they could all be manipulated.

Just as they were being manipulated now.

The Diva was playing the long game. Her plan, twenty years in progress but several millennia in the making, was playing out well. There were a few bumps in the road, and she was still not sure if the Advocate was fully committed, but all in all, things were working out just as she had hoped.

"Such a beautiful city. So many beautiful cities around the world," she said to herself. "It will be such a pleasure to sit atop the throne and watch them burn."

The Diva sipped her brandy and returned to the interview, smiling with the knowledge that she had set this chaos into motion.

She smiled, excited about what was to come.

CHAPTER SIX

"NO, THAT CAN'T BE RIGHT."

"Sir, I assure you, there is no secret book between books three and four of that series."

"No, I'm certain I read that there was," said the middle-aged businessman. "I'll pull it up on my . . ."

"Sir, I can appreciate that you are absolutely positive about this," Keiron started, "and normally I'm of the mind that the customer is always right. But I've been in this business a long time. Books are essentially my life. Trust me when I say it does not exist."

And there it was. That look. The look that silently assumes there's a reason for the separation in social status between a businessman and an independent bookstore owner who probably only makes enough to get the bills paid and keep a few groceries in the refrigerator. The look that said, "Mister, you don't live in the real world where real decisions are being made, so step aside and let me school you on some things." He'd seen it before, and he knew, as certain as bourbon had at least fifty-one percent corn, he'd see it again.

"Look," said the customer, "I know what I read. They said it's rare. Maybe it's just so rare you haven't heard of it. Maybe you're in the wrong business."

Another parting shot that simultaneously attacked Keiron's intelligence and his ability to navigate his own industry.

"I'm not sure where you got your information. Perhaps you're confusing it with another—"

"You know what, just . . . never mind. I should have gone to the other place."

You're in St. John, New York, Keiron thought. *There is no other place.*

As the irate customer left the store, Keiron considered all the things he could have said, perhaps even should have said. He mulled over the cutting remarks that could have put the man's ego in check. He could have just thrown him out. It was his business after all, and like most businesses, he reserved the right to refuse service to anyone.

But that was not Keiron's way.

"So, fuck that 'customer is always right' bullshit, huh?" asked a voice from behind.

Keiron smiled at the sound of the voice and chuckled at the question. He had not laid eyes on her in a couple of weeks. He hadn't been completely certain that he'd ever see her again after what had occurred. She was, understandably, angry. In the back of his mind, he prayed to whichever gods might be listening that she would see fit to forgive him, or at least make an attempt.

Perhaps today was the beginning of that.

"I'd never say that out loud," Keiron said.

"I'm happy to do it for you," Kassidy retorted.

"I'll put you on the payroll," Keiron started, "but if you say that to customers too loudly, I may have to let you go."

"No worries. I have two jobs to fall back on. Though, this new gig doesn't pay much."

"Probably need to talk to human resources about that."

"That's the thing, not many humans around for this one."

Keiron finally gave a slight turn to look at Kassidy. She

seemed . . . present. Whatever that meant. Perhaps he'd expected something more ethereal since her recent ascension. A month ago, Kassidy Simmons had been a PI who specialized in locating people, as well as a self-identified "former Reaper," a being that ushered souls into the afterlife. In the span of a few weeks, though, she discovered that Azra-El, the Angel of Death, was regenerating and coming for her, mostly because she'd tried to kill him twenty years before. She also learned that the Death God, Thanatos, was her father. Now, for all intents and purposes, after finally dispatching Azra-El, *she* was the Death God.

"You look good, Kass," Keiron said.

"Thanks. I, uh, feel good . . . I think."

Keiron walked toward her, apprehension thicker than a jar of molasses with a peanut butter base. He tried to calm his nerves, but so much had happened, so much had damaged their friendship, that finding calm was not possible. Standing in front of her, he took a tentative step forward to hug her, but she stepped back.

And there was nothing subtle about it.

"We'll probably get there," she said, gesturing with her hands to imply she was speaking of their friendship. "But— "

"I understand," Keiron said as he took a step back.

After an awkward pause, Kassidy walked slowly around the bookstore. She pretended to look at books. It reminded Keiron of the first time they'd met. Back when she was a teen, a new Reaper ordered by Azra-El to take Keiron's life.

"So, what brings you by?" Keiron asked.

"I just thought it would be a good idea to let you know that I'm working on rounding up Wraiths. I just can't see a reason to keep Azra-El's private army around anymore."

"Makes sense," Keiron said. "But why tell me? Do you need help?"

"Oh no. Not at the moment, at least. It's just that, considering how you helped me, and fought a few, I figured I'd give you a heads up, in case . . . you know . . . they tried to come after you. Either for revenge, or to get to me."

"Ah . . . yeah, I guess that's always a possibility since we're, well, friends and all."

"Yeah, exactly," Kassidy said.

"Probably should tell Octavia, too."

"Yep, I sent her a text."

A text? Yeah, she's still pissed.

"Good. She's capable. She can handle herself well in a fight. Gave her a couple of the daggers, too."

"Cool," said Kassidy. "Cool, cool, cool."

Again, awkward silence filled the room. Keiron tried to keep his guilt in check. With Kassidy's empathic powers, she'd feel everything he felt. His guilt was sincere, and she'd feel that, too, but he didn't want pity to be the reason for forgiveness. He'd screwed up. Both he and Octavia had screwed up. They'd kept the truth of Kassidy's lineage from her, and in her own words, Keiron's betrayal was the greatest. He had been more than a friend. He'd been a mentor, a father figure, someone she could trust with her life. Keiron should have been the one to tell her about her parents. He hid that, along with the fact that he too, was immortal—a son of Cronus, no less. Keiron wanted desperately to make amends. He just didn't know how.

"Kass," Keiron began, "can we just—"

"I've got a team looking into the souls, too," said Kassidy.

"The . . . souls?"

"It seems, when I dispatched Azra-El, some of the souls used to regenerate him were released."

"Oh my god. Did they—"

"Return to their bodies? No. At least not that we can tell. But they're out there, wandering. Some are even possessing. This is a problem above and beyond the Wraith issues and I can't tell you how much I'm looking forward to tackling that next."

Keiron wasn't sure how to navigate that. He had seen a great many things in several thousand years of life, including the devastation that soul possession can have. Not only on the person being possessed, but on the soul itself. Existing in a world you don't belong, being connected to nothing, had to be terrifying. He felt bad for the souls, and for the possessed, but mostly he felt bad for Kassidy. He knew she would find a way to blame herself for this. But how was she to know? In her mind, that question was irrelevant. All of this had happened on her watch, and so the burden fell upon her. And, considering the secrets he'd kept from her, he was a prime target for her anger over everything that was happening.

"Kass, look, you have to—"

Kassidy cut him off by holding up a hand. She closed her eyes and paused for a beat. When she opened them, they were glowing blue.

"There's a Wraith nearby. I need to go. He's one of the last two I need to find. Some of them have been possessing bodies, too. They're a little harder to manage when they attach to a human soul. I need to get to him before he tries."

"Um, yeah, okay . . . go . . . go. We can talk la—"

Keiron's words were cut off again, this time by Kassidy's abrupt departure. As a Reaper, she used to coalesce into a gray vapor and fly off. Now, as a god, she simply shimmered away.

Much like their friendship.

He pulled his phone out, scrolled through recent calls, and pressed a name.

"Hey," said the voice on the other end.

"Hey yourself," Keiron replied. "Listen, are you busy? Wondering if we could talk."

"I've always got time for you," said Octavia.

"I was thinking of taking a drive your way."

"Let me know when you hit the city limits, and I'll start the coffee."

"Probably gonna need something stronger."

"I've got that, too."

Keiron grinned then hung up. As he turned to prepare to close his shop, he saw a man waiting at the checkout counter.

"Hi," said Keiron. "I'm just about to close. Can I help you find something?"

"Actually, I'm here to help you."

Curious, Keiron walked closer. The stranger was a black man, tall, fit, in a beautiful tailor-made three-piece suit. His hair was close cropped, and his features had a familiar chisel.

Very familiar.

"Here to sell?" asked Keiron.

"Not quite," said the man, grinning.

"Are you here to talk to me about the Avengers Initiative?" quipped Keiron.

The man chuckled and pointed.

"Well played. I supposed I did just kind of show up all Nick Fury style. Truth is, I'm typically told I resemble Denzel Washington more."

That familiarity Keiron felt smacked him in the face like the wind in downtown St. James.

I'll be damned.

CHAPTER SEVEN

AWARENESS TRICKLED IN.

The pain of Jaxon's regeneration was nothing like the pain of death. Death was agonizing. Even when it didn't involve fire, it was gut wrenching and unpredictable. In all those other instances, knowing that he would come back didn't lessen the intensity of the fear—and fear exacerbated the pain. Being shot, stabbed, or drowning was one thing. Feeling your organs systematically shut down was another. Not knowing what was going to happen internally, or when, played with the mind to the point of madness. The sensation of swelling, internal hemorrhaging, and suffocation always overshadowed the assurance that he would return.

And in that return, there was some joy. It was the sensation one feels when intense pain finally subsides. There was something beautiful, almost elegant, about it. For Jaxon, it all began in his mind. It was as if he went through a series of checklists, immediately followed by a surge of electricity—a light, so to speak, at the end of the tunnel. The current tingled, starting in the center of his body, then it radiated out. His heart would beat, slowly at first. *Thump. Thump. Thump . . . thump.* before gaining a steady, strong rhythm.

Thump-thump, thump-thump, thump-thump.

Once that began, the sound was almost deafening as the rest of his body mended itself. In this instance, though, virtually everything needed to be reformed. Organs, tissue, and muscle, re-knit. Eventually, his lungs repaired themselves and filled with air. After regeneration, it never seemed like enough. As soon as he was able, he inhaled every molecule of oxygen he could, followed by that first, glorious exhale. The tingle of blood circulating in his extremities caused an itching sensation, but he was still unable to move. This was going to take considerably longer. Definitely longer than the first time.

The first time . . .

His thoughts quickly returned to his recent death. He wanted to forget the feel of it. The pain had been immeasurable. Over the course of his life, he'd been shot, stabbed, hit by vehicles, and pushed from high structures—and collectively the pain was a pin prick compared to the fire. The memory of the sound of flames dancing across his body seemed to mock him. As his senses returned, the scent of burned flesh and hair still lingered in the air. Or was that the memory of the smell? The sensation of his skin sizzling then slowly, painfully, melting off sent chills throughout his still reforming body. He tried to linger on those moments when there was no heat, no pain—no nothing.

Before the darkness came.

Continuing the mental checklist, he was able to recall his name, the city, his occupation and address, along with a few other essential elements.

Anna!

Electricity continued to run through him, his blood flow increased, and his extremities tingled more. First the toes, then the fingers, into the legs and arms. The process felt slow, slower than normal. Then again, he'd never had to recover from something so intense. Given that he'd never died by fire before, there was one thing he had not considered. His regeneration was happening within a suit of charred flesh. Charred flesh he'd eventually have to break free of.

I wonder if this is how baby birds and reptiles feel?

The shell cracked a bit here and there as he started to move his hands and feet. Even flexing a muscle or two had some effect. After a time, he was free of the cocoon. His muscles were sore, his limbs weak, his skin sensitive, but he was back. Though, something was still a bit . . . off.

He wasn't happy, though that wasn't new.

He was tired. It wasn't the normal tired he felt after regeneration, and there would no doubt be added fatigue from this particular rebirth given the nature of his demise. No, the type of tired he felt was of the soul. He'd felt that way for a while and when he drifted off into that dark abyss of nothing, a part of him was satisfied. Jaxon Burke had been ready to die and not return.

Jaxon Burke was *hoping* to die and not return.

But here he was.

Still though, something was off.

He lay on the concrete, shivering, uncertain what to do next. The gasoline had burning away from the ground, leaving only soot and ash between his flesh and concrete. He tingled still, but not from the regeneration. He tingled the way one does when they feel they're being watched. There was an undeniable presence looming. He hadn't attempted to open his eyes yet, and he was in no way prepared to defend himself, but he needed to do . . . something. Fear returned. Worse than when he'd been strapped to that pile of kindling that was once a chair.

"You know I'm here, don't you?" asked a male voice.

It wasn't the guy from before, the one who set all this in

motion. Of that, he was certain. The presence he felt, the voice he heard, was something . . . else.

"I have to say," the man said, "I've never come across anything like you before. I felt the pull of death in a way I'd never experienced. It was palpable. I almost choked on it. I was shocked that no Reaper had beat me here. Shocked, but pleased. Especially when I saw the life force inside you re-ignite. It was . . . remarkable."

Confusion swept through Jaxon. He heard the words, but the context was lost on him. Who was this guy? *What* was this guy? Another immortal maybe? Someone like him?

"A couple of weeks ago, I watched my Primus die at the hands of a girl. That damned girl. She was the key to his ascension. I watched that dream die as she severed his head. But now . . ."

The man's voice trailed off. Jaxon remained confused.

"Now, things may not be as lost as I thought."

With trepidation, Jaxon opened his eyes, just in time to see a dark figure lunge forward, grab him by the neck and hoist him into the air. Naked and afraid, he grabbed the forearm of the man holding him. He kicked weakly, wildly, struggling for freedom. He'd just returned from death, a death he wasn't even sure he'd bounce back from, to be greeted with . . . this.

Whatever *this* was.

"I think I need what you've got," said the man.

Jaxon's vision cleared despite the lack of oxygen, and his eyes widened as he saw the solid black eyes of a man with a wide grin. He watched as the man pulled back his free hand only to thrust it forward, violently, swiftly, into Jaxon's chest. It phased through, lingered a while, then retracted. When it was completely free, Jaxon saw a glowing orb, golden and pulsating, in the man's hand. Jaxon's eyes shifted from the orb to the man, and in that distorted face, there was shock.

"You definitely are something different. Whatever you are, whatever you have, it'll be enough to end Simmons and take what I deserve."

Both men stared at the golden orb and watched as it trembled, as if sentient. It rolled, then spun, and finally, slowly, rose into the air. It seemed to glow brighter, growing larger at first, before it collapsed on itself leaving golden particles of light in the air—which promptly returned to Jaxon's body.

"Impossible," said the man.

When the man reached in again, he was met with a surge of electricity, sending him flying back. Jaxon fell to the ground. Looking up, he saw the man convulsing as if electrocuted. Confused, Jaxon fled from the warehouse to a back room. Finding some old, dusty coveralls, and boots at least two sizes too small, he dressed and found his way out of the warehouse. He didn't know what that thing was. He didn't know what had just happened. But he wanted no part of it. He left and headed for the only place he could think of where he might find a measure of safety.

CHAPTER EIGHT

"YOU'RE HIM," SAID KEIRON.

"Well, I'm certainly someone. But yes, I think I take your meaning. Pleasure to make your acquaintance. I'm a big fan."

Keiron inclined his head in salutation, and his guest did the same. Kassidy had described him as resembling Denzel Washington, and he did, to some degree. More so in his speech though, the cadence and mannerisms. So much so, that if someone said this guy was Denzel's son, no one would think twice about it.

"Jacen . . . ?"

"Lucas. Jacen Lucas is my name."

"The so-called Advocate. Advocate of what?"

"That's a good question. I suppose, in many ways, I am an advocate of life. Of truth, justice—"

"And the American way?" finished Keiron.

"Well played," said Jacen.

"You are a strange visitor," said Keiron.

"True. Though, strange is quite subjective, don't you think? And I'm certainly not from a distant planet."

"Oh no?"

"Most definitely not. I'm from Chicago. Like our mutual friend," said Jacen.

"So, what can I do for you, Advocate?"

There was a subtle bite to the question. Not out of malice or animus. Mostly, because Keiron just wasn't sure what to do with this guy. He didn't know how to categorize him in the pantheon of supernatural beings. He'd only heard of Advocates. It seemed odd. After all the centuries that had passed, and with the power this man seemed to have, it seemed far-fetched that he would not have crossed paths with an Advocate much sooner.

Then again, perhaps he had. Would he really know?

"You're apprehensive about me? I can respect that. Given what I know of you, I fully expected that. Hopefully, in time, you'll see me as a friend, or close enough to it."

"Time will tell," said Keiron.

"Indeed. Anyway, you asked a question, so I'll get to it. There's a shitstorm coming," said Jacen.

"Subtle."

"I like to get to the point."

"You have my attention," said Keiron.

Keiron was still wary of everything. The shitstorm, as Jacen so eloquently put it, could well be this Advocate. What did they know about him? Nothing. What were the limits to his powers? His abilities could be greater than that of the Twelve. And if that were the case, and he were the big bad in all this, shitstorm would be a low-key descriptor of the days to come.

"There is rumor of a prophecy. If you ask me, it's more of a warning, but scholars and ancient types seem to love the mystery that surrounds the word *prophecy*."

"Ugh, tell me about it," agreed Keiron.

"Right? It's all so dramatic," said Jacen.

"Says the guy who pops in and out of people's lives, provides cryptic clues, and never fully answers questions posed to him," quipped Keiron.

"Touché."

Keiron appreciated that Jacen owned the description. He was a patient man, but one of Keiron's pet peeves was people not acknowledging their own character, flaws and all. That Jacen accepted his didn't make him more likeable, but it did, somehow, make him seem a little less malevolent.

"What's this prophecy?" asked Keiron.

"It speaks of the Four," said Jacen.

"Shit . . ."

"Yeah, pretty much."

When it came to modern religions, there was some semblance of truth in their respective scriptures. Keiron admired those who had faith, because in that faith was a pure love and trust that kept them safe from the truth of what was really out there in the world . . . and beyond. There were monsters out there. There was evil. There were things skulking about in the night that terrified even him, and he'd seen just about everything there was in the centuries he'd lived. But there was one thing that terrified everyone, even the most evil of entities.

The Four.

"So, what's in this prophecy?" asked Keiron.

"It speaks of the coming of the Four. Talks of escalating aggressions in the world opening a proverbial doorway through which the Four may enter. That, along with global sickness, drought, and a noticeable impact on the natural order—it seems the world may be primed for something devastating. I'm a little vague on the details, but essentially, it seems their time is at hand. Given what we've seen recently, what Kassidy just stopped—"

"Mass deaths?"

Jacen inclined his head in agreement.

"But that was to stop a would-be usurper. An abomination trying to bend the world to his will."

"I don't think the prophecy cares," said Jacen. "Just look at what's out there. War, terrorism . . . everywhere. There are countries bowing down to warlords and demagogues, and in the middle of it all, people are starving and dying from malnutrition and sickness. The world itself is in such dire straits that it's literally calling for the Four to come and take it out of its misery."

Jacen seemed to be on a bit of a soapbox, but he was right, and Keiron could see it. He could fight and make the argument that the world was resilient, that it could fight back with an abundance of love and hope. But there seemed to be so little of it these days that he wasn't even sure they'd make a dent. And in the end, wasn't that the purpose of the Four? To fight back on behalf of the world and force a reboot?

"What can we do?"

Keiron's question was met with a sarcastic gaze and grin.

Okay, so maybe he does look like Denzel.

"Have you ever heard of a prophecy not coming true?" asked Jacen.

Keiron's silence was the only response he could muster.

"On the bright side, we could be misinterpreting the prophecy."

"And the flip side?" asked Keiron.

"On the flip side . . . we have to keep in mind that our girl just ascended. Meaning—"

"It's probably already begun," finished Keiron.

The weight of this was a punch to the gut. Kassidy had just ascended. She was a Death God now. No, she was *the* Death God. Thanatos, missing or dead, was out of the mix, and now, a young girl born of the Nexus and raised in Oak Park, Illinois, was the—

"This could be wrong, right? We could just be seeing things that aren't there. I mean, there's a lot happening in the world, sure, but—"

"But it's at a fever pitch," said Jacen.

Again, he was right. The world had been on the brink countless times over the centuries, but it had never been as ripe for the Four as it was now. They needed to be certain though. At least more certain than they were. Prophecies were vague. Without oracles to assist in their interpretation, they were simply riddles with a different meaning for everyone who read them.

"Why are you telling me this? Why not tell Kassidy?"

"She's got a great deal to manage," said Jacen. "Also, even estranged, she'll trust you to tell her more than she'd trust me."

"I'm not so sure," said Keiron.

"I am."

Keiron turned to face Jacen, only to find that he'd vanished. He was unaccustomed to yelling, but he wanted to. He was unaccustomed to nervousness and fear, but he felt both. He was unaccustomed to not having the answers, yet here he was. The one thing that was normal was the knowledge that he had to act. He had to do . . . something.

The Four were coming.

The Four Horsemen of the Apocalypse.

And Death was already here.

CHAPTER NINE

KASSIDY AWOKE FROM AN UNEXPECTED NAP WITH A SMALL DEGREE OF brain fog. She'd fallen asleep on the couch again, which did not lend well to a restful slumber. Being in a home under remodel following the destruction that resulted from her battle with Wraiths, didn't lend well to a restful sleep either. The place was a bit drafty, and it was still technically winter, an unforgiving season in the Chicagoland area.

Since dispatching Azra-El she'd been working tirelessly to find the remaining Wraiths. That, coupled with her efforts to deal with the legal issues surrounding the Simmons family home and its remodel, left her exhausted. She was the Death God now, but apparently even gods tire, and for some reason that last Wraith took a lot out of her. It hadn't helped that she'd been distracted by having seen Keiron again. If not for that, the fight may have been a little shorter.

There were other nagging issues. Issues in the form of feelings, which Kassidy was all too adept at avoiding. Being an empath gave her the perfect excuse to ignore her own emotions. She could always blame what she was feeling on others, at least outwardly. Deep down, though, she knew she was the problem. Kassidy's ability to avoid dealing with her own emotions, fears, and anxieties was strengthened over decades of trauma. Her self-care was bourbon and sarcasm. There was a time when Vicodin rounded out the trifecta, but since her ascension, the physical pain she once felt from her overactive empathic abilities had lessened. Thankfully she'd managed to ween off Vicodin, slowly. Every so often she'd indulge, but not at the level she once had.

She placed her feet on the ground and struggled to adjust her eyesight. Everything seemed so . . . gray. Or green. No, greenish gray. And the ground was . . . moving?

"What. The. Fuck."

Kassidy rose immediately from the couch and confirmed her suspicions. Somehow, she'd awoke in the Nexus.

"This isn't possible," she said to herself.

She looked around but could find no one. There was no indication that someone had brought her here, and the only beings capable of doing that were the Primus and the Death God. The Primus was dead. She was the Death God and, to date, had not mastered the ability to summon anyone. If she had, rounding up the Wraiths would have been a hell of lot easier.

There was, of course, the Advocate.

Jacen Lucas had pulled her into the Nexus before. Kassidy was still uncertain about the extent of his power. She didn't really know whether he was friend or foe, either. His guidance had been sound, though muddled in riddles. But there was still something about him that didn't sit right.

It didn't help that she was also extremely insecure about her own role and abilities.

Kassidy's lineage may have made her the natural successor to the mantle of Death God but being the daughter of Thanatos—a fact she'd been ignorant of until a few weeks ago—didn't come with a manual. Kassidy had spent her entire life wondering who she was and where she'd come from. Having answers now only created more questions. Those unanswered questions fed her insecurities. Did she deserve this power? Did she have the right to just assume the role of Death God? What did it even mean to *be* a Death God? Kassidy had grown up feeling out of place and often like a burden. Without answers, without guidance, the power she had meant nothing.

She still didn't really know who she was.

"Lucas! Are you here? Did you do this?" she asked aloud.

Kassidy walked around, trying to make sense of things. She could certainly leave. She had the ability to transport herself in and out of the Nexus—even the newest of Reapers could do that—and she did not feel any barrier keeping her in the plane. But she was too curious about how she ended up there.

Kassidy shimmered out of the home, into the open environment outside. The Nexus, while on a different plane of existence, mirrored the real world. It was the gateway to the afterlife, the space where souls were ushered to the next phase of existence by Reapers. Outside the house, she saw nothing out of the ordinary.

"This doesn't make any sense," said Kassidy.

There was too much to do in the real world to dwell. The part of her that hated mysteries was at odds with the part of her craving to get back to business. In the end, the latter won out. As she prepared to transition out of the Nexus, she caught sight of a dark figure crossing between homes.

"There you are," she whispered to herself.

Kassidy ran after the figure. It ducked between homes and seemed to vanish around trees and bushes. At one point it shimmered out of view only to reappear blocks away. Kassidy kept up until it finally stopped moving. She walked toward it, standing in the open of a park wearing dark clothing and a hood. The figure was female. She was athletic, similar to Kassidy in height and build.

"Who are you?" asked Kassidy.

The figure turned around and stared directly at Kassidy. Or, at least, seemed to. Kassidy couldn't tell as the hood covered her entire face. It was not unlike the look of a fully cloaked Wraith. But whoever this was, she was no Wraith. Kassidy could sense at least that much.

"Answer me!" demanded Kassidy.

The answer she received was unexpected.

The figure crouched down then launched herself at Kassidy. They both went to the ground and rolled for several feet before coming to a stop. Kassidy rose immediately, turned, and set herself in a defensive posture anticipating another attack. Her attacker dematerialized into vapor then reappeared, standing in front of Kassidy. As she solidified, her right hand turned into a sickle.

"That's not fucking possible," said Kassidy.

In the Nexus, no Reaper or Wraith could manifest their sickle. Even Azra-El couldn't do it. Kassidy, somehow, had managed to do it once as a Reaper after Azra-El had returned. In hindsight, she assumed it was because of her bloodline. Only gods could create and wield weapons there.

Is this . . . a god?

The dark figure lunged at Kassidy again and attacked with her right hand. Kassidy threw up both arms to block the downward blow and pushed her opponent back.

"I don't know who you are, or what your beef is with me, but I'm probably not the one you want to be messing with," said Kassidy.

The attacker moved forward with a combination of kicks and punches that Kassidy easily blocked and side stepped. Kassidy countered with her own and was able to connect with a quick double kick. The first kick to the gut was blocked, but the second to the head was too fast. It caught her assailant off guard, and Kassidy took advantage of the opportunity. With a roundhouse, she sent her assailant to the ground and pounced. The sudden shock caused the assailant's hand to reform. Kassidy sent one punch to the face, then grabbed the woman, pulling her up and throwing off the hood. The attacker's face shocked Kassidy—and her shock left an opening. One punch to the face sent her flying back, and she landed hard on the ground.

The punch hurt, and probably would have hurt more if not for the shock.

Kassidy looked up to find her attacker standing over her. The woman's hair was long and black. Her face was gaunt, and her eyes a bright purple. Aside from those eyes, the woman was, in every way, a mirror image of Kassidy.

"Who . . . who are you?" asked Kassidy again.

"I think it's pretty obvious," said the woman.

"No. No the fuck it is not!"

The sarcastic grin was exactly the look Kassidy had given to thousands over the years. It spoke volumes, provided answers, and annoyed people—all at the same time.

"Like you, I was born here," said the woman, gesturing to the area around them.

Kassidy looked around and only then noticed that they were in Potter's Field. This was where she had first met Azra-El. The place she thought she'd died and become a Reaper. The place where she'd ended his existence with the Scythe of Cronus.

The place she'd become a god.

"Unlike you, though, I know who I am. I am at peace with who I am. I'm not some imposter flaunting a power I don't understand with my daddy's big knife in hand," said the doppelgänger.

"I don't . . . I don't understand," said Kassidy.

"And that is why you'll never be as powerful as Thanatos."

With that, Kassidy propelled herself from the ground to tackle her twin. She was met with empty air and ended up back on the ground. She quickly got to her hands and knees and searched for the woman.

"You're not ready," echoed the doppelgänger's voice. "You're not ready to face me. Until then, you will only fail."

Confused, defeated, and spent, Kassidy sat on her haunches and stared into the Nexus, stuck on that word uttered seconds ago. It haunted her in every plane of existence. It had loomed in the back of her mind ever since she took Azra-El's head. Now, it felt like a weapon against her.

Imposter!

Kassidy wanted to scream. A part of her wanted to cry. Normally, she felt safe in the Nexus. It was a source of comfort for her. Today, though, it was as comforting as the schoolyard bully she'd faced as a child. There was no peace today. No respite. Just a reminder of who she was. Not Krazy Kassie. Now, something worse.

Imposter!

CHAPTER TEN

AS HE TYPICALLY DID AFTER A HUNT, ALEX FROST ENTERED HIS BUILDING through the rear entrance, using the freight elevator that went to his apartment—and his apartment alone. The building was old but held its beauty well. Where others saw weathered red and brown brick and mortar, he saw . . . well, he saw the same, honestly. There was a simple, blue collar feel to it. This building was as much a part of the history of Chicago as the river, the museums, or Navy Pier. And it was in Lake View, right on Lake Shore Drive. People would kill for what he had.

In fact, that's how he got the place.

He opened the freight elevator and stepped into his apartment. Actually, it was more of a loft. Large, spacious, and with the vintage brick and mortar he was so fond of. He had a good blend of old and new here. The kitchen was modern, like showroom-on-Michigan-Avenue modern. The black juxtaposed against the stainless was a bit bougie, but whatever, he liked it. He dropped his things on the floor and made a beeline for the liquor cabinet. He gave himself a healthy pour of Johnny Walker Blue, closed his eyes, inhaled the sweet ambrosia, and took a sip.

His nirvana was interrupted by the sound of something hitting the floor.

"Holy shit! Dammit, Alex! You scared the shit out of me!"

He looked over to find his girlfriend coming out of the

bathroom. She'd dropped her makeup case upon seeing him.

"Next time I'll announce myself when I come home to my own place," he said with dismissive sarcasm. He knew that the whole startled act was less about him coming in quietly and more about her wanting to be gone before he got back. The look she gave to the two duffle bags by the door told the story.

"Heading somewhere?"

"Alex . . . I . . ."

She clearly wasn't prepared for this confrontation, and he wasn't in the mood. He'd had a busy few days hunting demonic undesirables. After exorcising a Wraith from a prostitute and watching the apparent Death God dispatch it with a sickle that was also somehow her hand, he was far too tired, physically, and mentally. So there was going to be no confrontation with her.

"Laura, don't bother," he said. "Seems clear what your intentions are. You done in my bathroom? I could use a shower."

He sipped more Scotch, then wiped blood off his eyelid. The wound on his head was dripping a bit. Occupational hazard.

"Oh my god, Alex! What happened?"

"Went a round or two with some demons and a possessed prostitute downtown."

"Did you kill her?"

"Thankfully, no. Fought a bit, but I was able to subdue her, then exorcise the thing in her. The honor of dispatching the evil fuck went to someone else."

"Someone else? You have a partner now?"

"Nope."

He saw Laura contemplate how far down the rabbit hole to go. His clear apathy steered her in another direction.

"So, she'll be okay?"

"She'll have a bit of a hangover and little memory of what's happened. But yeah, she'll be all right. As all right as a hooker in downtown Chicago can be."

There was genuine relief in Laura's posture. She knew what he did. They'd been together nine months, so he'd felt compelled to tell her. He could have lied, but what good came from that? It just added undue stress, and his life was stressful enough. Besides, he honestly thought she'd be the one. The one he'd been searching for, who would scare his own inner demons away and make him feel . . . safe.

"I'm glad you're okay, Alex. I'm glad you were able to help her."

Alex just stared at her. The tension between them had been high lately. Some of it was his fault, he knew that. His fault for not being open about his feelings, for letting things fester, for letting his resentment grow.

"So, you're leaving?" he asked, wanting to move this along.

"Alex . . ."

"Don't bother telling me that leaving me is hard, Laura. It's not."

"How can you say that?"

"How? That's an interesting question. Let's think about that shall we? How long have we been together?"

"Almost a year," she said.

"Nine months, but who's counting," he replied.

Laura crossed her arms and gave him that look she got when she knew he was hurt. A look of guilt and shame on a bed of righteous indignation.

"So here comes the part where you tell me all the things I did wrong, right? What about you, Alex? You're never here for me . . . for us. Yes, I'm leaving. But you left me first by choosing this calling over everything that we had."

"That's how you want to play this?" he asked. "We've been together nine months, and you've been cheating on me for eight of them. So, it's hard to say I left you, Laura, when you were never really fucking here."

The silence was deafening. He was thankful that she didn't deny it. Even more thankful that she'd stopped trying to defend herself. Alex wasn't looking to be right. He wasn't looking to throw all the problems of their relationship on her lap. He simply wanted to speak his mind, finally, and be done with things. He didn't need the hassle, and he was tired of loving someone that didn't even respect him, much less love him.

"There's nothing I can say to . . ."

"No, you're right. There's absolutely nothing you can say, Laura."

He downed the last of his Scotch, took off his shirt, and flung it toward the mass of junk he'd dropped on the floor when he came in.

"My god," she gasped.

He followed her eyes to his chest. The cuts and slashes were plentiful. They'd heal, but that didn't lessen the pain he felt.

"Can I, um, help you get cleaned up? You look like you could use some stitches."

Alex recognized this as a loose attempt at apologizing. She'd done it before. Hell, he'd done it before. Trying to ease the bitter tension with something sweet, without actually saying, "I'm sorry." He didn't need it. He didn't want it. Right now, he just wanted to be alone.

"No, I'll be fine."

"Alex . . ."

"I'm going to take a shower, Laura. Please don't be here when I get out."

He walked into the bathroom, closed the door, and leaned on the sink, staring at the guy in the mirror. He remembered when he was younger and a little more hopeful. He remembered being idealistic, scared, and excited. About everything. He remembered when he didn't come home with cuts or bruises. That seemed like a lifetime ago. And it was. Several, in fact. After today, he was feeling every bit of his age.

He heard the door close outside the bathroom, then turned on the shower.

"Amnesium," he whispered as he projected energy toward the departing Laura. Alex Frost was not a wizard, witch, warlock, or sorcerer, but his nature was rooted in something magical, preternatural, and otherworldly. Because of that, he was predisposed to some level of magic manipulation. It was slight, though—simple illusions, simple spells, like the one he'd just cast to cause Laura to forget about his occupation. She may have been a lying, manipulative, cheating bitch, but even she didn't deserve to carry the burden of his life. The knowledge of the existence of demons, werewolves, vampires, wizards, and every other supposedly fictional weird thing was definitely a burden.

Also, he still loved her.

He stepped in the shower and let the hot water cascade over his tired body. Holding his head under the spray, he watched the blood trickle down his legs, between his toes, and down the drain. He felt the cuts and slashes on his chest and torso close. The cut on his forehead healed, and he felt some of the energy he'd expended fighting the demon-possessed Jessi return. The water was a magical byproduct of the apartment he'd inherited after the death of its architect.

The water that flowed through the pipes had healing properties. The entire space was warded against intrusion, supernatural and otherwise. It also didn't hurt that he didn't have to pay rent.

The other units in the building were just normal Chicago apartments. Expensive apartments—it was the north side of the city, after all. But his was special, and he liked that.

Alex stepped out of the shower, dried off, and walked to his bedroom. He wanted sweats, a t-shirt, and some time on the couch with another glass of Scotch. As he walked to the kitchen, there was knock at his door.

Laura?

Knock-knock.

Okay, they'd leave after not getting a response this time. Right?

Knock-knock.

Dammit!

Alex stalked to the door and flung it open.

"Alex . . ." said Jaxon Burke before falling to the ground.

CHAPTER ELEVEN

"WHERE IS HE NOW?" ASKED THE DIVA.

"Burke's whereabouts are currently unknown," said Jacen.

"You've checked his apartment?"

"I have not. I don't actually work for you, so I'm not out there going full bloodhound."

The Diva sat calmly in a recliner, drink in hand, as she stared at the Advocate and absorbed his words. She had a reputation for being unforgiving when she received bad news. Most people never got the opportunity to disappoint her twice. It wasn't so much that the Diva was cruel or even vengeful. She was simply someone who liked things to go her way. The fact that things had not gone her way in the past was precisely why she was trying to hold the world by the balls now. She wanted obedience, she wanted results, and she wanted them when she wanted them. Not when fate found time to allow it.

She pondered the consequences of Jaxon Burke's disappearance. This wasn't the end of the world. That was hopefully coming later. But without eyes on him, the door was open for things to unravel a bit. A loose thread here and there was certainly manageable. Multiple loose threads were concerning. After all this time, the last thing she needed was an unraveling of everything she'd worked so hard to create.

"Do we think he knows anything?" the Diva asked.

"No, I highly doubt that. There's no evidence that any parts of his memory have returned."

"But we're not sure, because we don't know where he is."

"You're not sure, because *you* don't know where he is," Jacen corrected.

The Diva wasn't sure how she felt about the pushback. When she first met the Advocate, she had to convince him to help her. He'd been hesitant, but the fact that he was willing to contemplate anything at all was a victory in her eyes. Once he'd returned from his "walkabout" through time, though, he was fully on board with her vision—despite what it might cost him in the eyes of the Advocate council.

But that was twenty years ago.

A great deal had changed since then. Things most assuredly had taken a turn around the circumstances of Kassidy's ascension. The Diva was left wondering if Jacen Lucas was still on her side, or if he'd ever been on her side at all.

The Diva took a sip of her drink. She had been a wine drinker throughout life, as most gods were, but in recent years had taken to drinking harder liquors. Being locked away for centuries caused her to miss out on the advances of alcohol over the years. She had come to appreciate many things, but for some reason settled now on brandy. She found that she liked the taste and was pleased to find that some things in this world had been done right in her absence. Brandy was never far away now, and it matched this modern version of her well—this new self that was more professional and refined, but also more calculated and deadly.

Most people remembered her as a god who relished in mischief. She was a trickster. Not evil, but one that certainly did not care if her machinations affected people. She'd gone by many names before. Now, she was what modern man called a sociopath. The Diva was, to some, an enigma. She was respected by few, feared by most, and loyal to no one—save herself.

"Cartwright and his man are responsible for this?" the Diva asked.

"It would seem so. Their fear of Burke's knowledge may have caused them to move in a direction we'd not anticipated."

"Idiots!" the Diva exclaimed.

"Then there's the Wraith," said Jacen.

"Those fucking creatures! Had Thanatos paid more attention to what Azra-El was doing, we wouldn't have to deal with them now."

"They certainly came in handy when it came to imprisoning Thanatos," said Jacen.

"Three of them came in handy. And look at them now," said the Diva.

"In any event, this Wraith is a bit of a wild card. It seems Kassidy is hell bent on destroying them all, but this one may prove to be a challenge. Especially if he finds some way to use or align with Burke."

"Then we need to make sure that doesn't happen," said the Diva.

"I'd be happy to—"

"Oh, now you want to help?" asked the Diva with bite. "I will speak to him myself."

"As you wish," said Jacen. "What would you like to do about Burke?"

The Diva took a sip of her brandy and thought about it. Jaxon was out there somewhere, confused and possibly angry. He'd likely go after the group that tried to have him killed. If she could handle this rogue Wraith, they could simply keep an eye on Cartwright and his team, then wait for Burke to strike.

"Cartwright is the key," said the Diva. "Once Burke is back up and running, he'll go gunning for him, and we can follow from there."

Jacen nodded.

"Then we'll need to get him connected with Kassidy. Any thoughts on that?"

"I think there's someone in Kassidy's inner circle that would be the ideal conduit for that meeting," said Jacen.

"Perfect."

The Diva took another sip of her drink as Jacen shimmered away. She was still concerned about his loyalties. There were hiccups in the current plan. Small ones, though. Certainly nothing that gave her pause about her greater goal. Still, it might be wise to lay the foundation for a few other pieces to come together just in case Jacen turned on her. If he hadn't already.

The Diva stood and walked to the window of her hotel suite. She looked out at the city and saw the lights, the life, the energy, the excitement . . . and ultimately, man's arrogance. She often wondered what people would do if they knew the truth about their lives and the world they lived in. If they truly knew, perhaps people like Charles Cartwright wouldn't do stupid things like try to kill immortal assassins. Specifically, immortal assassins that were important to her goals.

The Diva contemplated killing Cartwright. But first, something had to be done about the Wraith. Maybe she could manipulate things to put them on a collision course. Cartwright's death would certainly step things up in the mortal world. Tensions were already high. His death could tip the scales further. More strife equaled more war, or at least the threat of more war. And that was the perfect playground for Jaxon Burke.

A smile flickered across the Diva's face as she contemplated the act. She saw her reflection in the window and found delight in the chaos.

"To the good old days," said the Diva as she held out her glass to the city and her reflection. As she did so, her blue eyes flashed. Down on the streets below, a car swerved and flew off the State Street Bridge into the river, taking three pedestrians with it. By the time she had finished her drink, the Diva heard the sweet orchestral sound of sirens, screams, and calamity.

"My kind of town," said the Diva.

CHAPTER TWELVE

"HOLY SHIT! WHAT THE FUCK HAPPENED TO YOU?"

"Mind if I come in?" asked Jaxon.

There were few people in the world that Jaxon thought of as friends. Fewer still that he'd feel comfortable showing up to their front door practically naked. Alex Frost was one of those people. When they'd first met, Alex was a soldier. Jaxon worked as a medic, a futile attempt to quell his seemingly innate thirst for war. Alex had been laid in front of him with a deep gash in his abdomen. Uncertain if he could fix it, Jaxon entertained Alex with stories of his European travels and the lavish parties he'd attended over the years. Such stories kept people engaged, especially the young, like Alex was at the time. Jaxon worked tirelessly to repair the damage that had been done to the young soldier, but with the limited medical knowledge of the time, there was little he could do besides clean and close the bayonet wound. The war was taking its toll, and General Washington had requested each medic do their best to save every wounded soldier.

Jaxon leaned on Alex, who led him to a spare bedroom. His limbs were still weak, and there was a burn within. It felt as if something had been ripped from him, violently. It was like an open wound, exposed and sensitive to everything. He sat on the edge of the bed, his head swimming with the question, "What the fuck just happened?" Sure, he'd been lit up, literally. Likely a clean-up effort by the folks that hired him for his last job. But that guy, that thing, that . . . creature, that was some next level shit that he couldn't quite comprehend.

"Here you go, brother," said Alex, handing Jaxon some clothing.

Jaxon took the clothes—a pair of blue jeans, a plain white t-shirt, and a gray hoodie. He stared at them absently, as if the concept of clothing was foreign. Ultimately though, everything about the day was foreign. For centuries, life, death, and rebirth, had been as typical as the sunrise. It wasn't as if death and rebirth happened often. He'd gone a century since his last death. He'd come close over the years, multiple times, but in the end they'd turned out to be only wounds that he could heal from. Still, aside from the manner of death, everything happened as it should have.

Everything but that thing, that . . . creature.

"I'm gonna make some coffee," Alex said. "You grab a shower, get dressed, and come out when you're ready. I'll heat up some food, too."

Jaxon heard the words and nodded instinctively. Seconds later he heard the click of the door, followed by the whispers. The loud, deafening whispers. Whispers, shouts, and screams. Horrific, agonizing screams. He covered his ears and rocked back and forth.

He'd come back wrong.

CHAPTER THIRTEEN

KASSIDY HAD ALWAYS BEEN A STRONG RUNNER. WHEN SHE WAS A CHILD, she often wondered if one or both of her birth parents had been athletes. Maybe that was why they'd given her up. Maybe her mom was on track to become a professional runner or an Olympic star when she got pregnant, and she wasn't ready for the responsibility. Maybe her dad was a top prospect, and his own parents forced him to choose career over starting a family. Dozens of scenarios like that ran through her head to try and justify why she'd been abandoned. Turns out she was a great athlete because she was born a demi-god whose father kidnapped her mother in retaliation for her aunt orchestrating the death of her older half-brother who was also in love with her mother.

As she put it, "My fucking life is an ancient Jerry Springer episode."

Some of those thoughts passed through her mind now as she chased a Wraith-possessed lawyer down the streets of downtown Chicago. She desperately wanted to teleport herself directly in his path, but there were far too many onlookers, even at ten o'clock on a Tuesday night. These possessors were becoming a thorn in her side. Thankfully, there were only a couple Wraiths left. With any luck, they'd be a little easier to deal with.

Her mind was unfocused. The shit that had gone down in the Nexus had her unnerved. She'd hoped tracking this rogue would be a good distraction. Plus, she desperately felt like she needed a win. When one of her Reapers reported this Wraith, she'd jumped on the chance to dispatch.

Kassidy followed the Wraith down State Street then up Lake Street where it barreled through people to cause further distraction. Kassidy had no time to check on them. Quick glances said they'd be okay as she leapt through an emotional wall of annoyance and confusion.

The Wraith hurried through the doors leading to the El train platform below the Thompson Center. Kassidy had had enough. She stepped into a darkened alcove and dematerialized into vapor. Her powers were upgraded now, but every once in a while, it was nice to call upon some old school tricks. Since the Wraith had possessed a human, the only true power it had was augmented speed and strength. It could not form weapons or vaporize to travel. Kassidy used that to her advantage, entering the station through a series of cracks and crevices only to reappear directly in front of her quarry on the platform below.

"Hey, sailor. How ya doin'?"

The Wraith stopped in its tracks, onyx-black eyes staring at Kassidy. It gave a sheepish grin, attempting to hide its concern.

"Well, if it isn't the slayer," said the Wraith.

"Is that what they're calling me? The slayer? Very Buffy-esque, wouldn't you say? There's gotta be a copyright on that. I mean, you would know, being that you've hijacked a lawyer's body and all."

"What, this old thing," said the Wraith with a casual wave. "Just a little something I picked up while shopping at Saks."

"Nice. Well, I'm going to need you to return it, or—"

"Or what? You'll kill me? Sugar buns, I'm already dead."

Sugar buns? This mother—

"Besides, the only way you can take *me* is to kill *him*. You've got no half-assed magician-slash-exorcist by your side this time. Oh, by the way, that girl you 'rescued'? Yeah, they found her this morning dead in an alleyway with a needle in her arm. So, you know, nice work."

Kassidy bristled. Jessi Trager was troubled, to be sure, but that didn't make her death less tragic. She wondered how much of what had happened with the Wraith had affected her. And what about the exorcism? Alex said it took a toll on the mind and body, especially for those that were already compromised. If she had killed Azra-El all those years ago, would Jessi be alive now? If she'd given in and let Azra-El go about his plan, the Wraiths would not have scattered. They wouldn't have possessed humans. They wouldn't—

"What's the matter, slayer? Realizing that maybe you're not cut out for this job? You're a poser, Kassidy Simmons. You've always been one. Nothing but a scared little girl playing dress-up and meddling in things you have no mind or talent for."

Imposter!

The word rang in Kassidy's head again. Was she? An imposter? Was she just an inadequate stand-in waiting for the real god of death to step in and take the reins? Since her ascension, almost nothing had gone right. Sure, she'd dispatched a few Wraiths, but in hindsight, that had taken a toll. Damage had been done. Humans had died because she was too late to save them. And now, Jessi—it was all just so much to accept.

Imposter!

"Are you . . . crying?" asked the Wraith.

Kassidy did feel tears welling in the corners of her eyes. She tried to focus through the confusion and the pain. She needed to get her shit together. If she could just concentrate . . .

The low rumble and high-pitched squeal of breaks signaled that a train was coming soon. Kassidy's concentration was broken just that easily. Letting her anger get the best of her, she summoned the Scythe of Cronus. Since securing the weapon, she'd learned that she could keep it in another plane of existence, not unlike the Nexus, the Beyond, or the Void. There it would stay until called upon. As it appeared in her hand, she felt a surge of energy. She didn't want to lose another life, but she saw no other way. She needed to sacrifice one life to save many.

"Ah, yes, the quick go-to. Guess you don't care about human life after all. You know, you're probably more like us than you care to admit," said the Wraith.

"I am nothing like you, you son of bitch."

As the Blue Line train approached, Kassidy stretched out her hand, allowing the power of the Scythe to flow through her. She didn't know what she was doing, but it felt natural, instinctive. The Wraith began to separate from the lawyer's body.

But not enough, and not in time.

The lawyer, still partially controlled by the Wraith, leapt in front of the oncoming train. As body and metal made contact, the Wraith skipped free, and floated in front of Kassidy.

"Damn you!" she screamed.

The Wraith laughed. It was deep and mocking. Crimson saliva dripped from its decayed mouth as laughter echoed through the station. Kassidy's red-hot anger raced through her body. Her eyes transitioned to an unearthly metallic blue. Her outstretched hand commanded the Wraith to come to her, and despite its protests, the shapeless entity moved closer. Stretching out further with her power, Kassidy forced the Wraith to take its human form. When it did, what she saw before her was a middle-aged, balding man with light facial hair and a scar that ran the length of his cheek. He looked just as he had in all the history books. Once the king of Chicago, the Boss, and now, about to bow down for his last trial. The irony of him having taken over the body of a lawyer was palpable.

"You can take me out, sweet cheeks, but I'm still gonna live forever in this town."

Kassidy plunged her hand into his chest, grabbed his life force, and retracted. She looked from him to the orb and back, disgusted. She dropped the orb to the ground and swung the Scythe down. The orb exploded in a rainbow of colors, and the Wraith quickly turned to ash that blew away with the soft rush of air in the subway.

As the ashes took flight, Kassidy heard the word *imposter* carried on the wind. She felt the sting of the word, and it brought her to her knees. As the few onlookers began to gather, she quickly shifted to the Nexus. She couldn't save the lawyer, but she could at least escort his soul.

Maybe that's all she should be doing.

All she was ever good at.

All she'd ever be good at.

CHAPTER FOURTEEN

"SO, THERE'S THIS MEDALLION, RIGHT? IT'S LIKE A MAGICAL PENDANT. SO, whoever possesses the thing, they can read minds. Then, well, this guy . . . not sure of his name yet, but this guy and his family, they're on vacation, and he finds it and he learns what it can do. But here's the thing—he's a presidential candidate. So, he starts using it to read minds to find out what people want so he can win the election. Then things just go really wrong from there. So . . . what do you think, K-man?"

Keiron stared at the young orderly, amazed that all of that had come out in a single breath. Sam was his name, Sam Winfield. Keiron was equally amazed that he kind of liked the premise of his story. While his bookstore wasn't internationally known, it was popular among the local crowd, particularly with young writers, poets, and lovers of certain genres. It was tied into a lot of writers' groups and clubs, and Keiron had close relationships with agents and publishers, indie and otherwise. Those in and around the writing community, for some reason, saw him as an excellent resource and, consequently, pitched ideas almost daily in the hopes that maybe, just maybe, he'd pass on some information that might help someone get recognized.

So this pitch was just a typical day.

"You know what, that's not all that bad. I'd be interested in seeing where that goes," Keiron said.

"Yeah? Really?" Sam asked.

"Seriously."

"Dude, thank you," Sam replied. "I figure, it's like, you know, a combination of that movie with Mel Gibson and that chick from the tornado movie where he could read chicks' minds . . . and, like, *The Manchurian Candidate.*"

Keiron let the two movies swirl around in his head for a minute and was able to see where Sam was going. He was tempted to ask if he meant the original *Manchurian Candidate* or the reboot. But, given Sam's age, Keiron answered his own question.

"Let me know when it's ready," he said. "I'd love to read it."

"I will. I definitely will."

Sam laughed out loud and gave Keiron a playful punch in the arm. It was lame, it was geeky, it was old, but it was totally him. Sam was a good kid. He was in his early twenties and naturally smart but socially awkward. He looked a lot like Luke Skywalker. Not older, wiser Luke, but a younger, eager, goofy, and energetic Luke from the original movie. He was, without question, a young man looking for his destiny but stuck working on a moisture farm. Only, Sam's moisture farm was the Morningstar Skilled Nursing Facility.

"You here to see Bobo?" Sam asked.

"Yeah, is he in his room or the lounge?"

"I think I saw him in the lounge. It's raining today, so he's sitting by the window."

"Okay, thanks, Sam. I'll catch up with you later. Get on that story," Keiron said, breaking away to head up the stairs to the third floor.

Morningstar was one of the nicer skilled nursing facilities in the city. There were so many facilities that seemed to be drowned in the stench of death, bleach, and urine with a side order of band aid adhesive and an intermittent blast of some generic lemon-scented something or other, making the overall atmosphere even more dreadful. Keiron imagined that Reapers hung out in the lobby like it was their own private social club. He wished he could see them the way Kassidy did. Well, sometimes.

Morningstar, on the other hand, smelled clean. As if every day was a spring-cleaning day. There were pockets of clinical scents, but they were not rampant or intrusive. The walls were clean, and it helped that the place wasn't monochromatic. It was almost pleasant to visit. Not enough to make a habit, but at least, if he did, it wouldn't feel so terribly gloomy and depressing.

He arrived at the third floor and moved quickly to the recreation room, or the lounge as the residents called it. Looking around, he saw all manner of activity. Some residents were playing cards, others were working out a ferocious game of dominoes. And others simply bided their time watching Judge Someone-or-Other on the mounted flatscreen. It probably didn't much matter to them though. Their focus was escape not intellectual stimulation. Keiron looked around further and found the person he'd been seeking sitting in a familiar spot. Tucked away in the corner, sitting in a beat-up leather recliner facing the window, was Bobo.

Bobo was a quiet, unassuming man. The staff didn't know much about him. He'd been dropped off from a local hospital after they'd determined there was nothing more they could do for him. Sam said that based on his belongings, they'd figured he was a veteran, a family man, and likely, hard-working. Keiron wasn't sure how they figured that last part. It was probably just a way to further romanticize the man's tragic story.

Another interesting thing about Bobo was that he never spoke.

Not so much as a nod or a shake of the head. He'd smile on occasion, but not in relation to anything happening around him. Whatever was going on in his head amused him at times. The orderlies had no trouble directing him throughout Morningstar. He never put up a fight and was certainly not a behavioral threat.

They didn't know what Keiron knew, though.

He pulled up a chair and sat next to Bobo. Keiron was immediately met with the familiar scent of worn leather, Irish Spring, and St. Ives lotion. The leather of Bobo's recliner was not unlike the man himself. Despite its age, the chair was soft and smooth with patches here and there but none so obtrusive as to tarnish its comfort and beauty. There was a small end table against the wall holding a thirteen-inch television. Bobo mostly looked outside, but occasionally he would look down at the television. Keiron reached down for the remote control on the table and handed it to Bobo. He kept staring out the window until he felt the touch of the device on his arm. Slowly, he looked down at it, reached for it, then looked up. There was a flicker of awareness in his eyes. It was faint, brief, but awareness, nonetheless. Bobo turned away slowly and powered the television to life. An episode of *The Rifleman* filled the screen.

"It's good to see you, Bobo," Keiron said. He knew there'd be no reply, but it didn't hurt to be polite. Also, it was genuinely good to see him. Keiron had few ties to the old world. At least few that were public like this. Most of his associations occurred behind closed doors or in the darkness of night. Visiting Bobo felt . . . normal.

Even if the reason for visiting was anything but.

"Some things have changed since I was last here," Keiron said. "We now have a Mistress of Death. Thanatos is . . . missing. His daughter has ascended. She's working to reset some things resulting from Azra-El's tenure. It's taking a toll, but she's managing. At least, I think she is. And now, my old friend, there's talk of The Four. I . . . we . . . need some guidance. Can you offer anything?"

Strangely, Bobo dropped the remote control. Keiron bent down to retrieve it, and as he did, heard the faint sound of cracked glass. Looking toward the television, he saw glass on the floor, then a broken windowpane.

"What the hell?" he said as he sat upright. "That's pecu—"

Keiron stopped mid-sentence after turning toward Bobo to hand him the remote control, only to see him slumped over in the recliner with a splash of crimson on his sweatshirt. There was a hole in his chest.

"Bobo!" he screamed. Pulling him down to the floor out of sight of the window Keiron scrambled to find something to stop the bleeding. Bobo's eyes were open, but they seemed vacant, even more so than usual.

"Can you hear me? Bobo?"

Staff scrambled behind Keiron. They asked questions, but he tuned them out, too focused on Bobo, on bringing him back from wherever he was. He kept calling his name while using his hands to put pressure on the chest wound to stifle the bleeding.

Then, out of nowhere, Bobo grabbed his arm and stared directly at him, his eyes completely white.

"*Death will change, and War will grow, his power veil soon shall cease. And when the sick and starving seek their vengeance, the Horsemen will be unleashed.*"

The voice was otherworldly. As if someone were speaking through him. This was the way of all Oracles. Bobo's eyes closed. His grip loosened, and his hand slowly slid down, falling to the ground. He was gone.

In the background, Lucas McCain carried on a conversation with Marshal Torrance.

CHAPTER FIFTEEN

ON THE OUTSIDE, CHARLES APPEARED CALM. HE WAS THE EPITOME OF poise. But on the inside, he was like an active volcano. His heart and mind were racing. The more he thought about what he'd seen earlier in the day, the more his anxiety rose.

"An immortal," he whispered to himself.

He had never been the type of child to fantasize, or play make believe with other kids. He didn't stand in line for hours on end for comic books, comic conventions, or blockbuster movies. With his family's wealth, he didn't have to, but more importantly, he had no interest. He cared about the things his father taught him to care about, the things that were important to his image and to the family legacy.

But he had found *him*.

At least, he thought he had.

As he sat in a rented office in a downtown Chicago high-rise, Charles thought back to the video he'd watched repeatedly hours earlier—the video of Jaxon Burke's demise. It was every bit as horrific as he'd imagined it to be. For some reason though, Charles could not look away. In the end, he was glad he hadn't.

He wasn't sure what had compelled him, but he kept watching the recording through the discomfort he felt at a man burning alive. He'd been tempted to turn the video off after Burke had stopped moving, but a shadow caught his eye. Seconds later, he saw a tall, sinister man appear and sit staring at the pile of char that was Jaxon Burke. The macabre scene continued as the man smoked a cigar. The morbid absurdity of it all was too fascinating to turn away from. Charles fast-forwarded through several hours of the nonsense—then there was movement.

First, the stranger stood, looking around, as if he'd heard something. Then there was movement in the space he'd been staring at. Jaxon Burke's body was reanimating.

"Son of a bitch," he'd murmured in disbelief.

Charles had no way of knowing if Burke was the soldier he'd seen as a boy, but the parallels were unmistakable. Could there be others? Could this man hold the secret to immortality? Could the man he'd ordered to be killed hold the key to everything he'd been searching for since childhood?

All of that ran through his mind as he waited for the Diva to arrive.

She'd sent for him, desperate to speak about the current state of world affairs. He indulged her because of her money, and because of his attraction to her. She was likely using her sexuality to manipulate him. But he didn't care. He'd just as soon take her money and carry out her plan as he would bend her over the desk. The way he saw it, he'd either end up inside of the White House, or inside of her. It was a win-win scenario.

The office had a waiting area, and there was a man, a gatekeeper of sorts, sitting at a desk. That man had let Charles inside to wait for the Diva and offered him a drink. In her defense, Charles was early. Normally he'd arrive right on time or a little late in an effort to assert himself as the "alpha" in the room. But his nervous energy needed an outlet, so he'd arrived early, hoping to end the meeting early too, so he could get back and figure out his next steps with Burke.

Charles heard the outer door of the waiting room open. *Finally!* He stood when he heard the office door open. He might be a lecherous, power-hungry pig, but he had some manners stashed deep in his blackened heart.

"I don't think you followed the rules the way you were supposed to, Mr. Cartwright," said a voice from behind him.

Charles turned to the voice and almost dropped the glass of whiskey he'd been holding. "Who the hell are you?"

"I am an associate of the Diva. I was sent here to remind you of the deal you both made and inquire as to why you've altered it."

"How dare you!" Charles said. "Everything I've done has been for her."

"Including killing Mr. Burke?"

"Who the fuck are you?" demanded Cartwright.

"My name is not important, as it's unlikely you'll ever see me again. But if such formalities please you, you may call me Jacen."

Charles stood motionless, staring at the strange man. He was unassuming in a tailor-made three-piece suit, well groomed, with the air of a proper gentleman. Charles had a way of filling a space. He entered every situation as if he were the smartest person in the room. His demeanor made others shrink down, and, when that happened, he assumed total control. The man standing before him now, this so-called Jacen, did not shrink down. The man's confidence commanded attention. In that, there was true power.

And that display of power made Charles uncomfortable.

"I don't know who you think you are, sir, but I answer to the Diva and the Diva alone. Now, if you'll excuse me, I have other business," Charles said.

Charles turned to leave, only to find that he could not move.

"I beg to differ," said Jacen. "Your business right now is with me. You were instructed to neutralize two key figures, which you did, and we thank you for that. Then, you altered the deal by going after Jaxon Burke, setting in motion a series of events that have jeopardized additional plans the Diva has in place."

Charles wondered how they knew about Burke, and further, why they cared. Those questions were supplanted by the returned realization that he could not move. It was as if some force had a solid grip on him.

"So, what's the problem?" asked Charles. "What do you care about a hired gun? If he's dead, then none of this can come back on any of us. I did us a favor, you son of bitch."

Charles tried to act as if nothing were wrong, but confusion and fear shot through him like a spark of electricity.

"The problem, Mr. Cartwright, is as I've already stated. Your actions have now caused the Diva to shift her plans. Thanks to you, we have a new player on the field, and it's making things complicated."

Charles could feel his anger come to the forefront. He hated being talked down to. He hated being told what to do. His anger was beginning to turn to rage, settling somewhere just below possible volcanic eruption.

"So, what is it that you plan to do? Beat me up a little, then go run back to mommy and tell her how you've spanked me to teach me a lesson?"

"My plan is to tell you to back off and follow your orders," said Jacen.

"Really?"

"Yes, really."

"And if I don't?" asked Charles.

"If you don't, the immobility you're experiencing right now will seem like a parlor trick compared to what the Diva will do."

Is he doing this?

Charles ran through a dozen scenarios in his head about how this was possible. He'd assumed it was some strange new tech. Maybe something the Diva was involved in. Some secret project. But something that powerful would have hit the rumor mill. Certainly, his Washington contacts would have told him. No, this was something else entirely. If a man could come back from the dead, then maybe a man could do . . . this?

"Your little trick doesn't scare me. Do you know who I am? You'd be wise to release me now before I call this whole fucking thing off and send the Feds after you both."

"I'd advise against that," said Jacen calmly.

Charles felt the grip on his body ease. Once able to move, he immediately walked up to Jacen. He said nothing, only stared. In those seconds, though, he saw his own death. He saw that he was dealing with forces he was ill prepared for. In the eyes of the man across from him, there was nothing. No concern. No fear. No doubt or hesitation. In Jacen's eyes, Charles saw someone unconcerned with the petty emotion of pride. Standing down, Charles took two steps back, turned, and headed for the door.

"Please offer my apologies to the Diva. I will proceed as we've agreed."

"She'll be thrilled to hear that, Mr. Cartwright. Thank you."

Charles Cartwright left the office with no intention of keeping his word.

CHAPTER SIXTEEN

A FEW HOURS PASSED BEFORE KASSIDY RETURNED FROM THE NEXUS. SHE hadn't fully understood her connection to the place, but there were some healing properties there. If for nothing else than her soul. The Nexus was a weighted blanket on a blustery winter day. It was the warmth and safety one normally sought out in a mother. It reminded her of those moments with Marlene after Kassidy would come home in tears when the kids teased her, calling her Krazy Kassie. Marlene would wrap her arms around Kassidy and hum a song. It was never the same song, and Kassidy never asked the names. Those moments were all about comfort, so it was enough to hear them, to feel Marlene's arms, and to return to some semblance of normalcy.

As normal as a girl with empathic powers could be.

She was grateful that she still felt some of that comfort despite the encounter with her doppelgänger the last time she was there. When she'd returned to the real world, she headed straight for the mini bar in the living room. The Simmons family was not one to shy away from libations, but they'd typically kept things in the kitchen. Wine was in an eight-bottle rack on the center island, and the hard liquor was kept in a cupboard above the refrigerator and pulled out only on special occasions.

Since she was having the house rebuilt, mostly as penance for having been a part of its damage during her battle with Senaya and some pretty boy Wraiths, Kassidy felt it was only fair that a mini bar be added. Could help with the resale value. At least it could offer personal comforts during the reconstruction.

She poured Blanton's into a rocks glass. She normally saved it for special events since it was so hard to get, but today it was calling her. Kassidy sipped as she walked upstairs. The Simmons home was modest. A two-story house with a detached two-car garage, a decent basement, and three bedrooms, it comfortably fit a family of four. Since she was staying there alone, she'd taken over the master bedroom. She didn't feel the ghosts of Dan and Marlene. Maybe it was because she knew where their spirits actually were. She also wasn't bombarded with memories of the past that kept her from walking into the space. Her sister, Sarah, couldn't say the same. But Sarah was mortal, not the Death God, and she just didn't see and feel things the same way Kassidy did.

Kassidy stripped off her clothes and headed straight for the bathroom. Taking her drink with her, she took a sip, then stared at her reflection for a long while as she leaned on the vanity. She blinked, and when she reopened her eyes, they were a majestic metallic blue—the color of the gods.

Imposter!

She heard the word in her head, and the color faded slightly. She ground her teeth, clenched her fists, and willed her power to manifest. The vanity and the mirror shook. Kassidy heard the pipes rattle, but she didn't care. She was determined to prove her power. To prove her worth. To prove she was no—

Imposter!

She shut her eyes hard. Not to stop the house from rattling, but to stop the tears from falling. God or not, she was still an empath, and she felt . . . everything. In a world where everyone called themselves empathic for simply having the heart to care, she was empathic because of her supernatural ability to feel. She didn't simply feel the emotions of others. Her own emotions were also amplified. Every loss, every broken heart, every bad joke at her expense resonated inside her tenfold.

So it was no wonder that a lost battle to an unknown Wraith had her at her wit's end.

Kassidy turned the shower on, waited a beat, and stepped into the hot stream. Leaning against the cool tile, she let the water cascade over her head and down the length of her body. On normal days, Kassidy showered to cleanse herself of the filth from a challenging day, and lately, that was the rule, not the exception. In other instances, her showers were attempts to wake herself up to face the day. Occasionally, though, there were times like today, where she did both—letting the shower carry away her tears.

"What the fuck am I doing?" she whispered.

Kassidy asked it of herself over and over. She scrubbed hard, as if hoping to discard the uncertainty of her life.

Scrub.

Rinse.

Repeat.

Imposter!

She finished, stepped out, and wrapped herself in a towel. Making a beeline to her drink, she sipped. Once. Twice. Three times. Then wiped the steamed mirror to stare at her reflection again. Her naturally brown eyes shone against the red and white matte resulting from an unprecedented crying session. When she heard the door open downstairs and sensed Traci, she ran her fingers through her hair, and patted down her wet skin with her towel.

"Babe?"

"Um . . . I'm up here," said Kassidy.

She heard Traci walk up the steps as she left the bathroom. Wrapping the towel around herself once again, she turned to see Traci walking in.

"Oh my," said Traci with a teasing lilt to her voice.

Kassidy giggled. It was forced. Somewhat. But she let it out.

"Hey, hon. How's your day been? I thought you were going to be out later?"

"Yeah, me too. But things went well right out of the gate, so we were able to wrap up early," said Traci.

Kassidy tried to hide her eyes as much as she could as Traci came up to kiss her. Diving in to avoid any questions, Kassidy felt the softness of Traci's lips and tried to let the failure of the day drift away. The kiss quickly turned from "hello" to "heeeey." And Kassidy felt Traci let go.

"I get the sense that maybe you missed me," Traci said lightly as she pulled away for a minute.

"Maybe."

Kassidy felt Traci's smile more than she saw it, and she went in for another kiss. This one was slower, deeper, and she let her towel fall to the floor. She pulled Traci closer. She knew sex wouldn't solve anything, but she needed to feel something, anything, other than what she had been feeling since leaving the Nexus.

She felt Traci's hand on her neck and shuddered a bit as it slid down and found her nipple. When Traci squeezed, a jolt of electricity shot through her body and settled between her legs. Traci lowered her head to take the erect nipple into her mouth, and the tingling continued. Kassidy attempted to let herself go because it felt good. Traci always felt good.

Traci's lips returned to Kassidy's mouth, and once again,

their bodies pressed against each other. This time, when Traci pulled away, the seductive grin quickly vanished, as a single tear betrayed Kassidy.

Traci said nothing.

They both stared into each other's eyes for what seemed like an eternity, then Traci led Kassidy to the bed, kicking off her shoes along the way. Kassidy followed, instinctively, feeling safer with every step. She *had* thought sex would help. She thought it would be the distraction her mind needed. In the past, that seemed to work. But times change. Kassidy had changed and was still changing. Sex was not what she needed, and she took comfort in the knowledge that Traci seemed to know that, too.

Once on the bed, she laid her head on Traci's chest. Traci stroked Kassidy's hair, and they held each other.

Traci said nothing.

Kassidy wept.

Rain began to fall outside.

CENTURIES AGO

With a final thrust, Ares released himself into her. He felt her shudder beneath him and her heart beat faster. In the past, when a woman climaxed, he felt it first in his ego, never his loins, and certainly never his heart. This woman was different. More so than any woman he'd known, she made him feel. With Aphrodite, it was simply lust and a general desire to cause discord among the Elder Gods. With other mortals, even those who'd given him children, it was momentary desire, often the residual effects of bloodlust after a battle. But with Octavia, something stirred in him. Something other than his cock.

Looking down on her, he was lost in her eyes. Perhaps he felt the kinship because there lived a similar pain . . . and shame. She was a skilled warrior, despite coming from privilege. Her abilities rivaled that of the fiercest Amazon. She said she'd learned from warriors here and there throughout her travels, but he knew better. He'd seen that fighting style before. She was quick and adaptable, but the basic tenets of Keiron's teachings were there. It pained him at times that she was not completely honest, but then, he had not been the most forthcoming when they'd met. Only tonight had she learned his true identity. Perhaps that's why their sex had been so much more intense.

They'd stopped in the small village after almost a full day of travel. They'd hoped to get a room with the local innkeeper, but he had nothing available. The innkeeper sent them to the home of a blacksmith, a man named Antolychus, who had a room in the space he worked, separate from his home. Antolychus was gracious and allowed them both to stay for no charge. Ares thought it strange, but Octavia convinced him to let it go. When she spoke, he listened. It wasn't supposed to be that way though. He was only supposed to use her to find Allesandra. Octavia was meant to be a means to an end. But she'd quickly become so much more.

"You are remarkable," said Ares, moving to lie by her side.

"For a mortal?" asked Octavia.

"For any breathing creature."

"Creature? Just what have you been up to?" she asked coyly.

Their shared laugh made him feel light. In the last few weeks with her, she'd been more an anchor to him than the pommel of his sword. He wondered what Athena would say if she knew her brother had found—

"What of Aphrodite?"

"What of her?" countered Ares.

"They say she is the most beautiful of all. They say one gaze from her and anyone, man or woman, god or mortal, is enchanted. They say . . . Ares is one of her lovers."

In the past, Ares was prone to lashing out at such questions, especially from a mortal. A mortal, any mortal, should feel lucky enough to have him. They should never think of things that did not concern them. If this were anyone else, he'd have her by the throat, not to kill her, but to show his brutal dominance.

Tonight, he simply smiled.

"She is beautiful, I cannot lie about that. But for her, sex is about power, and any admissions of love are deceptions, leverage used to get what she desires," said Ares.

"Did she desire you?"

"Yes."

"And you, her?"

"Yes."

"And now?"

Ares sat with that for a beat. But thousands of thoughts and feelings filled him. What *were* his feelings for Aphrodite? Had it been love? Lust? A desire to provoke a group that clearly hated him? His own father said that Ares was the most despised of all the gods, so perhaps his feelings for Aphrodite were a response to that pain and ridicule. A slap in the face to all because someone among them found him desirable.

"I don't know," he said.

He'd expected a pained look and perhaps some disgust at that answer. Instead, he got a kiss. It was slow, deep, filled with compassion and a hint of lust. And it quelled his anxiety.

Again.

Until the shouts began.

And the growls.

Ares and Octavia quickly donned their tunics and weapons and ran outside. The horror they saw stopped them in their tracks. There was chaos. Villagers ran, screaming, away from large creatures who attacked indiscriminately.

"What are those?" asked Octavia.

"Hellhounds," replied Ares.

"But . . . why? Why would they be here?"

"It's a message," began Ares, "from Thanatos to me."

"Are you feuding? Is this death and destruction the result of two gods angry at each other?"

"He's angry because I've not delivered on my end of a bargain we made. They're here to remind me of my mission. It's his way."

Ares looked to Octavia, then back at the vicious hounds stalking toward them. There were four in all, each the size of a horse. They were terrifying, red-eyed beasts with hard spiked ridges down their backbone. Razor sharp teeth protruded from dirt and blood-stained muzzles. Their large, clawed paws dug into the dirt . . . and any people that dared cross their path.

"What do we do?" asked Octavia.

"You redirect the people to safety. They're here for me. I'll lead them away."

Ares could almost feel a question forming in Octavia's mind. There was no time to sort through it. He wasn't prepared for her possible reaction to the truth either.

"Go!" he ordered.

"I love you," she said, as she moved quickly to help the villagers.

The words struck Ares in a way nothing ever had before. His feelings for her, his admiration, his affection, his . . . love, were overshadowed by his tremendous guilt. He needed to find a way to make this right without suffering the wrath of the Death God. To the side of the Hellhounds, Ares saw Antolychus, the man who hosted him and Octavia for the night. The man seemed unbothered by the beasts. He put a small flute to his lips and blew. As he did, the Hellhounds turned their heads to regard him, then he pointed toward Ares. The Hellhounds turned to the War God and lowered their haunches.

"Lord Thanatos tires of your games, Ares," said Antolychus.

Antolychus blew the flute again, and the Hellhounds sprang forward toward Ares. Confusion quickly morphed to anger. So, he did what came naturally when he was angry.

He charged and fought.

CHAPTER SEVENTEEN

JAXON WALKED INTO HIS BUILDING, HAVING RECOVERED ENOUGH TO FEEL anger flowing through him. That same anger kept him from feeling guilty about ghosting Alex. Frost was a good friend, but something was off about Jaxon's resurrection. With the way Alex responded to his story, Jaxon wasn't so certain his friend's home was the place to be.

The anger he felt was slightly quelled by a familiar scent in the air. He wasn't sure if it was related to his immortality or not, but for as long as he could remember, his senses had always been extraordinary, bordering on supernatural. Before the world became so technologically advanced, heightened senses had been a definite plus. Living in the old west, or Victorian England, or anywhere for that matter prior to the twentieth century was daunting. The perils were many, and emergency responders, such as they were, had been few. Enhanced sight, hearing, and smell were advantages, particularly for someone who'd made his living in war the way he did.

These days, he didn't rely on them as much. The world was more complex now, and there were so many competing smells, sights, and sounds, that he often felt overwhelmed. At times, it was difficult for him to discern the various elements assaulting his senses, and if he concentrated too much on them, it would affect his ability to focus on whatever his task or mission was.

There was a wonderfully comforting scent lingering in the air now, though. It was dissipating, but it was still there, just strong enough to hold his anger in check and keep him from going over the edge.

He stepped off the elevator onto his floor where the scent was stronger. Then he saw the source of the scent taming his growing beast.

"Oh my god, Jax! Where have been? Are you okay?"

Anna DeBartolo rushed at Jaxon and jumped into his arms as he cleared the elevator. He could feel her shaking. He could sense her nervousness, perhaps even a little fear. More than anything, though, he could feel her love, and that was exactly what he needed right now.

"Baby, are you all right?"

Jaxon felt bombarded with questions, but the caresses on his face and the look in her tear-filled eyes kept the anger he felt at bay. In fact, with the mix of emotion he was currently feeling, it was all he could do to not break down right there in front of her. He'd never been an overly emotional man, at least not as far as he knew. Perhaps in his other life he had been, but that was long ago. He didn't shy away from it, though, particularly in Anna's presence. With her, he felt a wave of peace. It flowed through him like no feeling he'd ever known. At least, no feeling he could fully remember. There was something familiar about how she soothed his fury, his bloodlust. He couldn't put his finger on it. Whatever it was, though, was irrelevant. What mattered was here and now. Anna DeBartolo was the light at the end of his dark, ominous tunnel.

Moving the hair out of her face, he kissed her forehead and said, "I'm fine. I'm all right."

"What happened?" she asked.

Part of him wanted to tell her everything. But a larger part of him stayed away from that. He'd not been entirely forthcoming with her to this point, so why on earth start now. He was frozen. He wanted to say so much. He wanted to continue to feel the good he felt in her presence. But his was a life of darkness and death. He couldn't burden her with that. He couldn't mar that beauty.

He loved her too much.

Instead of answering her, he cupped her face and kissed her. It certainly caught her off guard, but she seemed to roll with it. He kept kissing her, even as he backed her up toward the door to his apartment. Jaxon fumbled with the lock but managed to open the door without breaking the connection. They walked in, he closed the door with his foot, and pressed her body up against it.

To her credit, she didn't resist but he could sense some surprise and apprehension in his action. It wasn't as if he hadn't been this passionate and spontaneous before. He'd been much worse, and sometimes in public settings no less. Jaxon tried not to dwell and just went with things.

He raised her arms above her head and nuzzled her neck to breathe in more of her. He took one of her hands and guided it down to her chest making her cup her breast and squeeze.

"I can hear your heart racing," whispered Jaxon.

"You think?" she whispered back.

Jaxon looked deep into her eyes and saw a myriad of thoughts and emotions. Her body was betraying the confusion going on inside, and he listened to it. He was listening to his own urges, which weren't rooted so much in love and lust as they were in a desire to forget what had happened to him. He was lost. Confused. He wanted to die. But when he was with her, he wanted to live.

He bent down to kiss her lips again, and her mouth opened to accept him. Her lips were full and soft and tasted of strawberries. Her tongue moved in unison with his, and their kiss was deep and passionate. Jaxon's head swam. What he felt for her was genuine. It was real. A stark contrast to the death that he so desired, yet still so very real.

And familiar.

Anna replaced the hand on her breast with his and squeezed. With her free hand, she caressed the back of Jaxon's head, and drew him in for a deeper kiss. She shifted her legs and ground her pelvis into him.

Anna was exciting, intoxicating, and everything that was right in Jaxon's world. With her body against his, when they held hands, when she was just present, there were no snipers, no threats to anyone's existence, no contracts to take lives. There was only her—the heat of her breath, the taste of her lips, the beat of her heart and the feel of her body responding to him.

Her lips moved to his neck as her hands found the button and zipper to his jeans. She skillfully moved past each barrier and reached inside, grabbed him, then slowly, firmly began to stroke.

He could feel her heart rate increase. It was almost in tune with his own. Her breathing, like his, had increased. Their desire for each other was apparent in every touch and moan. The bloody thoughts of his past and present dimmed, and Jaxon allowed himself to live in the moment.

Jaxon struggled with the button on her jeans but eventually won the battle. In seconds he had her pants and panties down to her knees and he spun her around to face the door. Reaching down, he slid his hand between her legs to feel the warm, moist folds of her sex. Jaxon bent her over slightly and she braced herself against the door as he replaced his hand with the head of his cock and slowly slid inside her. She gasped, a sound met with a moan of his own. Anna backed up against him and they moved together, rhythmically, but furiously as lust and passion washed over them.

◆ ◆ ◆

Anna's head was on Jaxon's chest, one leg draped across his, and he'd never felt more comfortable.

Or had he?

The feeling of love like this was so familiar.

He just couldn't place it.

The previously clear night had clouded over, and a light rain was falling. He'd always loved the sound of rain. When the rain escalated, though, when thunder and lightning came, Jaxon felt uneasy. It wasn't fear. It was apprehension. His body was reflexively tense as he steadied himself for pain, guilt, and shame. And it wasn't that his feelings were projecting outward; no, when the thunder and lightning came, he felt that those feelings and that judgment was being directed at him. It was as if the storm spoke as proxy for someone who loathed him. After every storm, he felt inadequate. Then he felt angry. Then his bloodlust would arise because violence was the only satisfactory outlet he'd known for seven hundred years.

Anna was just what he needed. She was everything he needed. She soothed his anger and helped keep the bloodlust at bay.

"Thank you," said Jaxon.

"For what?"

"For making my world a little better today."

"Jax," she began quietly, "what is going on?"

"After the night we've just had, I'm not sure it's all that

important. It's so nice to just let the world pass us by for a while."

"So, we're just gonna stay in bed all night?" she asked.

"Shit, maybe all day, too."

"Well, hell, let's go for a week."

"Forever works, too," said Jaxon.

"That's a long time," she replied. "Who's gonna pay the bills?"

"No worries," he began. "I've got that covered."

With immortality came wealth. Undisclosed wealth, but Jaxon never worried about not having resources. It was one of the reasons why he was so sought after as a contract killer. He undercut the competition.

"Seriously, Jax, what's going on?" she asked, now sitting up in the bed, looking down on him. "I see pain in your eyes. You're trying to hide it, but you can't. Not from me. And you know damn well you don't have to. What happened today?"

Anna didn't know about his occupation, or his true age. She often joked about how good he looked for his age and how, over the last five years, he had not seemed to get any older. He reached up to touch her face and wondered whether this was the time to tell her.

He needed to.

He wanted to.

He was saved by an alert on his phone.

"You gettin' booty calls at one o'clock in the morning, sir?"

"I've already had my booty," said Jaxon with a sheepish grin.

Anna laughed out loud as he reached over to the nightstand to retrieve his cell phone.

"Hello?"

"Mr. Burke?" said the voice on the other end.

"Who is this?"

"This is the man with his finger on the button of the switch linked to the explosives under your bed."

CHAPTER EIGHTEEN

"DO YOU THINK THERE WILL EVER BE A TIME THAT YOU'LL TRUST ME enough to tell me what's going on in your life?"

Kassidy heard the question, but partly ignored it, choosing instead to pour her psychiatry session into a rocks glass. Traci meant well. She genuinely cared. There was no malice or judgment in the question, and to her credit, Kassidy didn't feel angry or offended. The tone was right, the emotion was right, everything was just so . . . right.

Why am I not telling her more?

"Look, I know this is a difficult time. I do. I guess . . . I guess I just want you to know that you don't have to experience this alone. You said parts of your life were hard, and you kept that secret from Lynn—"

"Don't. Just . . . don't."

And there it was.

Her Achilles heel.

The name.

Lynn.

The amount of guilt that Kassidy carried over Lynn's death could drown a pod of whales. She tried hard to push it out of her mind. And even though they'd made peace in the end, even though Lynn had forgiven her and urged her to move forward and accept her destiny, Kassidy hated that she, for all intents and purposes, had let Lynn die. She hadn't actively killed her, of course. Kassidy even had the presence of mind to recognize that there was nothing she could have done to stop what happened. She could have prevented it though. By simply telling Lynn the truth about her past, about who and what she was, she could have given Lynn the opportunity to decide for herself if she wanted to be a part of that world.

But Kassidy kept that option from her.

And now Lynn was gone.

"Kass, I . . ." started Traci.

Kassidy took a sip of her bourbon, then set the glass down and walked over to Traci. She loved looking into her eyes. When chaos surrounded her, when self-doubt engulfed her, those eyes set the world right. Kassidy brushed hair from Traci's face, caressed her cheek, and leaned in for a kiss. It was slow, lingering, but not lustful. It was a kiss that apologized while at the same time reminded them of the fire between them.

Kassidy pulled back, then rested her forehead against Traci's.

"I mean, if you're going to say you're sorry like that all the time, I'm sure I can come up with more dumb shit to say," said Traci.

They both shared a laugh, followed by a tight embrace. Kassidy felt Traci's anxiety, so she tried something she'd only been practicing in recent weeks. She tried to release her own calm and transfer it to quash the anxious feelings within. She wasn't sure it was working, but Traci held on tighter, so . . . something was happening.

"It's not you, love. It's me," said Kassidy. She pulled back from the hug and again looked into Traci's eyes. The anxiety was back, but now it was doubled.

What the fuck did I do?

"Oh my god," started Traci, "you're breaking up with me. Holy shit! Babe, I'm beyond sorry. I know you're going through some things but I never—"

"I'm not leaving you," said Kassidy, smiling, almost giggling. "You're just too damned cute. Babe, I'm not going anywhere. And in hindsight, I'm getting how that sounded, so I'm sorry for that."

The relief fell from Traci in an avalanche. Kassidy almost lost her balance.

"Whoa, you okay?" asked Traci as she reached out to brace Kassidy.

"Yeah, yeah, I'm good. Just got a little light-headed."

"Well, go sit down. I'll grab your drink, and we'll just sit and chill."

Kassidy walked to the couch. Traci handed her the bourbon, and she took a sip. That burn always felt so good. She still hated that it brought her comfort. It embarrassed her. She didn't want the crutch, and if she were to have a crutch, alcohol was not the healthiest. She was a god now, but still.

"Listen I—"

Kassidy was cut off by the buzz of her phone. Looking at the number, she saw that it was Alex Frost. Strange. They were a one and done duo. Though, maybe he'd come across another Wraith.

"Shit, babe, I really have to take this. I'll be right back, I promise," said Kassidy.

"Yeah, no, go ahead. I'll be right here."

She walked into the kitchen and answered the call. "Alex, what's up? You got another Wraith on your hands?"

"Um, no. Well . . . maybe. I'm not sure. A good friend of mine is . . . well . . . he's a bit special. Not unlike yourself."

"What do you mean?"

"He's got some pretty fantastic abilities."

"Like what?"

"Immortality."

"Hm, interesting. I'm not so sure *I* even have that, but you have my attention," said Kassidy.

"He thinks that with his latest resurrection, he was visited by someone who's right in line with the lot you're currently hunting down. In fact, this particular baddie mentioned you by name."

"No shit?"

"None indeed."

"You got a name?" asked Kassidy.

"No, nothing yet. My boy's asleep right now. Resurrection packs a big punch. Especially this one."

"Why this one?"

"He was burned alive," said Alex.

"What. The. Fuck."

"Yeah, we do things hard core in the Windy City."

"Where are you? I need to talk to your friend. What's his name?" asked Kassidy.

"Burke. Jaxon Burke."

"Well, when he wakes up, let me know. I wanna ask a few questions."

"He might not be so receptive to that. He's a bit of a private type, you know. Immortal and all."

"Yeah, well, I'm kind of the Death God, so that immortality shit can be wiped away pretty quickly if I'm having a shit day."

"All right now, easy, easy. I'll text you my address when he wakes up," said Alex.

"Appreciate that. See you soon," said Kassidy.

She stared at her phone and let her thoughts wander. Another immortal? What was he? The fact that he returned from being burned alive was both interesting and alarming. It was hard, however, to determine which was more interesting and alarming. The resurrection, or that a Wraith visited him and had a chat with him . . . about her.

Crash!

"Nooooo!" screamed Traci.

"Babe!" screamed Kassidy as she ran back to the living room. The scene stopped her in her tracks. Traci was pressed against the couch, a dark figure holding her down, with his hand inside her chest.

A Wraith!

"Oh, you came to the wrong house, mother—"

Kassidy's stopped, completely at a loss by what was happening. Traci somehow managed to push the Wraith off her, and with an outstretched hand, flung him against the wall where he was pinned. Traci got off the couch, hand still outstretched, and turned to face Kassidy.

"I think you're up, babe."

CHAPTER NINETEEN

"DON'T WORRY, MR. BURKE, IT'S NOT PRESSURE SENSITIVE. FEEL FREE TO get up for privacy if you'd like."

Jaxon didn't know what concerned him more. That there was a bomb under his bed, or that whoever planted it clearly had left some surveillance devices. His apartment had state of the art security equipment and, in the event someone did manage to get past them, counter measures to alert him of any possible breach. He'd received his hardware from the best in the business. Apparently, his supplier had competition.

Or the breach occurred courtesy of his supplier.

"Babe, it's a work thing, I need to take this," said Jaxon.

"A work thing? At this hour?"

"They're overseas. It should be a quick fix though."

Jaxon got out of bed and walked to his office. Closing the door, he pressed his palm to the back of it to activate a program to scan and secure the room.

"You should realize at this point that securing your office is moot," said the voice on the other end.

The voice was digitized, so Jaxon had no way of knowing who it was. He had some suspicions, though, so he tried to discern cadence and speed to help him identify the caller.

"What do you want?" asked Jaxon.

"I would think that's clear, Mr. Burke. We very much need

you to die. You're a loose end that we need to tie up. Not sure how you managed that little magic trick of coming back to life, though. That has us . . . intrigued. Perhaps, we can tie up these loose ends with a conversation and maybe . . . a new arrangement."

"A new arrangement?" asked Jaxon. "So, you found my trick intriguing, and you're thinking maybe you can use it to your advantage, is that it?"

"Something like that," said the caller.

Jaxon was certain he knew the caller now. At least, to some degree. He'd been hired for his last job by Damien LaVelle. But LaVelle was simply a middleman, some loyal lacky who did what he was told and likely survived by simply keeping his mouth shut. This guy was his boss, the real shot-caller. Jaxon had long suspected that the head man in all this had government ties. Jaxon was no fool. He was more than a hired gun. He understood strategy—battle strategy. He understood how to manipulate through disinformation and how to control a situation by taking out high value targets. And he understood the implications of his last assignment. His mark was closely involved with peace talks in the Middle East. With one shot, he'd further destabilized a region already in turmoil. In the big scheme of things, there were several beneficiaries of that action. The US Government was among them. Despite what they might say on the news, there was great benefit from destabilization—in the long run.

"So, what is it that you want me to do?" asked Jaxon.

"Mr. LaVelle will meet you tomorrow at nine a.m. to discuss what we think are some generous terms. In exchange for keeping your secret, you provide services to us, and perhaps even help us figure out how to replicate you."

"And if I say no?"

"Well, that bed exploding won't hurt you. But poor,

innocent Anna? Well, that's another story altogether, isn't it?"

Jaxon seethed. He squeezed the phone, tight. He heard it start to crack—once, then twice. It was the second that brought him back to some semblance of calm.

"Fine," whispered Jaxon.

"I'm sorry?" said the caller.

"Fine," said Jaxon, louder, through gritted teeth.

Jaxon's anger sent a surge of energy through him. The energy felt violent, primal, and urgent. He wanted to find this shot caller, and he wanted to hurt him. Badly. In his mind, he heard the sounds of bones snapping, of blood dripping, and the screams . . . oh, the screams. They were glorious. Like a symphony in which he was the maestro. His head ached right behind his eyes as the thoughts took on a life of their own. It was as if something was trying to break through. He couldn't place it, but there was a sensation, a familiar one . . . at least, it felt that way. Something inside told him he knew what to do, but his brain just would not zero in and fire. He found that he was squeezing the phone again, and that awareness calmed him once more.

"Mr. LaVelle looks forward to seeing you again tomorrow," said the caller.

"Can't wait," said Jaxon.

He ended the call, furious, and finished what he'd begun. Before leaving his office, Jaxon Burke left the plastic and metal remains of his phone on his desk.

He'd make LaVelle pay for a new one.

And a few other things.

CHAPTER TWENTY

INSTINCTIVELY, KASSIDY WALKED TO THE WRAITH, PLUNGED HER HAND into its chest and retrieved a purple orb. The life force of the Reaper. She ingested it, then allowed her eyes to turn blue and willed her hand into a sickle.

"You . . . you . . ." stammered the Wraith.

"Yeah, me."

"Your time is at an end, slayer," said the Wraith.

"I think not. You're the last of your sickly breed. My work is done."

"Oh, don't be so sure. Azra-El kept many secrets. Including the true number of Wraiths. Not even Senaya knew."

The Wraith bared blood-stained teeth. Kassidy wanted some answers, but she also just wanted to do away with the damned thing.

"Were you at a southside warehouse recently?" asked Kassidy.

"I was in the Nexus with your sister."

Kassidy gave a fake laugh, then her eyes glowed brighter.

"I'm not afraid of you, impost—"

The rest of his statement was cut short as Kassidy's sickle slid through his neck. It didn't sever his head. It didn't have to. Without the life force, the creature simply decomposed and withered away to dust and ash.

Of all the things that had occurred in the last thirty minutes,

Kassidy wasn't certain where to begin asking questions. She turned to stare at Traci, who remained silent. She walked to her, grabbed her drink from the end table, and took a sip.

"We should probably—"

"Talk?" said Kassidy. "Yeah. Let's do that."

CHAPTER TWENTY-ONE

DAMIEN LAVELLE WAS ONE OF SEVERAL DOZEN KIDS IN HIS SCHOOL diagnosed with ADHD. His parents could not control him, so they took him to a doctor, and just like that they had a month's supply of Ritalin to administer on a daily basis to help keep him manageable. At age ten he learned how to hide his meds under his tongue. By age eleven he learned how to hate his parents and their efforts to keep him sedated, so on his twelfth birthday, he killed them. He was careful about it, too. During his years of relative sedation, he'd spent a lot of time learning about crime, murder, and forensic sciences. He read books, he watched shows, and he learned enough in a relatively short amount of time to stage an apparent murder-suicide.

To call him unbalanced was an understatement. Following the demise of his parents, he bounced around from foster home to foster home and got in trouble every chance he got. Eventually, he ended up in a home for boys funded primarily by the Julia Cartwright Foundation. Things weren't necessarily better once he got there, but he was mostly able to stay out of trouble. And, after befriending young Charles Cartwright, any trouble he got into was quickly swept under the rug. In exchange for teaching Charles about the dark side of life, Charles taught Damien some refinement. Damien learned how to curb his turbulent instincts to focus on achieving an objective. In the eyes of those around him, he had improved so much that when people called him mature, they used the hard *t*. His association with the Cartwright family helped him get past several obstacles that allowed him entry into the military, where he further learned how to refine those skills and become a perfect living weapon.

After his term was over, he went into the private sector. His particular skill set was perfect for those who needed serious help and had the money to pay for it. In this city, his friend Charles Cartwright had the most money. And before long, he became Damien's primary employer. He'd worked hundreds of jobs for him over the years, but this latest project had been the most interesting. It had come with a lot of "what the fuck" moments during all the research and travel.

The vanishing of a man he'd burned alive qualified as the ultimate "what the fuck" moment.

Damien LaVelle wasn't used to failure. He had one hundred and twenty-five confirmed kills in the military. Two hundred and two unconfirmed kills in the private sector. The number of deals he had helped Cartwright negotiate over the years by applying the right kind of pressure was equally impressive. Failure was just not a thing he knew about.

And yet, here he was.

He stared at his phone contemplating whether he should call or text the Diva. He wasn't afraid of her or her response. He didn't even care that he was talking to her behind Cartwright's back. No, Damien LaVelle's hesitation lay in that he'd failed, somehow.

How the hell did that guy get away?

Damien pressed a button, and the line rang.

"It's me," he said. "We need to meet."

CHAPTER TWENTY-TWO

"WAIT, YOU WERE THERE?" ASKED KASSIDY.

Traci nodded.

Kassidy was not often speechless. It wasn't in her nature to have nothing to say. But the last month or two had been one shocking revelation after another. And now this from her . . . girlfriend? They'd never defined their relationship. Considering the way life was tossing curveballs her way, that was probably for the best.

"You were one of the girls in that basement?"

"Yeah. Me and my cousin, Lizzie. We were snatched up by this guy with black eyes about two weeks before you got there. Some of the other girls had been there for months."

"He was the first Wraith I'd ever encountered. I didn't even know they existed until that day," said Kassidy.

Shortly after Kassidy had become a Reaper, Azra-El began sending her out on her own for what he called "reckonings." He'd told her there were people in the world that needed to die because of the pain they'd caused others. Azra-El had convinced her that it was up to select Reapers like her to balance the scales of justice by reaping those souls and destroying them forever. On one such assignment, Kassidy fought a man who'd been targeting and kidnapping young girls. She'd found a number of those girls locked in a cage in the basement of his home.

"The only way I beat him was by using Wraith power myself. Not that I knew what it was at the time, or what *he* was. Honestly, it just manifested instinctually. Why didn't you say something?"

"Probably for the same reason you haven't told me about you and your abilities. Fear, maybe?"

"Of what?"

"Judgment."

"I'd have no place to judge," said Kassidy.

"Then why haven't you told me about what you can do?"

"Because . . . it's just . . ."

Kassidy had nowhere to go with her argument. And was it really an argument? Neither of them was upset. In fact, Kassidy felt an overwhelming amount of relief in the room now that all the cards were on the table. Well . . . almost all the cards.

"Hold on," began Kassidy. "What exactly are you then? How the hell were you able to fend off a Wraith? Why couldn't you do it back then?"

Kassidy moved to the couch as Traci sat down. There was an ease and comfort in Traci's demeanor. She did not seem apprehensive about sharing her abilities for fear of judgment in this moment. Nothing resembling nervousness or anxiety surrounded the woman. Like . . . nothing. Kassidy was looking at a woman who was in complete acceptance of who and what she was.

And she envied that.

"So, I'm a witch," said Traci.

"Sure. Why not," said Kassidy, throwing her hands up.

Traci chuckled, then continued.

"I come from a line of practitioners. Some practice more than others. Some are more powerful than others. But we all have some magic in us. My cousin and I were late bloomers. Our abilities didn't fully kick in until after you freed us."

"Why do you think that is?"

"I think we repressed it a bit. You know, fear of being different and all. But that whole experience, the kidnapping, seeing you and our captor fight, the experiments—"

"Experiments?"

"Yeah, babe. He was experimenting on the girls. We think he was trying to tap into our powers."

"So, all of you were practitioners?"

Traci nodded.

"But none of you were able to fight back?"

"Like I said, some of us hadn't come into our abilities yet. Others were just too new. They had no real understanding or control of their powers. If not for what happened to us, I'm not even sure mine would have fully manifested. It's like the trauma from it all sparked something within."

"For your cousin, too?"

"Yeah."

Kassidy sat with it for a while. Her lesson in the supernatural was stepping up another level. Reapers, Wraiths, gods, vampires, and now witches. Now, she not only envied Traci's acceptance, but she also envied her knowledge. If Kassidy hadn't spent so much time on the run avoiding who and what she was, she'd be better prepared for bombshells like this. And equally better prepared to deal with the challenges this life brought.

"So, you dove into studying?"

"For years. Both of us. Took the plunge and never looked back."

"This is just so—"

"Weird? Yeah, I know."

"What are the odds of us finding each other again?"

And there it was. For the first time since they'd known each other, awkward silence. Kassidy didn't need to stretch out too far with her senses to grab hold of the bitter taste of guilt that lingered in the air. She inclined her head and gave a quizzical look.

"What's that look for?" asked Traci.

"Us, meeting at Mullen's that night—that wasn't a coincidence, was it?"

The silence answered the question.

"How long? How long had you known about me?"

"I . . . I saw you once, in a coffee shop, about two months before that night at the bar. I couldn't believe it. Like . . . you were a part of my dreams for years and years, then suddenly, there you were. And I wanted to run in there and meet you, and hug you, and thank you, and . . . I just . . . froze. It's like when you meet your favorite movie star, and you don't know how to act. You don't know what to say. Then I started second guessing myself . . . like . . . it can't be her, there's just no way."

There was a strange tone in Traci's voice. It had never been there before. She was acting like a fan girl, and it made Kassidy uncomfortable. She'd always been ill at ease as the center of attention. This was different. There was genuine affection in Traci's words and behavior, but that didn't make Kassidy feel any more comfortable. She cared for Traci a great deal, probably more than she wanted to admit. But she feared giving in completely to those emotions.

"Then what?" asked Kassidy.

"Then, well . . . I'd stop by the coffeeshop every so often hoping to see you there. And a couple of times I did. One time, I overheard you saying you were meeting a friend at Mullen's.

So . . ."

"Oh boy," said Kassidy.

"Babe, I'm so not a stalker."

"Well . . ." Kassidy let the word drag out.

"I just . . . I just wanted to know you."

"You wanted to know the girl with the freaky eyes and weird powers."

"No. Oh my god, no. I mean, sure, I was curious. But it wasn't really about that. I wanted to know *you*. I remember thinking, that night you saved us, that you weren't much older than us. And there was something about you that seemed—"

"Off?"

"Scared. Like, you had this power, and you didn't want to use it, or know how to use it. And the way you just left us—it was like you didn't even want people to know you had it. And I thought, she's just like me. More badass, mind you, but still . . . so much like me."

Kassidy sat with those words for a beat and allowed Traci's sincerity, admiration, and . . . love . . . to fill her. She'd interpreted Traci's emotions incorrectly at some stages, perhaps allowing her own self-doubt to affect her. Traci meant every word she said. Which made her either a sociopath or just a genuine human being.

Kassidy chose to go with the latter.

"So, the night at Mullen's?"

"Purely coincidental. I'd stopped there to meet an old classmate before the party I was headed off to. I mean, I knew you *might* be there. I was certainly happy when I saw you, but I was there for a completely different reason. Then I saw you walking toward the bar, and I walked away . . . quickly. But after a few seconds I told myself to turn the fuck around and talk. I wondered if you'd remember me. But honestly, I hoped you wouldn't. I didn't want the trauma from that night to keep you from wanting to talk to me."

"I get that. I do," said Kassidy.

"I'm sorry. Maybe I should have said something sooner," said Traci.

"No. No, I think everything happened the way it was supposed to. I'm beginning to believe in fate much more these days."

"Yeah. Same."

"I suppose it's my turn for show and tell," said Kassidy.

As she took a breath to begin recounting her past, a knock on the door interrupted her.

"Oh, for fuck's sake!" she exclaimed.

Kassidy walked to the door and was surprised to see the source of the interrupted story.

"So, I guess we're just ignoring verbal and non-verbal cues these days, huh?" asked Kassidy, rhetorically.

"Seems the way to go," replied Keiron.

CHAPTER TWENTY-THREE

"WHAT ARE YOU DOING HERE?" ASKED KASSIDY.

"Well, hello to you, too," said Keiron.

Kassidy stared at him. She wasn't in the mood for witty banter or cutesy shit. She was still raw from events of recent weeks. She'd hoped he'd recognize that and respect her request for space. A request she'd made only days ago. Yet here he was, at her door.

"May I come in?" asked Keiron.

"Keiron, I—"

"I get that you need space. You made that very clear. But this is important."

Kassidy stood to the side, and Keiron entered. She was annoyed. Recently, she'd been spending most of her days like that. Which was understandable. She'd stepped into a role that she'd not anticipated and certainly hadn't coveted. Given the opportunity to turn back the clock, she would have made different choices. She had that ability with the Scythe of Cronus. She could control space and time. She could go back and change things.

But what good would that do?

Destiny always found a way.

"Hi," said Keiron.

"Hi, I'm Traci."

"Pleasure to—"

"What's so important that you couldn't text or email?" asked Kassidy.

"Wow. Really? We're there, now?"

"Keiron, what do you want from me? My world has been turned upside down. My life, everything I thought I knew, has been upended, and to top it all off, the person I trusted most . . . *you* . . . lied to me. So, you tell me how I'm supposed to feel."

"I'll just . . . give you two some space," said Traci.

Traci walked past Kassidy, touched her arm gently for support, and walked up the stairs.

"She seems—"

"Keiron!"

Her patience was wearing thin. Weeks ago, she would have soothed it all with a combination of bourbon and Vicodin. A part of her brain defaulted to that urge now. She was trying to be good. At least, good enough. But addiction was more powerful than she'd ever been as a Reaper, or a god. It called to her. She could feel her hands start to shake, so she instinctively put them both in her pockets. The stress was getting to her, but she was determined to hang on. She just wasn't sure how long she'd be able to.

"How many times can I explain and apologize, Kass?"

"I don't know. But it seems we're going to find out, because I'm not capable of sweeping this shit under the rug as easily as everyone would have me do."

"I don't think anyone is asking that of you, Kassidy."

"Then what? What is it that you're asking for?"

"A chance."

"To do what?"

"To make amends!" shouted Keiron.

Kassidy shook at that. Keiron had never shouted before. Even when she watched him fight, he didn't give so much as a battle cry. It just wasn't in his nature. For years, that calm had been her safety net. No matter how bad things got, no matter how many times she fucked up, no matter how chaotic her emotions and abilities became, he was always her calm, her center. He was peace.

He was not that now.

"Look, I understand that this is all bullshit for you. I get that all the revelations and the things that you've had to do are absolute fucking bullshit. And I completely understand and acknowledge that the choices that were made—that I made, that Octavia made—were not the best."

"Not the best?"

"But we did what we did because we *thought* it was best."

"Well, you were wrong."

"And how the fuck were we supposed to know that?"

There was that anger again.

"Look, be pissed," he said. "Be angry. I am right there with you. But if you can't see that we acted out of love, then frankly . . . fuck you, Kassidy."

Kassidy's jaw dropped.

"Yeah, fuck you. You don't have the monopoly on anger here. Yes, shit was done to you. Octavia and I have recognized that your entire life, and we have dedicated ourselves to being there for you in a way that no one else can. And if you can't see that our love is genuine, or that our efforts to help, to make amends, are pure . . . then fuck you."

Kassidy heard the words and felt their weight. She felt the emotion behind them as well. Despite the intensity, despite the bite, there was no malice. Keiron was angry, but it wasn't directed at her. He was mad at the circumstances that led to this moment. He was mad at himself. Kassidy had learned over time that anger mixed with guilt was the combination of emotion that signaled true sorrow and a yearning for forgiveness. She wanted to be mad. He'd essentially come out and said she was being a bitch, if she read between the lines. But he was also saying she had every reason to be that, and he wanted the opportunity to fix things.

"You realize that every therapist around the world would say that what you just did is wrong, right?"

"I'm not a therapist," said Keiron.

"No, you threw calm out the window," said Kassidy.

"If I were your therapist, I couldn't be your friend," said Keiron. "And I very much want to get back to being your friend."

The genuine love in those words squeezed Kassidy's heart. She felt a lump in her throat, made worse as she saw tears form in Keiron's eyes. She'd never heard him shout, and she'd never seen him cry.

"Uh . . . um," stammered Kassidy. She was trying hard not to let her emotion show. She was on the same page as him. She wanted that friendship back, too. She wanted it as strong, if not stronger, than ever. How could it not be now?

But she was still Kassidy.

She was still stubborn.

"You, um . . . said you had urgent news?"

"Uh, yeah," replied Keiron. "I um . . . saw him."

"Saw who?"

"Denzel."

It took Kassidy a moment, then recognition struck.

"No shit? Jacen? Why? What did he want? What did he say?"

"Seems he wanted the same thing he wanted with you. To warn me of things without offering much detail."

"Fuck."

"Yeah."

"I'm up to my neck tracking down Wraiths and trying to get shit squared away with this house, and now there's more shit coming."

"I suspect there will always be something," said Keiron.

"I just . . ."

"Yeah, I know. I want that for you, too."

Keiron wasn't a telepath or an empath, but he was smart, and he knew Kassidy. Often better than she knew herself. Or at least better than she would acknowledge. She knew all of that and felt the support in his words. She'd forgotten just how warm that felt, and how much she needed it.

"So, no specifics?" asked Kassidy.

"Just a warning."

"About?"

"The apocalypse," said Keiron.

"Oh . . . that. Sounds fun," said Kassidy.

"You may want to have a seat," said Keiron, gesturing to the couch.

"This is a sit-down conversation?"

"Very much so."

"Fuck."

CHAPTER TWENTY-FOUR

THERE ARE OBVIOUS PERKS TO IMMORTALITY. NOT AGING WAS CERTAINLY exciting, as was the ability to heal quickly. When Jaxon first awoke seven hundred years ago, it became apparent that he healed quickly from wounds. His metabolism and stamina were always above normal. He could run for hours, if necessary, at a fast pace. But most of all was the ability to learn about people. Jaxon was interested in learning about people to develop strategies to beat them. He was tactful. Every encounter with someone involved an intense study of how to evade, defeat, or kill them. He studied them physically and psychologically, often in a matter of minutes.

Jaxon had gleaned that Damien LaVelle was something of a control freak. He did not like it when others dictated his actions. Strange, because it seemed he spent his professional life taking orders from others. But even in those instances, he had some degree of freedom as to how he carried things out. He relished in controlling his environment. The key to beating him was taking that control from him.

"Let's do this," he said to himself, walking back into the warehouse where he'd been burned alive.

As nice as it was to learn that fire couldn't kill him, the pain that accompanied that revelation would be forever etched in his mind. The feeling, the scent, the sensation of never-ending agony, was all too overwhelming. But it triggered something else inside him—anger and a need for vengeance.

Jaxon was ready to die; he had been for some time. As much as he loved Anna, the all-consuming need to end his existence was palpable. He wasn't unhappy; he was tired. Tired of going on when others did not. He knew he'd have to eventually leave Anna or tell her his secret. He wasn't prepared for either. That added to his pain and fueled an anger welling inside that had no satisfying outlet.

The other pull for death, a final death, was the heartache of not knowing who he was. His persona over the last seven hundred years had changed with the times. He'd had dozens of names over the centuries. This latest name, Jaxon Burke, was chosen a couple of decades ago. He'd taken the last names of a couple of authors he liked, Shirley Jackson and James Lee Burke. He used the "x" in his name as a way of acknowledging his unknown self, the man he was before he woke up in the field outside Rome seven hundred years ago. There was a core self that he could not identify, and for all his bravado, it hurt to be ignorant of that knowledge. It was as if something had been stolen from him and it left him feeling incomplete. Living with that, year after year, century after century, and the recent nightmares that seemed more like blood-soaked memories, was just too much.

These thoughts ran through his mind as he walked through the warehouse looking for LaVelle. His heightened senses were blinded by memories of burning flesh and hair. The smell of gasoline was still thick in the air. Eventually, he heard a voice in the back office and moved toward it. He approached slowly and discovered LaVelle on the phone.

Jaxon stepped inside the office. The space was simple. One

metal desk, one dusty, rusty metal chair, one file cabinet, one stapler, and one phone . . . inexplicably a rotary phone. *Guess I'm not the only old school item in the building*, he thought to himself.

Damien LaVelle was tall, maybe six foot four or five, and built like a brick shithouse. The man was solid, even dressed in a suit. Jaxon knew LaVelle was ex-military. He still wore a military style haircut, high and tight. As Jaxon recalled, LaVelle carried a Glock in a shoulder rig.

He'd pull from the left.

Given the conversation with the mysterious voice last night, and the threat of being blown up, Jaxon was in little mood for conversation. He'd been hired to do a job. He'd completed that job. And for his troubles, he'd been burned alive. That wasn't an honorable way to do business. There was honor in battle and conflict—when it occurred between honorable people. LaVelle and his master proved that neither of them fit that description.

So, they'd pay the price.

Jaxon had arrived unarmed. It wasn't his smartest decision. He knew LaVelle would be armed, but with the rage he'd been feeling over the last few days, Jaxon wanted to engage in something more hand-to-hand. He wanted his hands soaked in LaVelle's blood.

"Excuse me," he began. "Would you happen to have the time?"

LaVelle twirled and smoothly reached for his weapon to pull it from his coat. For a big man, he moved quickly—but not as quickly as Jaxon. Jaxon grabbed a stapler from the desk and launched it. LaVelle dropped his weapon as he clutched his throat from the impact. Jaxon kicked the desk toward him to knock him off balance. LaVelle staggered back and hit the wall. Scrambling to the ground, Jaxon secured the Glock and shot LaVelle once in the leg.

Jaxon had three objectives. Control the environment, cause pain, and extract information. He'd relish in the first two for a minute.

LaVelle dropped to one knee and clutched his thigh with one hand while the other still held his throat. He was in pain, which was fine, but he wasn't going to be able to talk for a bit, which could make achieving that third objective a problem.

Feeding the anger a bit more, Jaxon elected to continue with his second objective for a while. At least until LaVelle's voice recovered. The only way to be sure of that recovery was to make the man scream.

The thought excited Jaxon.

So he went to work.

◆ ◆ ◆

"Hey, buddy. Listen, sorry about the whole stapler to the throat thing and the bullet in the leg, and all the other painful things I did. Fortunately for you, nothing I did was life threatening, unlike, say . . . fire."

LaVelle attempted to speak from the chair where he was bound.

"Rest that voice, LaVelle. You're going to sing a tune or two, then I'm going to kill you. I figured I'd tell you that now to save you the trouble of saying, 'Why should I talk, you're going to kill me anyway.' This way, the cards are on the table, we both know it's coming, and we can do our best to just be professionals about all this."

"Fuck . . . you!" LaVelle spat.

"Really?" Jaxon asked with a perplexed look on his face. "You burned me alive, and it's 'fuck you?' You don't think I have a right to ask questions and maybe be a little angry?"

"I don't give a shit what you think you have a right to be!"

LaVelle was in pain, but years of training and bottled-up hatred had taught him how to focus on other things. He was mad, but not because he was in pain. Because he'd been caught off guard by some . . . some . . . thing. He didn't know what to call this guy. By all accounts he was just a man. But coming back from the dead after being burned alive? Yeah, this guy was going to be a problem.

"Ah, big, badass soldier, eh? Not going to talk no matter how much I torture you?"

LaVelle looked his captor in the eye and gave him a crooked grin.

"That's fine. You don't have to talk. You can just listen. Feel free to jump in anytime you'd like, though."

LaVelle watched as his captor ignited the hand-held torch. It radiated a fine blue flame. He walked toward LaVelle with his new toy and looked at him, smiling.

"You know, LaVelle, I've been around a long time. So long, that there's a good chance I've forgotten far more than I've ever learned. Fortunately for me, though, I have guys like you to teach me new things. You see, I thought I knew the worst pain there was. I've been tortured before, and I've inflicted torture on others. I mean, who among us is truly a boy scout? Am I right?"

"You going somewhere with this?" asked LaVelle.

"Yeah," Jaxon said. "You instilled a fear in me that I thought had long since vanished. You showed me a new way to inflict pain that I never imagined. And now, I'm a little pissed. Your boss also threatened to blow me up last night in my own bed, so that's not helping my mood, either. I'm so pissed that I almost don't care if you answer my questions. I simply want you to taste of little of what I went through."

"Please," LaVelle said. "I've studied you, Burke. You're a pro. You don't resort to torture. You're all business."

"Well, you see, that's the thing. I wasn't always. And in recent days, I feel myself regressing, shall we say, into a life I thought I long left behind."

Jaxon could see the confusion in LaVelle's eyes. That look of confusion was quickly supplanted by a look of shock, likely from the sensation of white-hot pain on the top of LaVelle's right hand as Jaxon applied a torch to it. The blue flame tore through skin. LaVelle's hand turned red at first, then black before his skin blistered and bubbled.

Badass soldier or not, LaVelle screamed.

And Jaxon smiled.

"Trust me when I say, I can empathize," said Jaxon.

LaVelle's breathing was labored, and he foamed at the mouth as the agony set in. "What the fuck is wrong with you?" he screamed.

"Me?" Jaxon asked. "Again, we're back to me being the bad guy here? Hello! You burned me alive! That pile of rubble out there used to be me!"

It was registering with LaVelle more and more that maybe, just maybe, he really didn't know what he'd gotten himself into. Who, or rather what, was Jaxon Burke?

"I'm not in the mood to play games here," said Jaxon. "Give me the name of your boss, and we can jump right to your death. I have all the time in the world. But what I don't have is the patience. Coming back from the dead is exhausting. I'm tired, I'm hungry, and I'm anxious. Plus, there's that whole thing about not caring if you give me information or not, because I'm just going to enjoy this. You know, out of spite and loathing and all that. So, tell me why you did this to me. Tell me who you were talking to on the phone. Tell me if they're involved too. Then . . . I'll make it quick."

LaVelle said nothing.

The next round of pain came to LaVelle's left cheek. He couldn't see what was happening and frankly didn't care. The searing heat on his face caused him to writhe in pain and, consequently, kept the flame from staying concentrated in one spot. When the torch was pulled away, LaVelle could smell burning flesh. Being a combat veteran, the scent was recognizable. But he'd never expected to have it hit so close to home. His scream filled the cavernous warehouse.

"You stupid fuck!" LaVelle exclaimed. "You better hope I don't get loose! You better make sure you fucking kill me!"

He realized as the words came out that his death was the most likely end game. This guy didn't care one way or another if he lived. He wanted information. LaVelle knew only what he'd read about this guy, and even that was limited. But he knew that look. The look in Jaxon's eyes said a few things. First, that he was well and truly pissed, and second, that he did not care about anything but achieving his objective—vengeance. Getting answers was simply going to be a nice benefit.

"I can appreciate all the bravado, but we both know this only ends one way. It's up to you how quickly and how honorably you die."

"Honorably? You call this honorable?"

"I call this karma," Jaxon replied. "Honorable would be me making your death quick as opposed to turning this torch on your balls. I'm perfectly happy to do either."

"You're a sick son of a bitch," LaVelle said.

"Right," said Jaxon. "Because burning a man alive is so cosmopolitan."

LaVelle sat there, unable to do anything else because of the ropes, and pondered the situation. In all his years in combat and in the field and as a merc, he'd never been this helpless. Barring a last-minute rescue from some unknown cavalry, he was going to die. He had no men on standby, no team awaiting his contact. Hell, even Charles wasn't expecting a return call anytime soon. Definitely not soon enough to warrant someone crashing through those warehouse doors.

No one could accuse him of being a coward. He'd run into firefights with nothing more than a baton and a flash grenade. Didn't go as well as it could have, but he'd walked away. He'd always assumed he'd die in combat or on some job. He certainly never expected to die tied to a chair.

"If I tell you what you want to know, what do I get in return?" LaVelle asked.

"You get to die with your balls still attached and at normal body temperature."

"That's it?"

"You won't really need anything else where you're going," said Jaxon.

LaVelle looked at his captor, recognized that look again, and begrudgingly began to weave a tale. A part of him was disgusted that he would so easily spill his guts.

The story took several minutes to tell. It came complete with the name of his benefactor and the man's plans. He did not, however, mention the Diva. By the end, Damien LaVelle felt like that little boy who seemed to be a disappointment to his parents and every foster family he'd ever been to. That feeling made him sad, which in turn fed his anger. With a snarl, he looked up at Jaxon and said, "There you have it. Now, get it over with. Kill me."

The silent pause was deafening.

"Kill me, damn you!" LaVelle demanded.

"I will," said Jaxon. "I did promise you I would, after all. But first, why don't we make sure you're telling the truth and not leaving anything out."

LaVelle watched the flame on the propane torch reignite, and within seconds felt the heat on his inner thigh.

"Walk me through this story again, LaVelle."

When the screams subsided, LaVelle replayed his tale, again, leaving out the Diva.

Then Jaxon unleashed.

CHAPTER TWENTY-FIVE

"BUT THAT WOULDN'T WORK FOR ME? OR THE OTHERS?" ASKED Solomon.

"No, my old friend. It works only for the Death God, or someone with a bit of their power," said Azra-El.

"But we have a bit of *your* power, so by extension, don't we have some of his, too?"

"You have a much smaller fraction of Thanatos's power inside you. Enough to elevate you from Reaper, but no more than that."

As Solomon replayed this conversation with his Primus from decades ago, he thought further about what it meant. Azra-El seemed to trust Solomon among all others, even Senaya, so it didn't surprise him when his Primus explained his ultimate plan.

"Wait," began Solomon, "you can't be serious."

"I am as serious as the heart attack that young man over there is about to have."

Azra-El had pointed to a college age kid on the basketball court. They'd met in Barrie Park, one of the recreation spots in Oak Park, Illinois. It was a nice enough area, boasting a basketball court large enough for a couple of pick-up games. At the time, it was almost fall, and basketball season was around the corner. These kids were getting in a few games before going back to classes.

"Then you'll just absorb his soul? Instead of helping it transition?"

"I'll need a significant power boost if I'm to take on Thanatos, my friend."

"Will that be enough?"

"No. But I have other plans in the works that will help."

That was when Azra-El told Solomon about Kassidy Simmons and the unprecedented power he'd sensed in her. Azra-El had been certain that the girl was able to see Reapers. Apparently, she'd made something of a spectacle of herself at a young age following the death of a friend. Azra-El's plan had been simple. Get the girl to become a Reaper, allow her to take in souls to supplement her power, then take that power from her, along with her life.

That did not work out too well for the Primus. First, Kassidy tried to kill him when things became a little strange. Then, twenty years later, she succeeded. Somehow, though, she not only took his place, but managed to ascend and become a god herself. An ascension Solomon was certain she did not deserve.

She needed to pay for what she'd done.

Not just to Azra-El, but to Senaya.

Solomon let his thoughts drift to her. Senaya had been fierce, unforgiving, but given how she'd grown up, that was no surprise. Solomon had known of her before she became a Reaper, and he'd followed her exploits after her transition and beyond. They'd never engaged with one another. In fact, he was fairly certain she had no idea of his existence. That suited him fine. He went out of his way to avoid her and maintain some semblance of anonymity. Now that she was gone, some part of him regretted that intentional distance.

But he could change that.

Solomon needed to dispatch Kassidy. The only weapon that could do that was the Scythe of Cronus. He could use that weapon to kill her, and then, with its power, he could bring Senaya and Azra-El back. He didn't want to be a god. He was just fine standing in the background with the power to avenge at his command.

Right?

As Solomon stared at the empty basketball courts of Barrie Park, letting the memories of his time with Azra-El form in his mind, he allowed himself to wonder about the possibilities. If he could harness that power from Jaxon Burke, he might be able to collect souls and boost his power the way Azra-El had. He wasn't sure what Burke was, but he was positive he'd never felt anything like the power he achieved by just touching his soul.

In the distance, cars raced along the Eisenhower Expressway, and the Blue Line rumbled down the tracks toward downtown Chicago. When Solomon looked over and saw the sparks underneath the train, he flashed back to that moment with Burke. The feeling had been intoxicating. Solomon wanted it again. He wanted that rush of power. He wanted to feel like a runaway steel train that could roll right over Kassidy Simmons.

He needed to find Jaxon Burke.

He needed to find him now.

CHAPTER TWENTY-SIX

"IT'S COME TO MY ATTENTION THAT MAYBE I'VE BEEN A LITTLE UNFAIR to you and Keiron," said Kassidy.

"Who brought that to your attention?" asked Octavia.

"Keiron," said Kassidy.

"Of course."

Octavia gave a slight chuckle. She was on edge and felt confident that her efforts to stifle any anxiety was failing. She could even see that Kassidy was a little jittery. She felt bad about that, too. Yet another burden she was now placing on her niece. She was about to apologize when Kassidy put her hand up.

"I'm not here to fight or argue. I'm not here to toss blame around either. So, please, calm down. You want a drink? I'm gonna have a drink," said Kassidy.

"Um, yeah, I'll have whatever you're having."

"You sure about that?"

Octavia was perplexed until Kassidy reached for a rocks glass. Yeah, it was a little early for that. Or was it? What did she have to lose by having a drink in the morning? She didn't have to teach, and frankly, they were about to embark on a path that warranted some liquid courage.

"Yeah, I'm sure," said Octavia.

"Rock on, Auntie."

Kassidy gave a salute, and Octavia smiled back. As she sat

down and watched her niece, dozens of thoughts and hundreds of questions seemed to collide at once. Each one came back to the primary question on the table.

Did I do the right thing?

She'd honored her sister's wishes. By that alone, she had done the right thing. But, in the end, she had done it all to atone for childish and selfish behavior that turned deadly. So, was blind loyalty and penance the right thing? Maybe it was up to Kassidy to decide.

"Here you go," said Kassidy.

Octavia took a sip of her drink. The burn caught her off guard. But it warmed her, and she knew she'd likely need more to get through the conversation.

"So, do you have specific questions, or do you just want me to dive into the past?" asked Octavia.

"Probably more specific questions," said Kassidy.

"Fire away."

"I read my mother's journals. I didn't know they were hers when I got them, but I read them. Most of them, at least. Since all this Scythe of Cronus and my missing father shit, I decided to re-read some pieces, thinking that maybe it would give me a clue as to where my father is."

"Any luck?"

"Just more questions. Among them, though, is whether or not it's even a good idea to try to find him."

"Ah, yes. I suspect many of the things she wrote about him were . . . less than favorable."

"Less than favorable? He took her, blackmailed her into marriage, coerced her into having sex, then hunted her down after she got pregnant and escaped. Yeah, she didn't have nice things to say about that."

Octavia took a healthy sip of her drink to numb the sting of Kassidy's bite. She didn't blame her. To say that she came from a dysfunctional family was an understatement. And it wasn't her fault. She was allowed her feelings. In fact, if she didn't have those feelings, Octavia would have been worried.

"Did she indicate the reason for Thanatos's wrath?"

"Something about her boyfriend killing his son. So, I guess that would have been my brother? Weird."

"Anything else?"

"Well, she said Thanatos took the guy, Tyran, and like made him a slave or something as retribution for killing his son. My mother then decided to become some badass warrior to spring him."

"Well, yeah, that's the Cliffs Notes version. Tyran didn't just become a slave, though. He became a Reaper. Eventually, he became the Primus."

The cavernous silence in the room was interrupted by the sound of Kassidy choking on her bourbon. Octavia put her own drink down and tried to help, but Kassidy again put a hand up.

"You can't be serious," Kassidy said, still recovering.

"I am."

"Shut. The fuck. Up."

Octavia allowed Kassidy to recover from the shock and her coughing by filling in a few more details.

"I was always jealous of your mother. I loved her, but I envied the attention she got. So, when I found out she was sneaking around with Tyran, I told our father, and Tyran was discharged from his duties immediately. Father arranged a marriage with a nobleman, and once again everything was about Allesandra. My jealousy kicked in again, so I told Tyran what was happening and manipulated him into confronting this suitor. I had no idea that he'd go as far as he did."

"He killed him."

"Yes. Killed the nobleman and his entire party as they traveled to us to meet Allesandra and work out the terms of marriage. We had no idea he was the son of Thanatos. I mean, why would we even consider that? Anyway, Thanatos avenged that murder," said Octavia.

"So, he enslaved Tyran, then kidnapped my mother?"

"Yes. But not before your mother fought to release Tyran. She trained, learned from the finest warriors in the land, and attempted to free Tyran. In the end, it wasn't enough. Thanatos captured her, made her his bride."

"Made her?"

"Gods took what they wanted, when they wanted it," said Octavia.

She went on to tell Kassidy how she was eventually able to free Allesandra from Thanatos. Her hands were trembling. Would Kassidy hate her now, knowing that it was her actions that put things in motion? There was some relief when Kassidy only followed up with more questions.

"So, the two of you evaded Thanatos—"

"For a couple of months. But once your mother's pregnancy began to show, it became more and more difficult to continue to move around. So, with some help, we managed to hide her in the Nexus."

Octavia watched another lightbulb go off in Kassidy's head.

"In the Nexus? Then, the legend of the woman who gave birth to a child there. That was . . . that was . . . us. Me. I'm the Nexus baby."

Octavia nodded.

"How did he not know? How could you hide in the Nexus from the Death God?"

"Well, a couple of things happened. First, we secured a talisman that your mother could wear to keep her hidden. Similar to the one you used to wear to hide you from Reapers and Wraiths. Then, for some additional insurance, we uh, sort of locked him up."

"Wait, you're responsible for him being gone?"

"Oh no. No, no, no. Not this time. We managed to lock him up for the duration of Allesandra's pregnancy, but he got free soon after you were born. I have no idea how, or who, locked him up this time."

"You said you had help. Could that be the person who locked him up?"

"I doubt that."

"Why are you so sure?"

"He's dead," said Octavia.

"Who was it?"

Octavia gulped her bourbon.

"Oh shit. This must be big," said Kassidy.

Octavia let the burn continue down her throat. She'd thought about him a lot over the years. How could she not? His presence was awe inspiring to be sure, but in their brief time together, they'd loved a lifetime. Even beyond his betrayal, she loved him. So yes, she'd thought about him. But she hadn't said his name. Even when she taught her class, she never said his name. It came out now in almost a whisper.

"Ares."

CENTURIES AGO

As a War God, Ares was used to looks of devastation on the battlefield. They tended to manifest on the faces of the soldiers losing comrades at every turn. He expected to see those looks. He relished them. They fueled him as much as the feel of his sword running through the heart of an opponent. The only thing better was the look in a soldier's eye when his light was extinguished. Ares's bloodlust had few limits.

But this was different.

He could almost feel his heart shattering as he looked upon Octavia. Her quivering lip and the tears forming were dagger cuts against his skin. Her silence spoke volumes, and the weight of it was greater than the heavens.

"How . . . how . . . could you?" she asked.

Ares could say nothing. In the part of his mind that was the War God, he owed her nothing. What he'd done had nothing to do with her. She was a mortal, after all, and as such, should not concern herself with the will and the whims of the gods. But that part of him had been virtually dormant since they'd met. She was his heart. She ignited things within him that no other woman, divine or human, had ever been able to.

It was that side that spoke to him now.

It was that side that failed her.

"Octavia, I—"

"No! Don't you dare come near me!" she screamed.

In the background, Ares heard the low laughter of Thanatos. The Death God stepped forward, arms behind his back, with the air of authority Ares had witnessed only in the presence of his own father, Zeus.

"Silence, mortal!" said Thanatos. "The only reason you're still breathing is so you can tell me the location of your sister. She carries my child. My child! Tell me where she is now, and I'll spare both you and her."

Ares tensed. The hair on his neck stood at attention. Had Thanatos just threatened the woman he loved? Adrenalin shot through his body as he turned toward the Death God. Thanatos was powerful, certainly more so than he was. Moreover, Thanatos was the only being capable of killing a god. The Scythe of Cronus was the ultimate power. Despite being a descendent of the old Titan, Ares could not wield the weapon. Now, only Death or his offspring could do such a thing. Annihilation loomed, yet Ares could not let the threat against Octavia stand.

"You . . . you will not harm her, Thanatos!"

Thanatos's grin flattened.

"You dare challenge me, Ares? You are no match for me. None of you are."

"You cannot take my life without majority rule from the Twelve. Even you won't go against that oath."

"For my child, I would defy any oath," said Thanatos.

His voice was low when he spoke. Low but righteous. Ares felt no doubt in those words. Thanatos would defy his oath and challenge the Twelve for his child. If he was willing to start that war, neither he nor Octavia would survive without giving up the location of Allesandra.

Ares moved to shield Octavia. He closed his eyes, concentrated, and called his own power forth. A rush of fire sprang from the ground engulfing the War God. As the flames dissipated, he was left standing, armored, with the Glade in hand. His eyes glowed an ethereal blue, and his rage was channeled through his blade in the form of a low hum.

"You fool!" said Thanatos.

"Run!" shouted Ares.

He'd expected to hear Octavia's feet in quick retreat from the coming battle. Instead, out of the corner of his eye, he found her inching next to him, her own sword and dagger brandished, ready for battle.

"What are you doing?" asked Ares.

"Is this what you meant to tell me earlier?"

"Yes," said Ares.

"Because you love me?"

"Yes."

"Then I am doing the same thing you are. Fighting for those that I love. I will not tell him where my sister is. I'd die first."

She did not mention her love for him. It stung his heart, so he used that pain. He needed the fury of war to fill him if he had any hope of surviving this fight.

"This is your last chance, Ares," said Thanatos. "Hold back the mortal and tell me what I need to know . . . or die."

Ares charged.

CHAPTER TWENTY-SEVEN

RETURNING HOME, JAXON MADE HIS WAY TO HIS BATHROOM. HE WAS running on autopilot as his thoughts were still on the events that had just taken place in the warehouse with LaVelle. Jaxon had always taken pride in his work. He was, for all intents and purposes, a surgeon. Only, he didn't save lives, and his operating tools were vastly different. He didn't have a favorite weapon when he worked. Everything he used felt natural in his hands. From handguns to combat knives to sniper rifles, Jaxon was at home. When he wanted a little more finesse and distance, poisons suited him. When he wanted distance, but needed to make a statement, explosives were the way to go.

But today, he hadn't used any of those.

Today, he hadn't wanted distance.

Today, he wanted to feel every sting, hear the snap of every bone, and watch the will to live slowly drain from a person's face.

Vengeance wasn't his thing. Not really. Certainly not in a long time. But there was something about being burned alive that just rubbed him the wrong way. He'd never experienced pain like that before. The memory of it, the feel of it, the . . . smell of it, just lingered. His life had been as violent as it was confusing. He couldn't remember who he was, what he was, or how he came to be. But he knew that he was drawn to violence. He'd tried to trick himself over the years into thinking that he was drawn to conflict out of some altruistic need to serve, to use his gift of immortality to help and potentially save others. But that was all bullshit. He loved battle. He loved war. And he'd embraced that love today.

Jaxon watched the red water swirl in the sink as he washed his hands and face, and he wondered how many times scenes like this had played out in his life before he had woken up seven hundred years ago. Was the old Jaxon some warlord perhaps? A gladiator? Or just some bloodthirsty soldier who got off at the sight of death and destruction?

He didn't know.

He'd never known.

But today? Today he was filled with something he'd not felt in decades. Satisfaction. He had the name of the man who'd ordered his death. The same man that had hired him for his last two contracts using LaVelle as proxy. He suspected there were more people involved. No, he was certain there was at least one other name to share. But LaVelle had only given one name, a famous name. It made sense that he'd want to tie up loose ends. Killing an ambassador and an international leader within weeks was bound to bring some heat. He'd warned of it when he accepted both contracts. In the end, neither he nor his clients cared. At least they hadn't seemed to care, until the other day.

There was blood splatter all over his clothes. He hadn't noticed until he'd dried his face, taken a deep breath, and let it out.

"Fuck it," he said.

Jaxon undressed completely and took a shower. When he was done, he put on fresh clothes, threw the old ones in a bag to be discarded, and poured himself some Scotch. It had been raining for a while now, and the storm seemed to intensify. Jaxon hated storms. Perhaps a holdover from his former life? Who could say?

Jaxon settled in on his couch and turned the television on. Every channel seemed to be about the escalating tensions overseas. His last two contracts had certainly turned the tide on peace talks. Each image showed some war-torn area of different countries. People running here and there to escape gunfire, martial law declared, tanks and troops mobilizing. War was coming, and soon.

None of it seemed to bother Jaxon. Whatever concerns he had were belayed the moment he took LaVelle's life. In fact, the only thing that bothered Jaxon was how much he was loving the carnage manifesting in the world. It seemed to fill him. Energize him.

Jaxon turned the television off and sat in his darkened living room staring at his reflection in the screen. He closed his eyes, swallowed, and savored the sweet burn of the Scotch in his throat. When he opened his eyes, his reflection stared back at him again—only now his eyes were blue.

A bright, metallic, pulsating blue.

There was a pull, a compulsion, something in his mind urging him to leave. Amid the sensation, he heard voices and screams again. He covered his ears and rocked back and forth. The confusion he felt only increased his agitation. Jaxon took a pillow from the couch, buried his head into it, and screamed. It was a woeful desperate scream. He just wanted everything to stop.

He felt no better once he was done, so he tossed the pillow to the side, stood, and left his apartment. Something was compelling him to leave, guiding him. If he focused on it further, the voices were silent. Leaving his building, Jaxon took off, hoping to find salvation in the end.

He never saw the dark cloud overhead moving with him.

CHAPTER TWENTY-EIGHT

"SO YOU'RE TELLING ME THAT ARES, THE WAR GOD, WAS YOUR boyfriend?"

Octavia shrugged.

"Any chance my grandmother was banging Zeus? I mean, that could be a cool story. But . . . ew! That could mean Ares was your brother, then . . . ew! Of course, what's a little incest among immortals, am I right?"

Kassidy was almost disgusted with herself at the sarcasm she was laying down. It was tempered by the rising frustration and anger in Octavia, though. A small part of Kassidy was curious where this could go. At this point, she'd experienced her aunt feeling only sadness, happiness, and guilt. She wondered what anger would look like on this one-time warrior. Maybe they could fight and both blow off some steam.

Kassidy gave Octavia credit. She may have been boiling on the inside, but she did not show it. In fact, Kassidy could sense a deliberate attempt at self-regulation. She'd noticed over the years that when people purposely attempted to calm down, she'd sense the change in emotion much in the way a car experiences a speed bump. The anger would be at cruising speed, they'd attempt to slow it down before escalating to something large, but they'd hit that bump and they'd be angry again. The pattern would repeat, until the speed bumps were gone, and a new equilibrium was in place.

Octavia didn't have many speedbumps.

"I recognize how difficult all this has been for you. And believe me when I say, I am so terribly sorry for the role I played in making your life what it is. But it happened. Whether we like it or not, it happened. And it happened to more people than just you. So, while it's easy for you to sit in judgment and be pissy and bitchy about the way your life turned out, recognize that lives were lost, hearts were broken, and loyalties betrayed. So be angry or grow the hell up and help deal with the cards we've been dealt."

There were few people in Kassidy's life who dealt with her behavior, sarcasm, and all-around bullshit in a way that acknowledged her feelings but also established boundaries that told her just how far she could go. Her best friend, David, was a master at it. In part because he was a trained therapist, but more so because he was a real human being who'd dealt with his share of BS growing up. Keiron was another. Kassidy realized early on that he was as cool inside as he was outside. He operated on a logical plane guided by emotion, very different from most people.

And now there was Octavia.

It wasn't as if the woman was angry when she said her peace. Well, she was, but it did not come out that way. She was controlled. Kassidy could sense that compassion, that guilt, and some genuine love within Octavia—all directed at her. But she also felt some of Octavia's pain. It was a real thing. As real as if it had just happened yesterday. Kassidy's sarcasm had been salt on wounds that, despite the passage of centuries, had not healed. Hell, they apparently hadn't even closed. Kassidy was finally starting to realize that she wasn't the only victim of Thanatos's vengeance, and that her issues were just that . . . hers. They weren't more important than anyone else's. They just seemed that way because they were hers and consequently hit harder. David had been trying to tell her that for years, encouraging her to learn how to cope with her problems beyond pouring bourbon into a glass. So had Keiron. Perhaps she just needed to hear and experience it from another perspective.

"I . . . I'm sorry," said Kassidy.

Octavia placed a hand on Kassidy's lap. She jumped, a little. She wasn't expecting the contact, but also, the physical touch made the emotions even more real. The anger was gone, mostly, but in its place was an undeniable and unconditional amount of love and compassion. From a woman she barely knew. She took a deep breath, inhaling the feelings, and when she let it out, tears came with it.

Followed by a hug.

And then they both cried.

CHAPTER TWENTY-NINE

JAXON APPROACHED THE WAREHOUSE THAT HAD BEEN THE SCENE OF nothing but death over the last few days. He entered with trepidation, the impulse he felt earlier guiding him to this spot.

"You ran off last time," said Solomon.

Jaxon whirled to find the man he'd run from standing there. He was calm, confident, and displaying a grin that was nothing less than sinister. Jaxon's instinct was to run again. But that other impulse compelled him to stay.

"Yeah, well, you did some pretty weird shit to me," said Jaxon.

"Perhaps. But . . . let's not dwell on the past. Let's focus on the here and now. Next steps, as it were."

"Can we get on with it?" asked Jaxon.

"Why the rush? You clearly have nothing but time."

"Listen, you saw what I can do. Seems to pale in comparison to what you can do, which makes me wonder why the fuck I'm so interesting to you. If it's my life you want, you're welcome to it. I have one more score to settle, then I'm more than ready to check out."

"Check out? You mean, die?" asked Solomon.

Jaxon inclined and tapped his head with his finger.

"Why would you want to do that? You're immortal. Do you know what you could do with that ability? With that time?"

"I do. And I've done it. Now I'm tired."

Jaxon took a deep breath and let it out. Sometimes it calmed him, sometimes it didn't. At this point in his life, it had become habit just before he was about to walk down some dark memory-filled path. A path filled with blood, death, screams of agony, pleads for mercy, all the things that gave him nightmares—all the things that energized him. It made him sick when he realized how much he enjoyed the carnage. He cringed at the feeling of joy that came when he snuffed a life out with his own hands. What kind of man does that?

Was he even a man?

It all confused him, and the confusion added misery. Century after century of misery. So he took a deep breath each time he stood upon this threshold, the outcome a mystery like every roll of the dice.

"How long have you been around?" asked Solomon.

"I honestly don't know. My first memory is waking up in a field in some village outside of Rome."

"When?"

"A little over seven hundred years ago."

"That's . . . interesting," said Solomon.

"I suppose that's a word for it," replied Jaxon.

"You truly are remarkable. And you have no memory of life before that?"

"No."

"How old were you when this happened?"

Jaxon raised an eyebrow.

"Sorry, I should clarify that. Were you a child when you woke up? Or were you fully grown?"

"I was grown. I was . . . this," said Jaxon with a reflective hand gesture.

"You have the gift of immortality, and yet, you want to end it?"

"Gift? *Gift*? Living a lonely life, watching people die generation after generation, and having this thirst for death and carnage bubbling just under the surface is no gift," said Jaxon.

"I suppose that's a matter of perspective," said Solomon.

"Perspective? Whose? You have . . . gifts. Why covet mine?"

"Because yours comes with life."

"What life? What life do I have? I can't hold a relationship because I know they'll die. And what do I do for a living? I take the very thing I've taken for granted for the last seven hundred years."

Jaxon paced out of frustration. Thinking back, he remembered a time when immortality felt like a gift. In those days he wanted to see the world. He wanted to learn. Learn about people, about life, about himself . . . and he had nothing but time on his side. He absorbed languages, martial arts skills, knowledge of math and science, everything a man would need to be a true force for good in the world. But beneath the surface, taking the occasional peek over the horizon, was that drive for blood and war. He used all he'd learned to make himself the ultimate warrior. Where there were battles, he was there. Where there was strife, he lingered until the scales tipped to armed conflict. He fought and fought, then he specialized. He sold his knowledge and skills to the highest bidder. He instigated. He assassinated. He became the one to control the balance.

And it fed his soul.

But now? Now, there was a shift within. Those things fed him, but he didn't know why, and the dissonance it caused hurt more than the hundreds of times he'd died and been reborn. For all the knowledge he'd gained, for all the skills he possessed, for all his so-called gifts . . . he still had no idea who he was or what his purpose was. All he knew was that he despised himself, that he wanted it to end. He just didn't know how.

"You are distressed. You truly don't want this life anymore?"

"And yet I can't stop it."

"Well . . . maybe I can."

Jaxon turned to face Solomon. When he did, he found himself staring at the black-eyed being he'd awoken to in the warehouse. It didn't scare him. Not then and not now. After dying in all the ways he had over seven centuries, not much scared him.

Except the moment Solomon transformed into a wretched cloaked creature.

"What the fuck?"

Jaxon stepped back, uncertain of what to do next. For the first time in hundreds of years, he had no idea how to proceed. The tattered cloak did little to hide the creature's face. It was old, wrinkled, with sunken eyes. Its teeth were yellowed, jagged, descended from bloody gums.

It floated toward him.

Jaxon again staggered back only to stop after two steps. This was a no-lose situation. If this creature could kill him, he'd finally have the one thing he'd sought. If it didn't kill him, he'd be just as he was when he woke up virtually every morning.

Inches away from the cloaked figure, Jaxon stared it down.

"Do your worst."

Solomon plunged his boney hand through Jaxon's chest.

◆ ◆ ◆

Power exploded from Jaxon's chest like a shaken carbonated beverage, and Solomon Steele drank from it like a dehydrated puppy. His fist almost didn't phase through the chest this time, but Solomon would not be denied. He would retrieve this man's life force, his soul, and transform himself. This power had to be enough to make him stronger. At least strong enough to defeat Kassidy Simmons. He could then take his rightful place as Primus. Why bother bringing back Azra-El? Why settle for Primus? With the Scythe of Cronus, he could ascend. It was his duty, his right, his destiny.

He was, after all, the first Wraith created.

Solomon removed his hand from the Jaxon's chest, opened his fist, and his eyes widened.

It was empty.

"I . . . I don't understand," said Solomon after shifting back to human form. "I felt it. I had it in my hand. This makes no sense."

"What are you talking about?"

"Your soul, your . . . life force . . . I can't remove it," said Solomon.

"Yeah, I kind of mentioned the whole immortality thing, right?"

"Even immortals have a life force, though. I . . . I am a Wraith, created by the Primus, the First. He was created by Death himself. I should have the ability to—"

Solomon stopped as he felt a tingle. Waves of energy ran along his forearm, up to his shoulder, crackling like electricity. It stunned him, and he opened his mouth to cry out, not from pain, but from the exquisite sensation filling his body.

He shuddered in delight.

"This . . . is incredible!" he shouted.

Solomon's body felt alive with power. Ripples of energy leapt from his body. He threw his head back and let it flow.

"What the fuck is happening?" asked Jaxon.

"I don't know," said Solomon. "But I feel more powerful than I've ever felt before. I . . . wonder . . ."

Solomon's right hand shifted into an onyx sickle. He watched Jaxon's eyes widen in astonishment.

Lifting his arm, Solomon, in one swift motion, swept his sickle through Jaxon's neck.

The sickle of a Reaper or Wraith didn't sever physically but metaphysically. Once a life force was removed, it severed all remaining life from a being. When done to a psychopomp—a being that helps souls transition from life to the afterlife—what was left was dust that simply blew away with the breeze. When done to a human, what was left was a meat suit filled with bones, blood, and organs.

Jaxon Burke was clearly neither. He stood before Solomon just as he had seconds ago. Very much alive. Confused, from the look on his face, but alive.

But what was the deal with the power surge Solomon felt?

"What did you just do to me?" asked Jaxon.

"Apparently nothing," said Solomon.

"What were you hoping to do to me?"

"Well, kill you. It's what you want, right?"

Jaxon nodded.

"Then I think we need to look at some other avenues," said Solomon.

"Like?"

As Solomon spoke, his entire body hummed. He couldn't take Jaxon's life force, but he could siphon off some of his power. That was unexpected but welcomed. He knew, instinctively, that he was no longer a Wraith, at least not entirely. He'd not ascended yet either. Still, perhaps this power boost, along with Jaxon's skills, could get him just what he needed. Perhaps there was still a way for him to become a god. No, that's not what he wanted, was it? He wanted to bring back his Primus, bring back Senaya. He didn't want to be a god himself.

Or did he?

"You wish to die. I wish to see someone else die. That one person alone can serve both our purposes."

"Who?" asked Jaxon.

"The new Death God. Let me tell you about Kassidy Simmons."

CHAPTER THIRTY

TENSIONS WERE RUNNING HIGH IN WASHINGTON, DC, IN THE WAKE OF THE assassination of United States Ambassador Hassan Davis. He'd spent four months identifying key issues to address in negotiations between the Shihadi and Jen'ai regions of Ki'lal. Both regions were laying claim to a small piece of land that was a gateway to resources that could benefit a number of countries, including the United States. The precious land, at this point, served as nothing more than a weigh station for terrorist groups and warlords. Without the ambassador in play, negotiations had stalled.

Long enough for another assassination to have taken place.

Kareem Nasir, leader of the Shihadi region had been visiting Chicago on a good will mission. The Windy City sponsored a number of refugees from his country, and, in good faith, he'd agreed to meet with them personally to assure them that under his leadership things were different and they were free to return home. He'd expressed great understanding in their defection from their homeland. The previous dictator was cruel, vindictive, and many families paid the price for the actions of the men and few women who'd left.

Nasir had arrived to right that wrong.

A single shot to the head from a high-powered rifle derailed that effort.

With the assassinations of Nasir and Ambassador Davis occurring so close together, all eyes turned toward Jen'ai. Protests called for swift action against Jen'ai and its leadership. Citizens demanded retribution. The President and Congress, in agreement for once, urged stakeholders to await the completion of joint investigations into the murders. All signs may have pointed to Jen'ai given the open hostilities, but there was little proof to back the assertions. Even the intelligence agencies heard no chatter. No claims of responsibility. Everything had simply been dark.

The unrest in the Middle East gave rise to aggressions across the globe as world leaders were unable to agree on how, or if, to proceed. Most were concerned that the world was on the brink of a third world war.

◆ ◆ ◆

In a cave on the island of Crete, an ancient weapon was responding to world events. In this cave, lost to the eyes of man, rested a true weapon of mass destruction. The weapon had been secured centuries ago by Thanatos himself. Initially, a select group of Reapers, hand-picked by Thanatos, were charged with guarding it. Their sole purpose was to ensure that no one ever learned the whereabouts of this weapon, and if they did, they were to dispatch them immediately. They were to protect it with their lives if necessary.

Over the centuries, the weapon simply remained there, embedded in a large altar. To the Reapers, it meant nothing. But to Thanatos, it was everything, so they vigilantly fulfilled their roles and stood guard, even in the absence of the Death God.

Recently, though, guarding the weapon had proved to be eventful.

Months ago, it began to hum. Low, at first, but steady. It unnerved the Reapers, but they remained on task. Within the last few weeks, the weapon began to glow. A low reddish hue emanated from the blade. It pulsated, lightly, in time with the hum. Some days, both would be more intense, but eventually, they would power down.

Today, though, was not one of those days.

The glow, the hum, both in sync, lasted for hours and became only more intense.

"What does this mean?" asked Dyson.

"I've never seen this before," said Cyrus.

"The altar . . . it's . . . cracking," said Dyson.

"Indeed."

"Shouldn't we alert someone?" asked Dyson.

"Our job is to keep this weapon hidden. If necessary, we'll move it. But no one is to know of its continued existence. That order comes from Thanatos himself."

As he finished, the cracks in the altar spread like an intricate spiderweb. It was not as beautiful as a spiderweb, though. The delicate patterns of nature's eight-legged artist spoke to the wonder of life. The web-like fractures in the stone altar spoke, most assuredly, of the certainty of destruction.

Of all the Reapers charged with protecting the weapon, only Cyrus knew its origin and original master. If the weapon was coming to life, it likely signaled that the god meant to wield it was doing the same. Cyrus knew that something was happening out there. Something was happening in the world that nurtured death and destruction, just as the weapon's master had.

The Gladius de Bellum, also known simply as, the Glade, weapon of Ares, powered down to a lowered hum and subsequent glow.

CHAPTER THIRTY-ONE

"NICE PLACE," SAID KASSIDY.

"It is. Good atmosphere. Good coffee. Good food. Lots of boxes checked off for me," said Octavia.

Kassidy sat down at a table with Octavia and Keiron. Looking around, she decided the place checked off some boxes for her, too. It was out of the way, but Third Wave Coffee was certainly a gem of the West Loop. It smelled like a coffee shop should. Like people busted their butts to make sure everyone felt comfortable and happy to be there. You had all walks of life coming through the doors. It was easy to tell who the regulars were. They simply made themselves at home. The occasional customers, probably like Octavia, knew what they wanted, ordered, and stayed long enough to get things done. Then there were the first timers. Folks who came in curious. They spent a great deal of time checking out the menu, looking for prime real estate to sit, and always asked questions. And the folks that worked there treated every one of them like they were old friends who'd stopped by for a visit.

Kassidy decided she liked the place. Especially when Keiron slid over a French vanilla cappuccino.

"You don't have to buy my love. I think we're cool again," said Kassidy.

Keiron grinned and she returned a smile. Things were tense,

but mostly because she had to swallow some pride and take some verbal licks. She wasn't happy . . . still . . . about the choices they'd made. But she was in a place to at least understand their reasoning now and accept that they could not have possibly foreseen events playing out the way they had.

"So, where are we with things?" asked Kassidy.

"Well, not completely fucked," said Octavia.

"That's promising," said Kassidy.

"Based on the prophecy Keiron was told, it seems that what we're dealing with is a possible unification of The Four," said Octavia.

"Right. The Four," said Kassidy. "Still struggling with why they're just the Four and not the Four Horsemen. Is it a marketing thing? Saving character space on social media?"

"Because, my dear, not all of them are men," said Octavia.

Kassidy let that sit with her. Did it matter that the Horsemen of the Apocalypse weren't all men? For some reason, she'd always had it in her mind that Pestilence and Famine were women. It didn't make much sense to her as she dissected it further in her mind. Maybe it was sexist. Why should War be a man? Athena was a War God as much as Ares. Maybe she could have been a horseman. And Death, hell, *she* was Death now. She could be just as—

"Oh. Shit," said Kassidy.

"You see where this is going?" asked Keiron.

"Where it's going? Wait, you can't possibly think that I'd be helping to usher in the end of the world. That's . . . that's . . ."

"I don't think either of us think that," said Octavia. "Right now, it's a matter of the players we have on the board."

"Well, all we've got is Death," said Kassidy. "And she ain't playin' the apocalypse game."

"We may have more than just you," said Octavia.

"Like whom?"

Octavia looked to Keiron, and Kassidy sensed some tension. The two of them were best friends. Kassidy once thought, given their respective ages and what they'd seen and experienced over the centuries, that they might be more. If not now, perhaps at one time. But both maintained it had never gone beyond friendship. This current tension was likely due to a difference of opinion. Centuries of friendship made it easier to agree to disagree without physically fighting and hurling insults.

"Well?" Kassidy asked, impatiently.

"We think—"

"You think," corrected Octavia.

"Fine. I think," Keiron began again, "that War is upon us."

Kassidy sat back in her chair, crossed her arms, and sighed. Given what Octavia had said about the War God, it was no wonder they disagreed on this particular subject. Kassidy gave a silent fist bump to her aunt for not jumping down Keiron's throat at the mention of her lost love. Betrayed or not, it was clear Octavia still held a place in her heart for him.

"Why would you say that?" asked Kassidy.

"Look around us. Look at what's happening in the world. A US ambassador killed? The leader of a small country assassinated? Both men were in prime position to end hostilities in a region that, while outwardly insignificant, plays a pivotal role in the distribution of resources to major superpowers. The instability their deaths have caused will only escalate. We've also seen an escalation in threats from countries in Asia and Eastern Europe. There is global unrest to say the least."

"There's always global unrest," said Kassidy.

“Not in such concentration,” said Keiron. “And not in the wake of a prophecy given by the Oracle, who, I might mention, was also killed.”

Kassidy looked to Octavia, who made no eye contact with either of her tablemates. There was some unrest right in front of her. The tense feeling shifted to confusion and doubt in an instant. As Octavia sipped her coffee, Kassidy realized that a part of her aunt believed that perhaps Keiron was right. The tension Kassidy had felt before was Octavia’s own dissonance. She didn’t want to think it was possible, yet everything seemed to point to one inescapable fact.

The War God had returned.

Or perhaps someone had simply assumed the mantle, just like Kassidy had.

“So, let’s say you’re right. Let’s say the War God is here . . .”

Kassidy trailed off as she felt a stab of pain shoot through her abdomen. She knew that wasn’t her. Octavia was going through an emotional roller coaster right now. Kassidy felt bad for her, but they needed to have this discussion.

“If there is one here, it can’t be Ares. It just . . . can’t,” said Octavia.

“Okay, okay,” began Kassidy, “for argument’s sake, let’s assume it’s someone who’s taken the title. Perhaps someone has ascended the way I did. Maybe one of his children?”

The intensity of the stab of pain increased and Kassidy doubled over.

“Kass, are you all right?” asked Keiron, reaching out to brace Kassidy before she hit the ground.

“Yeah, yeah, I’m fine,” replied Kassidy, catching her breath. “One of us though . . .”

Kassidy let her words trail off as she looked to Octavia. There was concern on the woman's face. Then the proverbial light bulb went off.

"Oh my god. That was me. Oh sweetheart, I'm so sorry. I . . ."

"No worries," said Kassidy. "Look, I get that this is a touchy subject for you. But right now, touchy subjects are totally our thing right now. We need to look at all possibilities, and as much as possible, we need to keep our emotions in check. At least for my sake."

Kassidy gave a light chuckle as she tried to ease the mood. Keiron followed with a smirk, and Octavia finally gave a reluctant smile.

"It seems like we've got multiple issues," said Kassidy. "We need to deal with a few things to clear the way for us to address this apocalypse issue."

"The rogue Wraith?" asked Keiron.

"The rogue Wraith," said Kassidy. "We need to find him, dispatch him, and end this fucking bounty he put out on me. I honestly don't know why he thinks that's going to work, especially since my ascension, but it is, at best, a nuisance."

"So, what's the plan?" asked Octavia.

"I'm thinking we finish coffee. Then, you two go see Frost and talk to our assassin, and I'll go after the Wraith. I'll give Alex a call and let him know the two of you are on your way. The Wraith, well, that's my cross to bear. Besides, I'm the only one that can dispatch him."

Octavia and Keiron looked at one another, then turned to Kassidy and nodded in agreement.

"And once that's accomplished, how do we go about finding the War God?" asked Octavia.

"If we can find the Glade, we can use it to locate him," said Keiron.

"Yep. What he said," replied Kassidy.

"That damned sword," said Octavia.

Their shared laughter was interrupted by a pulling sensation. Kassidy felt the tug and recognized it as a call through the Nexus. This wasn't a death call, though. Someone was trying to contact her. Would the rogue have the audacity?

"I need to go," began Kassidy. "Let's check in with one another this afternoon to see where we're at with our respective assignments."

After getting a nod from both, Kassidy took one last sip of her coffee and left the shop. Rounding the corner, she found a quiet spot to transition into the Nexus. Once there, she was met by a Reaper. Months ago, she couldn't have told you his name if the fate of the world was stake. Now, though, she had a matriarchal connection to them all. It frustrated her that she did not have the same connection with the Wraiths.

"Cyrus, right?" Kassidy asked.

"Yes, that's right. Thank you for coming."

"What's happening?"

"I need to talk to you about your father . . . and about the Gladius de Bellum."

"The what now?"

"The Glade," said Cyrus.

Kassidy held back her shock so as not to look less like a deity and more like a freshman in high school on the first day.

"That damned sword."

"You are not the only one to feel that way lately," said Cyrus.

"What do you know about it?" asked Kassidy.

"Well, it's . . . active."

"Active? What does that mean? You know where it is?"

Cyrus nodded, then went on to explain his connection to

sword as its guardian. Kassidy listened carefully, then felt a punch to the gut as Cyrus explained how Thanatos came in possession of the powerful blade.

"This is insane," she said. "How could he do that?"

"I understand this may be a shock—"

"A shock? The more I find out about Thanatos, the more I'm disgusted," said Kassidy.

"Nevertheless, something must be done about the weapon," said Cyrus.

"And what exactly do you expect me to do?"

"I think it's powering up now because of tensions in the world and a possible reawakening of the War God. If he awakens fully, the Glade will find him, and the consequences could be . . ."

"What?" asked Kassidy with impatience.

"Incalculable," said Cyrus.

"So, in other words, you don't know?"

Cyrus responded with a slight shrug.

Kassidy felt her frustrations rise. Frustration over so many things. So much weight on her shoulders. The weight of her decisions had affected so many, and she felt as if everything she'd done was wrong. Being a god, this powerful entity, was supposed to be easy, right? That it wasn't only made her feel even more inadequate. A failure. Completely unsuited for the role she was in.

She *was* an imposter.

"The Glade is safe, for now, right?"

"Until the Death God calls for it, or until you remove it from the altar, it's safe," said Cyrus.

"Until I remove it?"

"Yes. A Death God embedded it, so it takes a Death God to liberate it."

"Or its owner can call to it?"

Cyrus nodded.

"Get back to it, then. Continue to guard it. There's too much happening now, and I can't deal with yet another issue. Contact me with any updates. Otherwise, wait until I reach out to you."

"But—"

"Cyrus, please!" shouted Kassidy. "Just do as I ask."

Cyrus gave a quick bow and left the Nexus. Kassidy took a deep breath and tried her best to gather her thoughts and calm down. Within the Nexus, in the distance, she saw a dark figure that seemed to be looking at her.

"To hell with you!" shouted Kassidy.

Then she shimmered away.

CHAPTER THIRTY-TWO

"WHAT DO YOU MEAN HE'S GONE?" ASKED KASSIDY.

"What do *you* mean, what do I mean? I mean he's gone. Left. Bolted. Ghosted. Gone," said Alex.

His sarcasm was on par with hers. Any other time she'd be just fine with that. But given that this possible immortal had a possible run-in with a possible Wraith, sarcasm was not on the menu. Kassidy needed answers, and she needed them now. Her pot was beginning to boil over, and if she didn't find peace soon, she feared for the safety of those around her. She was the Death God now and experiencing a psychological meltdown would not be a good thing.

"Tell you what, Frost, I'm going to extend professional courtesy and assume you've checked his home and usual hangouts already. Before I start pounding the pavement, can you think of any place off the beaten path he could end up?"

"I appreciate the courtesy, death lady. But I've checked those places, too. Even talked to his girlfriend"

"His girlfriend?"

"Yeah. Anna. Anna DeBartolo. She said he left early this morning. Didn't say where. Just that he had to tie up some loose ends on his last job."

"And what job was that?"

"Fuck if I know," said Alex. "Jax plays his life close to the vest. Probably best in his . . ."

As Alex's voice trailed off, Kassidy's curiosity went to high alert. Apparently, Jaxon Burke had secrets beyond being able to recover from injuries and seemingly death itself.

"His what, Frost? What is he into?"

"Look, it's not really import—"

"Don't give me that shit. You know as well as I do that it could be the key to his current whereabouts. What is it? Guns? Dope? Girls?"

The silence on the phone seemed to last a week. Kassidy was doing her best to be calm and patient. Frost did do her a solid the other night. The least she could do was hold in her frustration and anxiety. Finally, he spoke.

"He's a shooter."

"Private or government?" asked Kassidy.

"These days, possibly somewhere in between."

"Uncle Sam isn't too keen on competition," said Kassidy.

"True. But Jax is not one to give a fuck. So, there's that."

Maybe this guy wasn't so bad then. Kassidy liked people who didn't give a fuck. Made things . . . interesting. Though, an immortal assassin roaming the streets of Chicago was interesting enough for the time being.

"Look, I'll put some feelers out, and see if he pops up on someone's radar. But Jax is about the best there is. If he doesn't want to be found, he won't be. He doesn't just go off the grid. The entire fucking grid disappears with him," said Alex.

"You're a fan?" asked Kassidy.

"I owe the man my life, many times over."

"Got it," said Kassidy. "Look, I'm not trying to jam him up or dig into his shit. I'm more interested in the Wraith he may or may not have encountered. That's it. If you find him, let him know that. A few questions, and he'll never see me again."

"I'll pass it on," said Alex.

"Thanks. Listen, I got a guy that may know something. When I lived here before, he had eyes and ears virtually everywhere. Maybe he points me in the right direction."

"Good luck."

"Back at you," said Kassidy.

Kassidy ended the call with Alex and felt no more confident than she had been when it began. She hoped that this Jaxon Burke guy had not encountered a Wraith. That would be ideal for a few reasons. Well, maybe just one reason—she would have less on her plate. Although, if the damn thing was not a Wraith, that could bring an entirely new strain of problems that she just did not need.

She needed to lay eyes on Burke, and fast.

Kassidy grabbed her coat and shimmered out of view.

It was time to go see the Big Man.

CHAPTER THIRTY-THREE

"OH, HE GOT KNOCKED THE FUCK OUT," SAID THE BIG MAN AT THE END of the bar.

"Yeah, he did. Good thing that contract is guaranteed," said the bartender.

Kassidy missed the bar talk of her city. They talked shit in St. John bars on football Sundays, but it was nothing compared to what came out in Chicago. Chicagoans were more invested. They had a team, after all. But it was more than that. The city and sports just fit together like a well-tailored suit. She'd put money against anyone who said their city had a better fan base than Chicago, in any sport.

"I mean, I hope he's all right, but I need a field goal to win this quarter," said the big man.

"How many squares did you pick up?" asked the bartender.

"Just two. Twenty bucks each."

"Couldn't you spend your money a different way?" asked Kassidy.

The big man turned toward her. Recognition flooded her senses, and she felt the warmth of a friendship long passed.

"Holy shit," said the big man. "You really are here."

"Yeah. It's me, Herb. I'm back."

Kassidy walked to him as he got out of his chair and fell into a hug. Herb Jones was indeed the big man. At six foot four inches, he towered over almost everyone he knew, and he was solid, a force to be reckoned. Despite his size, he was quick when he needed to be. He'd been a counselor at a camp Kassidy attended in River Forest when she was younger. Her empathic abilities were strong even then, and she knew immediately that this man would be a friend for life if she allowed it. Aside from her adoptive mother, Marlene, she'd never met anyone with a bigger heart than Herb.

Pulling back from the embrace, she sat in the chair next to his. When he took the seat next to her, they just stared at each other for a minute. The feeling that she'd finally reconnected with her big brother washed over her. He wasn't her brother, of course. But he acted that way. He was like that with everyone. It made coming home that much more comfortable for her.

At least, as comfortable as she was capable of feeling these days.

"What's your drink?" asked Herb.

"Um, how's the bourbon here?"

"I mean, they've got it," said Herb, laughing.

"I won't be too picky, then."

"Hey, Kev," said Herb, gesturing to the bartender.

"Still know everybody, eh?"

"Pretty much."

"What's up, buddy?" asked the bartender.

"Kevin, this is an old friend of mine. Shit, what's it been? Twenty years? Damn. Anyway, this is Kassidy. Kassidy, this is Kevin Lowe."

Kassidy gave a wave and exchanged pleasantries. They were distracted by a collective groan, and all heads turned toward the television. Another brutal hit—at least, in the world of sports. The hits Kassidy had taken in recent months made these seem like pin pricks.

"Kassidy, what can I get for you?"

"I see some Woodford in the corner over there. I'll take that."

"On the rocks?"

"Neat."

"Coming up."

"And a Jamo," said Herb.

"Still shootin' Jameson, too? Has anything changed around here?" asked Kassidy.

"Ownership."

They shared a laugh. It felt good to laugh. No, it was more than that. It felt good to have a safe and genuine laugh.

Kassidy and Herb toasted each other after their drinks arrived. The Woodford Reserve warmed her, as it always did. Though, in the back of her mind, she realized she should have ordered a double.

"What are you doing here? Why now? Where the hell have you been?" asked Herb.

After a laugh and another sip, Kassidy laid out the twenty years for her old friend. She left out the part about being an empath and a Reaper. She absolutely left out the part about being the new Death God. But the important pieces of the puzzle were there, and it seemed to satisfy Herb's curiosity. Though, it also ignited some sadness.

"Damn, kiddo. That's some crazy shit. I'm sorry to hear about your girl. Lynn, you said, right?"

"Yeah."

"That's tough. And your dad, too. Shit. I heard about Mr. Simmons, but I wasn't sure if you knew. Last I heard, nobody could reach you."

"Yeah, it was a whole . . . big . . . thing," said Kassidy, absently, trying hard not to get into specifics.

"Well, what can I do? Anything? Just say the word," said Herb.

She knew he'd say that. There was little the guy wouldn't do for his family and friends. She wasn't even sure he differentiated between the two. Bound by blood or heart, Herb Jones fought hard for those he loved. She was happy to still be among them.

"I could use some info, actually."

"What's up?"

"I'm looking for a guy named Jaxon Burke. I hear he's in the game," said Kassidy.

She felt Herb's reaction before the look on his face spoke to her. He gave a heavy sigh, threw back his whiskey, then asked Kevin for another pour.

"What are you into besides simple PI work?" he asked.

"A lot of things I can't go into," said Kassidy.

"Gotta be something big if you're asking about a guy like Burke."

"He that good?"

"The best."

Kassidy had been away from home for over twenty years, but that didn't mean she was oblivious to what some old friends had been up to. Herb, with all his networking, had become a Concierge. He wasn't a criminal, he wasn't a cop, he was the one both sides went to when they needed something. She wasn't certain how he'd come into that role. There were some gaps in his background that even she couldn't shine a light on. Likely meant he'd been involved in some things off book for Uncle Sam. She knew for certain he'd been involved in dealings with the Outfit. Probably one of the few black men to do so, in fact. In the end, it all made him the perfect go-between—a living Switzerland.

"I got a tip that he may be working with a guy I'm looking for," she said.

"Who's that?"

"I'd rather not say."

"You know I'm probably gonna find out later anyway," said Herb.

They shared a grin then took a beat.

"Maybe. But if there's a chance I can keep you out of it with the other guy, I'd like to try. Burke may be badass, but the guy I'm on the hunt for . . . he's on an entirely different level of lethal."

"All right, if you say so. I'm not sure exactly where Burke is, but there's a guy that might know. Name's Frost—"

"Alex Frost?"

"You know him?"

"Yeah, I just did a job with him the other day."

"Well, there you go," said Herb.

Kassidy took a sip of bourbon and allowed her thoughts to wander. She wondered now, if the rogue Wraith was working with Burke, did that mean Frost was in on it, too? It couldn't be, could it? No, there was no way. He'd come to her by way of London, and there's no way London was setting her up.

"Frost already lost him. Any other thoughts as to where he might end up?" asked Kassidy.

"The only other person he might reach out to is his lady, Anna. She works out in Itasca. Has her own publishing business called First Person Plural," said Herb.

"Interesting name," said Kassidy.

"No doubt. Anyway, you'll probably find him if you keep eyes on her."

Kassidy took note and sent a text message to Octavia and

Keiron. She stayed for several minutes, finished her bourbon, and turned to her old friend. His concern was palpable, yet it felt tempered with understanding. It was as if he knew she could take care of herself. Hell, if he knew the kind of work Alex Frost did, maybe he had some sense of what she was involved with too. They'd have to explore that another time. Now, she had to go.

"It was good to see you, kiddo," said Herb.

"You, too."

They hugged, and as she pulled away, a flash of light caught her eye. It wasn't in the normal human spectrum, though. Shifting her vision, she saw the glow of Herb's life force. It seemed to dim a little. It was strong, still. He had miles left in the tank. But it was not as bright as she would have liked.

After a kiss on the cheek and a wave goodbye to the bartender, Kassidy walked away. The dimmed life force didn't concern her as it once had in the past. She was the Mistress of Death. As long as she lived, Herb Jones would never be gone from the world.

CHAPTER THIRTY-FOUR

SOLOMON LOOKED OUT AT THE CHILDREN PLAYING IN MILLENNIUM PARK recounting everything he'd told Jaxon. In some ways, Jaxon was like these children. Impressionable, malleable, easily manipulated with the right words. Solomon felt certain he'd convinced him of the need to kill Kassidy. Felt even more certain he'd help if for nothing more than to allow Solomon to take his life once done so he could finally find peace.

As he thought about the future, memories of the past came to him. Memories of his time with Dominique. He could recount their conversation about their own child, word for word.

"I'm . . . going to be . . . a father?" Solomon had asked.

"Yes," replied Dominique.

He didn't know what to say. In some ways he wasn't even sure how he should be feeling. This was supposed to be a blessed moment. He was going to be a father. The woman he'd loved since he first laid eyes on her was going to have his child. It was a moment he dared not dream of. Not here. Not in this place. Not in this time.

But here he was.

It had been a couple of months since he'd seen the strange man in the woods, the one who called himself, Azra-El. The promises he'd made to Solomon sounded too good to be true, and clearly they were. Solomon was still on the plantation. Still working his fingers to the bone. Still carrying the weight of his people on his shoulders.

Still being beaten and whipped.

It had been a while since the latter, but he'd taken a punch to the gut just the day before for not walking fast enough. His shoes had holes, and he'd cut his foot and big toe on a rocky path. Every step was excruciating. He tried to keep up as best he could. He even requested a chance to return to the slave quarters to fix the problem. That was when the punch came, along with the order to get it together and the threat of others sharing a beating since he wasn't feeling up to working.

"Oh lord," said Solomon.

He looked everywhere except in the eyes of the woman he loved, and when he finally did, he saw sadness. He saw despair. But he knew her well enough to know that it was not because she was with child. It was because he wasn't elated. He'd allowed his fears to take away this moment from her. She wanted this. He knew it. As sure as Solomon knew that he loved Dominique, he knew that she wanted this child.

His child.

Their child.

"Baby . . . I . . . I," he stammered.

"I know you're scared," she said.

"Yeah, but not for me. For you. And for him."

"Him? What makes you think this is a *him*?"

The smile that came with that question gave him a reprieve from the tension. He felt relief in the deep breath he took. His jaws unclenched. His muscles relaxed. And with lowered shoulders, he let his own grin take shape.

"I don't make girls," said Solomon.

"Oh really? You got a bunch of boys out there I don't know about?"

"I might."

"You better watch yourself, Mister Steele," said Dominique.

Solomon held up his arms to guard his face against her soft playful jabs. The light laughter they shared gave rise to happiness and hope despite their chains. His son could know this happiness and love the way Solomon did—or his daughter, though he hated to think of the things that could happen to her. As difficult as it was for negro men, the women had it exponentially worse. They were beaten and whipped, like the men. But . . . the other thing. The brutality of it. The humiliation. He could not bear the thought of his daughter having to experience anything of the sort.

He'd burn down the entire plantation if that happened.

"I know this is going to be difficult—"

"Difficult?" he asked.

"Yes. Difficult. Because it damn sure ain't impossible," Dominique said. "Hattie had a baby last year. Letty had twins six months ago."

"I'm not thinking about them. My concern is you. You . . . and our child," said Solomon.

He was not always inflexible, except when his passion ruled him. He would not have his child raised in that place. He would not have his love subjected to whatever possible punishment could come while pregnant. He wanted his child born free. He wanted Dominique to give birth free.

"I understand that. But we have to do our best with what we've got."

"No. We can do better. I'll see to it," Solomon promised.

He closed his eyes as Dominique caressed his face. Her hands were soft. All of her, so soft. He hated that his skin was so rough. His scars, his calloused hands, his sunbeaten face—she deserved to feel something better against her flesh. He told her how it pained him, often. And each time, she kissed him.

The frantic and excited screams of the children playing brought Solomon back to the present. How he wished Dominique was with him now. But she was in the Beyond, where she deserved to be. He hoped that one day he'd join her there.

As her face took shape in his mind, he felt a tingle in his fingers, in his toes. Then he felt a tickle across his skin. He felt himself being taken, transported. It was nothing like transforming to vapor. His body was breaking down, entering a void, and in a split second he was no longer at a park in the city. He was in a room surrounded by windows with a view of Chicago.

"Thank you for bringing him here, Jacen. You may leave now," said a woman from the shadows.

CHAPTER THIRTY-FIVE

"PLEASURE TO MAKE YOUR ACQUAINTANCE, MR. STEELE."

Solomon allowed himself to get acclimated to his new surroundings—and to the fact that he was clearly not the alpha in the room. Ever since he'd been turned, the only person he ever saw as more powerful than himself was his Primus. Solomon new there were beings with more power. Azra-El spoke about them all the time, but he never had reason to believe that he would need to come into contact with them.

Apparently he'd been wrong.

"We're on the Skydeck?" asked Solomon.

"It's my unofficial office," said the woman standing in the shadows across from him.

"You've appropriated the Skydeck of the Willis Tower for meetings?"

"Willis, eh? I know you're not a native Chicagoan. But you've clearly never lived here for any stretch of time, either."

"I'm a little older than this city, as you seem to already know. I don't care what they call the place, I just know the name that's on it now. What I'm most concerned about is why I'm here."

"That's fair," said the woman.

Solomon watched as she stepped out of the shadows into view. She was stunning, to be sure. But beauty had a way of being overshadowed by attitude. And he did not like this woman's attitude. She walked with an air of authority, but as far as he was concerned, that authority wasn't earned.

"No, I think not. The first thing you're going to want to know is my name. You may call me, Diva."

Solomon bristled at that.

"And as to why you're here, it's quite simple."

"You have me waiting anxiously," said Solomon.

"I need you to leave Jaxon Burke alone."

She said it plainly.

Over the centuries, Solomon had taken great pleasure in the knowledge that he did not have to take orders from anyone. Even when Azra-El directed him, it was less of an order and more of an assignment between partners. They were not peers, but there was a level of respect between them. Perhaps it was due to the similarities in their backgrounds. Both men were seen as nothing more than slave labor before their respective ascensions. Both were treated as "lesser-than" throughout their human lives. That type of shared experience went a long way toward building respect.

This woman was coming at him out of left field, and he was not a fan.

"And why exactly is that?" asked Solomon.

"Well, because I've asked," said the Diva.

"And why should I acquiesce to this request? I don't know you. You don't know me. Perhaps if you were to tell me more about your interest in him, we'd find that we had common goals and could work together."

She laughed.

She laughed . . . at him.

The woman had no respect for a cordial request either. She was flippant, dismissive, and emasculating. Things that Solomon hated. Did she know who he was and what he was capable of?

"Mr. Steele, I don't actually need you. Your very presence, all you've done to interfere in the last few days, is affecting my plan for the future. I don't need your help. I need you gone. Go off and do what you Wraiths do."

She did know.

Solomon wondered how someone, anyone, who knew what he was and what he could do could not fear him. Who was this so-called Diva?

"Yes, Mr. Steele, I not only know who you are, I know what you are. I've had dealings with your lot before, and I have to say, I'm most unimpressed, at best."

Anger shot through Solomon, and in a flash his eyes turned black. He stepped forward to take an offensive posture, but instead found himself flying through the air, pinned against the window. Fear ran through him for the first time in centuries as he found himself unable to move or even dematerialize so he could escape. His heart was now beating so fast that it was visible in his chest. He could not speak, he could not cry out, and he could not believe what was happening.

"I'm sorry, did I frighten you?" the Diva asked with a not-so-subtle hint of sarcasm.

"Wh . . . wh . . . what are you?" he asked.

"Well, that's an interesting, long, and old tale. You see, in the beginning . . . well, you know, that's truly not important right now," said the Diva, smiling. "What is important is that you and I come to an understanding before you leave here."

Solomon had the look of a man who was seeing all the ghosts of victims he'd laid to rest throughout his lifetime come to exact their revenge. He'd known for years that there were ruthless beings in the world. Beings more powerful and cunning than he could ever be. He'd chosen wisely to stay away from those people. He was perfectly content to "stay in his lane" as it were.

Then Kassidy happened. She'd returned to finish what she'd started twenty years ago. She'd taken the Primus and Senaya, and that demanded retribution. He wasn't sure how he'd get it, until Jaxon Burke. Now, he was being threatened and robbed of his right to vengeance by some . . . thing. He didn't know the extent of her power, but perhaps she didn't know the extent of his either.

Solomon closed his eyes and concentrated. He thought back to the night Senaya and Azra-El were dispatched. He thought back to when his wife had died. He thought back to all the times he'd been beaten as a slave. He allowed that anger to fill him. Saturated with rage, he opened his eyes.

His red eyes.

Solomon dematerialized into vapor and quickly reappeared directly in front of the Diva. He struck her, one punch to the face, then another. He spun and kicked, connecting with her head and sending her to floor. He let his hands turn to vapor, willing them to reappear as two sickles, and he prepared to strike.

"Now, ask me again to back—"

The rest of the words never came out. The Diva had cut him off, only this time, it wasn't with words, it was with a gesture. The Diva held her right hand out and simply squeezed. The tighter she squeezed, the more Solomon's throat constricted.

She stood and walked over to him. Solomon went to his knees, his reformed hands clutching at his throat. His anger replaced with fear, Solomon stared into the metallic blue eyes of the Diva.

She's a god.

"Understand this," the Diva began. "Whatever you believe

you can do, you do so only because I wish it. Whatever it is you think you are entitled to, you get only if I allow it. You are nothing to me, Solomon Steele. You are not even a means to an end. You could be useful, but only if you follow my directives. If you cannot do that, or simply choose not to . . . then you are no good to me. Nod if you understand."

Solomon clutched at his throat and gasped for air. He understood the words and nodded as he felt his death approaching.

The Diva opened her fist, and the invisible grip released. Solomon breathed in deeply, taking in air as if it were the scarcest among natural resources. He coughed, bracing himself on all fours on the floor of the Skydeck. He looked up slowly at the Diva and found her still staring at him.

"Now, Solomon, do I have your word that you'll leave Jaxon Burke alone?"

With a loud, violent crack and sizzle, thunder sounded outside, as a storm that seemed to be never-ending raged on. Instantly, the lights were out. That fear that had welled inside Solomon gave way to adrenalin. He launched himself toward the Diva, striking her in the face again to send her toppling. Then he quickly dematerialized and sought the nearest exit from the Skydeck.

After all these years, he finally realized—he had no idea what true power was.

Had it not been for the power boost he'd received from Jaxon, he might not have survived his encounter with the Diva. He needed to reenergize. With some of Jaxon's power still remaining, Solomon took to the skies and sought out some souls to recharge.

A reckoning would come soon enough.

CHAPTER THIRTY-SIX

KASSIDY'S ANXIETIES WERE OVERWHELMING HER. BETWEEN JAXON BURKE and the rogue Wraith, she just could not deal. No, she could. She was just in that space again where she didn't want to. So, she took a slight detour to Malibu after hearing about a suspicious death.

Kassidy had been bouncing around the planet, one step behind the rogue Wraith as he was taking souls. It was Azra-El all over again. As a Wraith, he had a portion of Azra-El's power, but certainly not enough that he'd be able to increase power by taking souls. At least, he shouldn't have had enough. Something else was happening here. Something was giving him additional abilities that he should not have. He was also able to block her ability to track him, and that pissed her off even more. Now that she was the Death God, she was connected to every Reaper, but not this Wraith.

"Being a god fucking sucks," she said to herself.

Kassidy knelt and checked the pulse on the body at her feet. There was nothing, of course. She knew he was dead just by looking at him. But she always checked. It was habit. Perhaps, deep down, it was the hope that she'd be wrong. After all, London had no life aura either, yet she had a pulse. London Jaymes was a vampire, so there's that. But hell, why couldn't this guy be a vampire or something, too?

Sleeping.

On the beach.

In shorts.

During a rare southern California rainstorm.

"I'm sorry, my friend. Sorry I wasn't able to keep this from happening. I promise you, though. You, and the others, will be avenged. I'll make this right."

She didn't know how, but she knew she was the only one who'd be able to, so she needed to figure something out, and soon.

"What the fuck is this asshole after?"

"I'd have thought that would be obvious," said a voice from behind.

Kassidy knew that voice. It hadn't so much startled her as it annoyed her. Or added to her current annoyance. As the rain fell, pelting the sand and blending with the crashing waves of the Pacific, she stood, turned, and faced a perfectly dry Jacen Lucas.

"Are you even here?"

"Are you trying to have a conversation on existentialism? The theory of self perhaps?"

"I really hate you sometimes," said Kassidy. "How. The fuck. Are you dry?"

"Oh," began Jacen, "I don't want to get wet. So, I'm choosing not to."

"You can just do that?"

"Clearly," responded Jacen.

It wasn't his answers that bothered her. Well, yes, it was his answers that bothered her. He was evasive. More than that, he was a smart ass. Kassidy was good at giving the smart-ass answers, but she wasn't too appreciative of them coming back and slapping her in the face. She was trying to be better at that. Hell, people had been putting up with her shit for years. When talking to Jacen Lucas, she finally empathized with the hell that her smart mouth put people through.

"What can I do for you, Mr. Lucas?" she asked.

"So formal," he replied.

"I'm a little busy, so . . ."

"Yeah, busy chasing down rogue Wraiths. Seems a job that's a bit below your new pay grade, wouldn't you say?"

Kassidy stiffened at that. First of all, what the hell did he know? He'd never been a Death God. Second of all, *how* the hell did he know? When she ascended, she felt an automatic pull toward caring for all things related to the afterlife. The sense of responsibility filled her as much as her godly power did. She *wanted* to be out cleaning up messes made by those before her.

"This is my job. No one else is able to dispatch Wraiths."

"They could be able to," said Jacen.

"Then I'd be no better than Azra-El," said Kassidy.

"There are larger challenges facing you, Kassidy. There are things in this world that require your attention. Chasing angry rogues is a distraction, at best."

"Yeah, well, unless you're going to do it, this is my life right now. What do you want? Why are you here? If you're not here to help, I'd rather you take off so I can get back to work."

A crack of thunder emphasized her words.

"Can I assume that you received my message from your mentor?"

"You can."

"And yet you're still here, chasing a rogue?"

"I'm chasing a rogue who's killing people prematurely. We're legit going through the same shit that occurred when rogues were trying to heal Azra-El. The rogue is powering up. Once I'm done dealing with this ridiculousness, I'll be more than happy to jump on board the apocalypse train. So, unless you have something helpful to tell me that can assist with any of my current issues, I'd just rather you leave me and my friends alone."

"I'm not your—"

"Enemy. Yeah, yeah, I heard all that before. You're also not an ally either, because you literally have nothing to offer me but smart-ass comments, which, we both know, I'm more than capable of providing myself."

"That's a fact," said Jacen.

Kassidy rolled her eyes and sighed. She was starting to feel a chill in the air and being soaked from the rain was not helping. She absently tried to read the Advocate, but just as before, had no luck. Whatever he was, his power trumped all of hers. She wondered if any of the twelve Elder Gods could take him. Hell, she wondered if any of the twelve even knew of him.

"Your current issues are intertwined, Kassidy," said Jacen.

"Meaning what?"

"Meaning that if you focus on the apocalypse issue, you'll be able to deal with your rogue."

"What? Like, he's involved?"

"As much as a fly is involved when the smell of sweets is in the air."

"Dude! Come on!"

Jacen held his hands up and chuckled.

"Your rogue is amassing power in the hopes he can best you. By extension, he's attracted to power . . . and there is a great deal of power amassing in the wake of this apocalyptic prophecy. He'll be drawn to it, and that will be your chance to stop him."

"So . . . what? Until then, I should just keep letting him kill people?"

"If you don't get yourself focused, it won't matter how many people he kills, because everyone will die."

There was a certain power in those words. It sounded very "needs of the many versus needs of the few" or however that quote went. It made sense. And in her new role, she recognized that until Thanatos returned, she was responsible for providing balance in the world. Balance that was already precarious in light of the prophecy of the Four.

"I can't just let him do this," said Kassidy.

"And yet, you must," said Jacen.

Kassidy stared at him, then threw her head back, letting the rain hit her face. She took a deep breath, held it, then slowly let it out as she lowered her head, only to find Jacen Lucas gone.

"Of course," she said to herself.

Kassidy retrieved her phone and called 911 to alert them of the body on the beach. She couldn't save him, but she wouldn't leave him to the elements either. She didn't bother to leave her name. She'd be back in Oak Park in seconds anyway. After providing details on the location of the body, Kassidy hung up, kneeled again, and placed her hand on the dead man's chest to give a silent prayer.

She felt a tingle in her fingers as she did. There was some sort of residual power in the man. Kassidy kept her hand there because it felt . . . familiar. It was not unlike the power she felt when she first held the Scythe of Cronus. In fact, it was similar to what she felt when she'd ascended. It was faint, but it was there.

"This is . . . god power," she said. "That can't be."

Had the rogue ascended in any way, Kassidy would most certainly feel that. No, this power residue was a byproduct. The Wraith had it, but it wasn't his. Somehow, he'd come into contact with a god. She wondered if it could be Thanatos. But then she remembered what Keiron had said about thinking the War God had returned. Then there was the report Cyrus provided on the Glade.

"Shit. Ares *is* back."

She wanted to scream, but that would accomplish nothing. She wanted to run and hide in the Nexus, but the problems would still be there when she returned to the real world. Jacen was useless, and she needed guidance, strength, and most of all comfort.

She shimmered away to the one place she could get all three.

CHAPTER THIRTY-SEVEN

FIGHTING OFF THAT . . . WHATEVER SHE WAS, DRAINED A LOT OF THE power Solomon had siphoned from Jaxon. It was disappointing, but he was thankful that was the only thing he'd lost. He'd never encountered power on that level before. As Primus, Azra-El was powerful, but not like that. The Diva was a god. He'd fought a god and lived.

Imagine if that power was mine.

Solomon found sanctuary in an unused apartment overlooking Lake Michigan. It had been used by Azra-El for a time, right before he was destroyed. It still pained Solomon to think about. That night was devastating. For so many reasons.

He needed to push that out of his mind now. For weeks his focus had been on destroying Kassidy Simmons for what she'd done. She needed to pay. He needed to wrap his hand around her neck, look her in the eyes, and end her. He needed to find a way to ensure Burke would follow through.

That man was another enigma. So much power, so much potential, and he just wanted to snuff out his own existence. Sure, there was something to be said for spending century after century watching friends and loved ones die. But there was also something to be said for having power and long life. The ability to right wrongs, to punish the guilty, to pave a new world where things were better, where people were not used and discarded as property, had been Solomon's initial motivation. In his own, distorted way, it still was. But ultimately, he truly enjoyed the power.

A world where those that did so were punished and dispatched immediately.

"How could he not want that?" Solomon silently asked himself.

Solomon let his thoughts drift away to a time long ago. He'd said yes to Azra-El, so when his death came, the Primus was there for his transformation. The sensation was surreal. It was as if he lived between worlds. It felt much more natural now, but back then, he was a newborn babe learning to hold his head on his own, then learning to roll over, crawl, walk, and finally run. When he was able, he was elevated as promised. He was the first Wraith. He remembered what Azra-El said to him:

"Like you, I come from a world where I was treated as lesser-than. I wasn't bought and sold, but those above me made certain I knew of my station. I carried buckets of piss and shit, cleaned things most foul, all for the privilege of a night in a barn away from the elements. I dared to love someone above me. Dared to dream. Dared to make that dream a reality. And for that, I have become this."

"But this is so much more," said Solomon.

"Oh, my friend, it is indeed much more. And I have several lifetimes of it ahead of me. But a part of me would trade it all for her. In time, I may find a way to bring her back. And that is what keeps me going."

"Then what?" asked Solomon.

"Then, my dear friend, we create a world in our image. Where everyone has a chance. Where everyone is equal. A world in which we decide who's worthy and unworthy. Where we are free to love who we choose."

Solomon let those words vibrate through his being again. He'd said yes to Azra-El all those years ago for just that chance. Loss was not just a human tragedy. Even as a Wraith, he had a heart and soul. He'd had to watch his beloved Dominique die. He'd had to watch his daughter grow and become a cruel woman. He was embarrassed by what she'd become. Ashamed of the way she shunned her own child. In his granddaughter, Solomon saw traits of Dominique. She was a spirit that loved life and the people in it. A bit naïve, she saw the potential for good in all. But that was early in her life. She was unloved by a jealous mother and seen as nothing but a means to an end by her father. Solomon's granddaughter had become a commodity—it hardened her heart, and it broke his.

From the Nexus, he watched her die, alone. He planned to take her to the next plane, but then his Primus arrived at her bedside. From the Nexus, Solomon watched Azra-El transform her to a Reaper. Shock and gratitude filled him. He wanted to rush to their side, but she'd never known him. And Azra-El . . . well, he'd not been aware of their connection.

Or had he?

Solomon never knew. He never asked. He simply carried on, happy in the knowledge that the last link to his beloved Dominique was still with him.

Until Kassidy Simmons dispatched her.

Solomon had arrived early enough at the park to provide his Primus with additional power to help him battle Simmons. He'd arrived early enough to see her kill his granddaughter with ease before beheading Azra-El with that damned Scythe of Cronus everyone coveted.

Looking out on the city, watching the lights and the people, Solomon absently wondered about all the battles raging among the men and women of Chicago—of the world. He wondered if they'd be so consumed with trivial wars if they knew there was a battle brewing that could change everything. He quickly let those thoughts go because in the end it didn't matter. Kassidy would die, the Scythe would be his, and he would ascend. The needs of the insignificant specks walking the streets of the Windy City and beyond were moot. He would be a god. He would succeed where Azra-El had failed. He would bring back his love, Dominique, and he would resurrect his granddaughter.

"I'll see you soon, Senaya. And together, we'll dance on Kassidy's ashes."

CHAPTER THIRTY-EIGHT

KASSIDY PLACED FLOWERS AT THE GRAVES OF DAN AND MARLENE Simmons. She kissed two fingers then touched both markers. There was a chill in the air, but it was otherwise sunny. The cemetery was near major intersections in Westchester, Illinois, just west of Oak Park, but fortunately, the Simmons plot was well within the maze of graves and away from the squealing tires and honking horns of angry and impatient drivers.

"Hi, Mom. Hi, Dad. It's me," said Kassidy. "I'm uh . . . I'm getting the house fixed up. Sarah and I worked through logistics and money and all that. I am staying there, too. I might even move back, maybe stay there permanently. Still kind of up in the air, but . . . you know . . . we have talked about it, Sarah and me, so . . . that's happening."

Kassidy's words came out like soup on a fork. She felt love, guilt, anger, and embarrassment as she sat with her adoptive parents. They had been so good to her, and all she did was cause them worry and get them killed. Well, at least Dan. Marlene was killed by a scumbag gangbanger who more than paid for his crime, thanks to Kassidy. Dan's killer had been dispatched as well. Avenging both deaths meant nothing, though. At least, not the way she had hoped. The guilt had not lessened. The pain of their loss was not any easier to bear.

Because it was all coupled with the knowledge of who she was.

Kassidy Simmons was a god now. Not just any god, but the one whose domain was death. With her new powers and abilities, and with the Scythe of Cronus at her command, she could easily bring them back. She could turn back time on their decayed bodies and bring them home with her. Alive. Happy. Thriving. But at what cost? She'd fought Azra-El to stop him from affecting the natural order. The rampant death across the world as rogue Reapers and Wraiths tried to resurrect their Primus had more impact than she had realized. She was still cleaning up the mess. God or not, she could not meddle. The repercussions could be disastrous. Her job was to maintain.

"I've got a new job now," said Kassidy. "Doesn't pay well. Benefits are good. You know, weird, almost limitless powers. I can legit teleport instead of turning into mist. You cannot believe how much I've saved on gas."

She laughed. She had to. She was hurting. Kassidy had not realized just how much she missed Marlene and Dan. When she left to become a Reaper, she really thought it was for the best. The challenges of being an empath had never been easy for her, and by extension had not been easy for the family. Yet, they all stood by her, supported her, defended her. Leaving meant that they would never have to do that again. Kassidy had truly thought it was the best way to pay them back.

But she missed them every day.

She missed them still, even more so now.

Kassidy was smart enough to know that it hurt more now because she had the power to make the pain go away. Her pain, Sarah's pain, even little Kassidy, her niece's pain. She could make all the heartache vanish in an instant. The devil on her shoulder told her to do it. The angel reminded her of her greater responsibility.

"This sucks, you know?" she said aloud. "I can straight up 'Superman' all this shit and bring you back. I don't even have to fly around the fucking Earth. I've got the Scythe now, and I can easily use it to resurrect you or rip a hole in space and time and make changes to the past."

Her eyes watered, but tears did not fall. She held onto them. Taking a deep breath and letting it out, she found herself centered . . . at least a little.

"I know what you'd both say. I know you would not want the world to suffer just so I could have you back. I know you understand . . . and I know . . . I know that . . . I know that you forgive me."

Then tears fell.

Kassidy had never understood their capacity to love unconditionally. She admired it, envied it, even. But she could not understand it. Marlene and Dan had nothing but unconditional love for her, for Sarah, for so many. It was that knowledge that convinced her that they had nothing but forgiveness in their hearts for her.

Yet she struggled to forgive herself.

On some level it was the result of having so much to forgive. Kassidy had been a hot mess for a long time. But more than that, Kassidy did not *know* how to forgive herself. She had seen forgiveness in action, but she had never practiced it. So, she held onto her guilt and her anger. For all these years, she held them close to her. They were as much a part of her as her new powers.

"I'm sorry," she said, wiping tears away. "I'm so sorry. So sorry that my crazy life, my crazy past, came here and landed on your doorstep. You will never know how much I appreciate and love you both. I should have said it when you were here. So many times over. But I was selfish—*am* selfish. Life is just all about me. God . . . how did you stand it?"

She knew how. She knew it was out of love. That unconditional love that deep down she hoped she would one day be able to give.

Kassidy stayed longer, despite the chill in the air, and talked to her parents for the first time in decades. She laughed, she cried more, but she talked and got them caught up on recent happenings and plans. It felt good. Bittersweet, but good.

Kassidy stood, looked down, and blew a kiss to each marker.

"I'll be back soon, guys. I love you," she said.

As she turned to walk away, she was met by a man . . . with black eyes. With a loud yell, he swiftly pivoted to deliver a side kick to Kassidy's chest that sent her flying back into a solid marble marker. The shock of the attack and the initial sting of the impact left her dazed. Looking up, she saw her attacker standing above her.

"It's time to pay for what you've done," said Solomon.

CHAPTER THIRTY-NINE

KASSIDY SPUN AND DELIVERED A KICK TO THE ABDOMEN, SENDING THE Wraith flying backward into a headstone. The marble monument disintegrated into dust and rubble. Trying to take advantage of the Wraith's disorientation, Kassidy shimmered out of view and reappeared directly in front of him. She sent a knee to his chin causing him to topple over to his side. Stretching out with her senses she called to the Scythe of Cronus. When it appeared in her hand, she held it over the Wraith.

"Don't you fucking move," said Kassidy.

The Wraith turned his head, wiped his bloodied lip with the back of his hand, and gave a look of sheer hatred. Kassidy couldn't sense anything from him, and this concerned her. Since her ascension, she was tuned into every Reaper. Tracking some of the Wraiths had proven to be problematic. Some had found ways to possess humans, thus hiding from her as they used the souls of humans as a shield. Without that shield, they were easy to sense.

Not this Wraith though.

He was directly in front of her, but according to her senses, he didn't exist. She felt nothing from him. He was hollow. Vacant. A singularity with no explanation for existence. He was a Wraith, that much was certain. But there was something so different about him.

"Before I dispatch you, why don't you tell me who you are," said Kassidy.

"Fuck you!"

"Oh, that's so the wrong response. You know I'm like your boss now, right? I mean, you're about to get fired, in the worst way possible, but you could at least respect the title before you go."

Kassidy touched the Wraith's chest with the tip of the Scythe, giving birth to a crackle of electricity. It caught her off guard. That shouldn't happen. That shouldn't happen at all. She was certainly no expert yet, but she'd never encountered that before when using the weapon. The surprise was enough to give the Wraith a moment to collect himself. Off guard, Kassidy was thrown to the ground by an invisible force emanating from the man. She watched as he dematerialized into vapor, only to reform standing, brandishing two sickles. Regrouping, she shimmered out of view and reappeared standing in front of him, Scythe in hand.

"What the hell are you?" demanded Kassidy.

"I am going to be your undoing, imposter," said the Wraith. "The power you wield should not be yours. It was not meant for you."

"I suppose it was meant for you instead? Well, come and get it."

Deep down, Kassidy knew that baiting him was probably the wrong move. She was now the Death God, but even gods knew they shouldn't go into battle against a foe they had no knowledge of, didn't they? She felt like a substitute teacher with a lesson plan for first graders in a classroom with doctoral students.

Imposter!

She lunged at the Wraith, her Scythe coming down in a wide

overhead arc. He rolled to the side, avoiding contact, sprang up to his knee, and turned to slash, but Kassidy blocked the blow in time and backed up. The Wraith stood and took a step forward.

"You're nothing without that weapon, girl."

"Jealous?"

"Not at all. I'm going to enjoy licking your blood off the blade after I take your head with it."

"Awfully ambitious," said Kassidy.

"I was trained by the best, and I've been around a lot longer than you."

Kassidy let those words sink in a bit more. She didn't know enough about him to risk using the Scythe. What if he *could* beat her? What if he took the Scythe? Calling on her will, she sent the weapon away. Back to a nameless void only she knew. A place from which only she could recall it. She may have been out of depth in some areas of this new job, but at least she'd gotten that right.

"Tell you what," she said, "let's test that training of yours and see how well you do."

The Wraith smiled, allowed his hands to reform in place of his sickles, and immediately threw a punch.

Kassidy blocked the jab and countered with a punch to the gut followed by a quick uppercut topped with a spin kick to the chest. The combination and speed seemed to catch the Wraith off guard and sent him to the ground. Kassidy pounced, straddled him, and sent one punch after another to his face. After a short volley, she held him down by the neck with her left hand and sent her right hand into his chest.

"So much for experience," said Kassidy.

The Wraith struggled, trying to throw her off. After a beat, he stopped. He stopped, and he grinned. Then . . . he laughed.

Kassidy, her hand phased inside the man's chest in search of his life force, felt a buildup of pressure then an explosion of power as she was propelled through the air. She landed hard, ten feet away, and in pain. Electricity coursed through her body. Her vision dark, she felt an intense weight on her chest. Her attacker was kneeling on it.

"I told you, little girl, you're not ready for this," said the Wraith.

Kassidy then felt the point of a sickle at her neck. That familiar tingle from the metal adding to the electrical current coursing through her.

"Now, you wanted to know my name. It's Solomon. Solomon Steele. I was Azra-El's first . . . and now, I will be the last. Call back the Scythe of Cronus or die."

Imposter!

The word reverberated in her brain. Worse than the taunts from children when she was a kid. She'd just been bested by a Wraith. That wasn't supposed to happen to gods, was it? No, it definitely wasn't. It couldn't. It . . . shouldn't. Right?

As the sensation from the electrical charge within subsided, Kassidy was focused a little more. But only a little. Her mind was everywhere. The pressure on her chest increased as Solomon bore down. He pressed his sickle in further and she felt a trickle of blood slip down her neck. She needed to escape. She needed out.

She needed . . . home.

"Call to it, damn you!" Solomon demanded.

Summoning her will once again, Kassidy allowed herself to transition into the Nexus. In this world, this between space, she was able to roll from under the weight of Solomon, shimmer away, reappearing in her home without leaving the spectral plane.

For her, the Nexus *was* home, despite everything.

And home she stayed.

CHAPTER FORTY

CARTWRIGHT TOWER WAS A TALL MONSTROSITY OVERLOOKING Chicago. It was considered an architectural wonder, but in the eyes of many, it was just a lot of steel and glass that didn't seem to fit the old style of the city. There was an original building, built by Jefferson Cartwright, Charles's grandfather. It sat along the river and was viewed as a "working building," which was another way of saying the company and people within it worked for the city. The old Cartwright building was more in line with the feel of this city. If Charles had opted to work there instead, he'd likely have had more respect from the people of the Chicago. Instead, he relegated the old building to serve as a dusty warehouse that housed nothing but the ghosts of hard-working men and women and the dreams of his grandfather. It was off limits to the public, and, as Jaxon Burke had recently found out, was the site of many horrific business deals signed by Cartwright and his security guard, Damien LaVelle.

Well, his former security guard.

Jaxon entered the architectural wonder and checked in at the front desk. He didn't bother to hide his identity. He was an elite soldier, tactician, and assassin with seven hundred years of training. If he wanted to get inside the building without being seen, he could certainly accomplish that. But there was no need. Jaxon had the upper hand here, and he was going to milk it.

"May I help you, sir?" asked the burly security guard.

"Yes. Jaxon Burke for Charles Cartwright."

"Do you have an appointment, Mr. Burke?"

"No."

"I'm sorry, sir, Mr. Cartwright does not meet with anyone without an appointment."

"You'll probably want to tell him I'm here. Trust me when I say, he'll want to see me."

The security guard stood, his posture making it clear he was trying to intimidate Jaxon. The man was bulky, but more muscle than anything else. He stood about six and a half feet tall and weighed every bit of two hundred and sixty pounds. It was easy to see how that would intimidating for most people.

But Jaxon was undeterred. Size just didn't matter. He'd learned a number of fighting styles from the very people who'd invented them, and there were few opponents who could best him. This guard, with all his posturing, would be down in seven seconds.

"Sir, again, Mr. Cartwright does not see anyone without an appointment. Now, I would suggest that you make one and come back another time."

The guard was holding fast to that no appointment thing. Cartwright had his people trained well. Jaxon wondered if LaVelle had any part in that training.

"I think you're misunderstanding me," began Jaxon. "I don't need to see Mr. Cartwright. Mr. Cartwright needs to see me."

"It doesn't matter how you say it, sir, without an appointment—"

"Yeah, yeah, yeah . . . I heard you the first time."

The guard wasn't going to give in, and Jaxon was still hell bent on not causing a scene. Things were probably going to get ugly later anyway. So, Jaxon opted to go with some truth.

"Let me ask you a question. Were you guys trained, by chance, by Damien LaVelle?"

The guard looked down at his partner who had been watching the cameras. Their eyes met, then they both looked at Jaxon. The second guard stood, as if to protect their pride leader.

"Yes, sir, we were," said the first guard. "Do you know Mr. LaVelle?"

Jaxon smiled.

"Know him? I just killed him. You see, this is why I need to speak with Charles. I bet—in fact, I guarantee—that if you let Mr. Cartwright know I'm here and that I killed his boy, he'll buzz me right up."

"Sir—"

"The other option is that I put you two down, then open fire on everyone in here and cause a terrible scene," said Jaxon, opening his coat slightly to reveal a holstered SIG Sauer P226.

The guards again made eye contact. Odds were good that they'd been trained for something like this. Odds were even better that they were just the first wave of security. They'd likely send him up and tell him to get off on a "trouble floor"—a floor with no offices and no personnel, except more trained guards who would be in position to neutralize whatever threat was coming. He'd likely be told to take Mr. Cartwright's "private" elevator. Jaxon was perfectly okay with that.

The second guard sat back down and made a call. The standing guard redirected his focus to Jaxon. After a few seconds of whispers, the second guard stood again and handed Jaxon a key card.

"Sir, Mr. Cartwright would be happy to see you. He's asked that you take his private elevator to meet him in his office. This card will open the elevator located on the left side of the elevator banks, all the way at the end."

Jaxon smiled wryly, then followed the guard's finger as he pointed to the elevators.

"Thank you," said Jaxon with a slight nod.

As he walked off, he imagined those guards were giddy at the thought of him getting roughed up by the B Squad. If only they knew what awaited them.

Using the key card, Jaxon entered the elevator, pressed the top button, as there were only two, and let the doors close. As he did, his eyes turned blue.

◆ ◆ ◆

"I had to let a counselor go a few months ago because of budget cuts. We haven't been able to give our staff raises in over five years, yet we continue to acquire new properties and we hire new staff that, from the outside looking in, seem completely unnecessary. So, I guess my question is, how am I supposed to justify those decisions to my staff?"

Charles Cartwright sat in his chair at the head of the conference table and listened carefully to the question posed by the young program director, Rick something or other. At least he thought it might be Rick. From what Charles had heard of him, he was a bright man and an amazing counselor. He had a great deal of confidence and patience and straddled the lines between counselor, supervisor, and administrator with great ease. Today, though, Charles sensed a little bite in his tone. Charles didn't like little bites in people's tones. Charles didn't like feeling as if his words and decisions were being challenged.

Charles also hated dealing with the petty bullshit of his late mother's pet social service project.

He kept this agency and its efforts alive because of optics. It made him and his company look good when he was involved with the community. It also made him look like a loving and caring son honoring his mother.

Beneath the surface, he could not have cared less.

"Let me start by saying that I'm sorry that you had to make those cuts," said Charles. "It sounds like he was a valuable member of your team."

He used terms like "sounds like" and "what I hear you saying is" to shut them up. They loved that shit.

"Unfortunately, we are in a position where we've lost a significant revenue stream from the state due to the cuts they've been forced to make to their budget. Consequently, we've got to dig in deep if we want to continue to get things done the way the charter mandates."

Although forked, Charles Cartwright had a silver tongue. The only reason he hadn't gone into politics was because he didn't want to have to disclose his finances. Some of his millions were made by, well, applying pressure to certain things and certain people. For Charles, the ends justified the means. There were no grey areas. There were only two ways to get things done: the wrong way and his way. The people at this Rising Phoenix agency were going to do things his way.

Whether they liked it or not.

"Well, is there some way that we can communicate that to the staff?" the program director asked. "Is there some way that we can be proactive in explaining the changes instead of us being reactive to their questions and frustrations?"

"Rick, is it?" Charles asked, getting an affirmative nod. "Rick, we can absolutely do that. The problem is that I'd have to hire more unnecessary staff people to get something like that out to everyone. We are all in positions here to do a specific job and we all have to trust that the people in those positions are doing what they're supposed to be doing to keep this Phoenix rising."

He got smiles and a bunch of words of affirmation for that. Charles ate it up. He knew he had these folks in the palm of his hand. Touchy feely morons like the ones gathered at this meeting loved a good "inspirational" play on words. He wanted out of here. This was painful.

"Folks, I hate to end this, truly I do, but we've run out of time, and I have a conference call with a prospective donor in twenty minutes. But if you have anything additional to ask or suggest, please email me. I promise they won't end up in my trash bin." Charles smiled as he arose to shake a few hands, give a few waves, and walk out the door amid applause.

The beauty of these wastes of time was that Charles could get away by simply walking down the hall to his office and locking the door. He had Trish, a competent and ruthless administrative assistant. There was no better gate keeper in the city. She was fairly no nonsense like he was, which made it easy for her to accept that they wouldn't be sleeping together anymore, unless he wanted it. At the same time, she could charm people into doing just about anything she needed, which typically mirrored exactly what Charles needed.

As he neared his office, he saw Trish talking to a man who was not at all familiar . . . at least not from the back. Walking closer, Charles caught her line of sight and saw that she seemed a little concerned, as if she were uncomfortable with the conversation or the man, or both. Charles was certainly in no mood for further bullshit, particularly not after the meeting he'd just come from. He needed to focus on this thing with the Diva, and he needed to determine if Burke was still alive. He'd flex a muscle or two to get this guy to move on. If that didn't work, he'd call security, although the odds were Trish had already done so. She was that good.

"Is there a problem, Trish?" asked Charles.

"This gentleman insists on seeing you, but I explained that he'd need an appointment," she replied.

Charles looked to his right and observed two security guards walking toward them. They were from downstairs, though, not the thirteenth floor. Where were those guards?

"Sir, I'm afraid she's correct, we are very busy, and as much as I'd like to meet with everyone, I don't . . ."

Charles lost his train of thought as the man turned to face him. He'd studied those chiseled features almost daily before sending Damien to meet, negotiate, and kill him. Normally, Charles had a world class poker face, but not this time.

Not with this.

Not with him.

"I was explaining to Miss Watkins here that you'd probably make an exception for me," said the man, extending his hand. "Jaxon Burke. But you already know who I am, don't you, Charles?"

CHAPTER FORTY-ONE

"WHAT IS IT THAT I CAN DO FOR YOU, MISTER . . . ?"

"Please," said Jaxon. "This conversation will go a lot smoother if you don't act like you have no clue who I am."

Jaxon watched Cartwright as he walked around him dismissively to sit at his desk. Cartwright leaned back, crossed his right leg over his left, and looked at Jaxon.

"Very well, Mr. Burke, we'll keep our cards on the table."

"LaVelle is dead," said Jaxon.

"I see. And how did he die?" asked Cartwright.

"Poorly, and in great agony."

Jaxon noticed a slight shift in Cartwright's posture. It was enough to let him know that the man was unnerved, and that knowledge sent a rush of excitement through Jaxon's body.

"And now you're here to do what? Scare me? Intimidate me?"

"Kill you," said Jaxon, plainly.

Cartwright shifted again, and Jaxon felt another surge. In his mind, the screams and cries started again. He heard voices begging for mercy. He heard swords clanging against one another and the rush of a man's last breath as a blade entered the chest. His mind's eye envisioned rivers of blood flowing down battlefields. Cartwright's shift was one of fear, and that fear was throwing gasoline on Jaxon's bloodlust.

"As I said on the phone, I think we can come to some type of arrangement. I mean, especially if Damien is gone. You could take his place. You'd be head of security here, and—"

"I don't think so," said Jaxon. "Most of your security is either dead or in serious to critical condition on the thirteenth floor, which means I'd have to spend my first several months on the job hiring and training a new team, and I gotta tell you, Charles, I don't have the patience for that."

Cartwright shifted again.

"Let's keep this simple. LaVelle gave me your name as the one who called for my death. In some respects, I can appreciate that. You're a businessman, and you were trying to tie up loose ends. It is, however, dishonorable, and a slap in the face to a professional like me. So, I'm going to ask a question, and I want you to think long and hard about how you respond. It could be the difference between a long, agonizing death, like LaVelle's. Or an even longer agonizing death for pissing me off and threatening to blow up a bed that my girlfriend was in."

"And that question is?" asked Cartwright.

"Who are you working for?"

Jaxon initially thought that the meeting might be a battle of wills. Cartwright had already tipped his hand a few times, so that battle was already won. His death was a foregone conclusion. With any luck, he was bright enough to see that, so Jaxon could get back to other business with Solomon and this Kassidy Simmons woman. He needed this name though. LaVelle was hesitant to give up Cartwright's name, yet he did. By the time he'd alluded to someone else being involved, he was already too far gone. Jaxon was going to have to rely on Cartwright to spill his guts.

"And what makes you think I'm working for someone?" asked Cartwright.

"Well, LaVelle told me as much," said Jaxon, lying to get a reaction.

And there it was.

Every human being reacts in their own way. Whether it's good news, bad news, or painful news, they all do it. For some, it's overt and over the top. For others, it's tiny micro expressions that reveal levels of deceit or discomfort. Cartwright's micro expressions spoke loudly to Jaxon.

"I can assure you, whatever he said was wrong," said Cartwright. "Listen, I am a powerful man. I didn't get here by being the nice guy all the time. I have my finger on the pulse of all the major dealings in the world. They've been orchestrated meticulously. I can manipulate outcomes for world events, and I can assure you, that does not happen by working with others in a committee."

"You're lying," said Jaxon.

"How dare—"

"Stop. Just . . . stop. Please," said Jaxon. "I get that you want to be seen as the ruler of your own little kingdom. I also see that you want to influence and control the world from a tiny little booth like the all-powerful wizard. You may even have aspirations of entering the White House as more than a guest. I get all of that. But I care about none of it. If you don't want to give me the name of the person you're working with, that's fine. For right now, my beef is with you, and I'm perfectly content to end it here with your death. If your silent partner wants to come after me for taking you out, that's fine. I'll deal with it. As you know, I'm hard to kill, and I have nothing but time on my hands. So tell me, or don't . . . your life ends today either way."

Jaxon was having fun. His adrenalin was pumping. The screams in his head were louder. There were more of them. He hated them because he didn't know why they were there. He hated them because they gave rise to this rage inside. But right now he needed them to fuel his revenge.

"We agreed to put all our cards on the table, Mr. Burke, and I have done exactly that. I can assure you, I am working with no one. With that in mind, I would welcome an opportunity to work with you. We can find a way if you open yourself up to the possibilities."

Jaxon loathed the arrogance of the rich and powerful. They always assumed that nothing could touch them, that there was a solution to everything, and that the solution came in the form of green paper, zeroes, decimal points.

"I am currently working on other projects, Charles. And I'm not taking on any partners."

Cartwright shifted.

Jaxon rose.

Any chance of negotiation ended.

CHAPTER FORTY-TWO

ANNA DEBARTOLO SAT IN HER OFFICE WAITING FOR HER INTERN TO arrive. Today, they were going to practice interviewing, and Anna would be the subject. She did this annually, provided she had an intern with the interest and skill in being a writer. As the editor of First Person Plural, an online magazine that catered to writers of all genres and disciplines, most of her interns came from schools dedicated to communications or the arts, but a good number of them were still trying to figure out what they wanted to be. Grace Childs was a little different. She'd been writing since before she could walk. At least that was the word in her family. Anna had a chance to meet Grace's mother during the FPP Family Day last month, and she got a lot of background on the intern. Anna found that she genuinely liked Grace and was happy to help her further her career and explore her interests. Grace reminded her a bit of her younger sister, Sage.

While FPP was not necessarily rolling in money, it made enough through advertising and donations to rent office space in a nice building in Itasca, away from the nonsense of downtown Chicago. Anna had been told many times to move and settle down where the action was. But in the digital age, that wasn't necessary anymore.

Anna's office was modest. The wooden desk was the most elaborate thing she had. Her father had made it for her as a gift.

Like Grace, Anna had been writing since before she could walk. Her father made building that desk his mission, so she'd have something nice to pen her great works upon. He worked on it a little bit every day and several hours on the weekends to get it right. The project began with she was eight, and he'd finished it and presented it to her on her fourteenth birthday. The desk's beauty was unmatched. It was hand-carved hardwood, and he'd etched literary themed designs into it. There were quills, fountain pens, typewriters, notepads, and even a few quotes expertly carved into the wood. He'd built it to last and built it for an adult so that she could take it with her wherever she went. Anna had it with her in college, grad school, and for a long time, in her home. But when she'd founded FPP and began spending more time at the office, she opted to move it in to her brand new space so she'd have a piece of home with her.

It fit well in her office. She decorated the place to match the desk. Her chairs were dark brown leather as was the loveseat next to the wooden bookcase to her left. She'd hung some beautiful pieces of art that she'd acquired over the years. Several were from friends she'd gone to school with; some were from people she'd interviewed. Her favorite was an oil painting of the Parthenon, a gift from her boyfriend, Jaxon. He once told her that he didn't fancy himself an artist, he simply put on paper or canvas what he saw in his head. Anna's mother was Greek, so she identified with the culture.

Anna heard a knock at her door. "Come in," she said.

"Hey, it's just me," Grace said. "Are you free? Ready to do this interview?"

"Absolutely. Get in here and shut that door. Let's do this."

Anna was enthusiastic about the interview. Not because she enjoyed talking about herself, but because she enjoyed helping other writers. Jaxon always said it was one of the things he loved most about her.

The interview went well from Anna's perspective. Grace's questions were well thought out and allowed for good follow-up. The most important aspect of the interview was that Grace was genuinely engaged. Over the years, Anna had observed that many people conducted interviews seemingly for the sole purpose of getting to the next question. That wasn't the case with Grace. She asked a question and actively listened to the answers. Her follow-up questions were organic, and that put Anna at ease because the interview was more like a conversation.

If she'd had a doubt that she'd offer Grace a job after graduation, that doubt was certainly gone now.

"Okay," Grace continued, "enough of the business. What does Anna DeBartolo like to do for fun? Reading and writing don't count."

Anna laughed because anyone who knew her well understood that those two things were just as fun for her as going out for dinner or traveling.

"I like getting out there and discovering new things, meeting interesting people. I love going to ballgames or hanging out in sports bars. I mean, you see so many interesting people, you know?"

Grace nodded in agreement.

"I guess, though, I'm the type that's up for anything, because the way I see it, I'm going to get a story or story idea out of it, or I'm going to flat out enjoy it for the sake of . . . well . . . whatever it is."

"Give me an example of the last fun thing you did," said Grace.

"Um, well, my boyfriend and I went whale watching. And I

mean, this guy absolutely loves the sea. I think in another life he may have been a dolphin," Anna said with a grin. "But, seeing the joy on his face, seeing him relaxed, made me happy. He works hard and rarely takes time for himself, so when he does, it's always a treat."

"It sounds lovely," said Grace.

"It was. You know, we are just as happy spending a day at home doing nothing. But yeah, when we're out, we enjoy having fun. Which is good, because I think it took him a long time to get to that point. He's a little shy. Well, in the sense that he focuses on others so much that he sometimes doesn't think about himself."

Just then, the phone rang. Grace glanced at Anna with a look of understanding. They were in the middle of a workday, and interruptions happened. She smiled politely as if waited to be put on the backburner, but Anna was having none of it. She'd been that girl before. The girl looking for an audience from a mentor, a friend, a lover only to be put on hold as the person opposite her responded to an e-mail, text, or phone call. She'd vowed to not be a person who did that. This was a big moment for Grace. It meant the world to her, and Anna knew that. So, she reached out for her desk phone and pressed a button that sent the call to voicemail.

"What else you got for me, Grace?" she asked.

"You . . . you don't need to take that?" Grace asked.

"You're doing an excellent job, and I don't want to stop the momentum. This is fun. And more importantly, this is time that I've blocked off for you. So, yeah, they'll have to wait."

Anna saw a sparkle in Grace's eyes. The young girl was good at what she did, and she was only going to get better. Though that would depend a great deal on the examples she followed.

A knock at the door interrupted Anna's thoughts. She was tempted to ignore it as she had the phone call, but this one probably wouldn't go away as quickly. The first few knocks were normal, but the second round was much more intense, rapid, and followed by her assistant calling her name.

"Good grief," Anna said to Grace. "Yes, come in."

Anna's assistant, Sarah rushed in the door. Her face, normally calm but bright and cheery, was now flushed, and her eyes watered.

"My god, Sarah . . . what's wrong?" Anna asked as she rose from her chair to walk toward her assistant. The girl was in shock, unable to speak. The seconds seemed to last hours as Anna struggled to get Sarah to at least look at her.

"An . . . An . . . Anna," Sarah stammered. "You have to turn on the TV."

"What? Why?"

"It's . . . it's . . . it's Jax."

CHAPTER FORTY-THREE

OCTAVIA WATCHED ANNA DEBARTOLO FROM ACROSS THE STREET AS she rushed out of her office at First Person Plural. She let the name of the business bounce around in her head. Wouldn't have been her first choice for a company name, but Octavia wasn't a writer.

Octavia had lived a long life, cursed by Thanatos for the part she played in the death of his son at the hands of Tyran, who went on to become Azra-El. She'd seen the world as a traveler and historian. Often, as a student and warrior. But always, in every lifetime, alone. No one had captured her heart since him—since Ares. It wasn't that she was closed off to love or taking lovers. She'd certainly had her share over the centuries. But the things she'd felt and experienced with him, in such a short amount of time, left a lasting mark on her heart and soul. So even when she took a lover, man or woman, they already had an insurmountable obstacle to climb. Octavia tired from keeping those walls up. After so long, though, she didn't know any other way to live.

As Anna practically sprinted to her car, Octavia scanned the parking lot. Thankfully, it was fairly wide open. There were few places to hide. If Jaxon had been there, she would have spotted him quickly. She was grateful that the young woman worked in the suburbs as opposed to the city. Itasca was a nice area. There was a time when Octavia had considered living there. It was some distance from the city, but the interstate was close by, and if traffic was light, she could be in the city in a decent span of time.

Octavia enjoyed Chicago. There was nothing more spectacular than the view of downtown at night. The people, the food, the culture . . . it felt like a true melting pot, and despite some clear cultural divisions, she could not imagine being anywhere else. Like Anna, she lived in the western suburbs, but she would visit the city for various events, and sometimes, just to be surrounded by the people. Still, even after all the centuries, she missed her true home, her family . . . and him.

As Octavia followed Anna from her office to her home in Elmwood Park, she wondered about the girl and her relationship with Jaxon Burke. Kassidy said he was a gun for hire, something Anna was not aware of. It seemed strange to be with someone and not truly know them. Perhaps Anna DeBartolo didn't want to know. Even that prospect was foreign to Octavia.

Pulling to the side of the street and parking as Anna turned into her driveway, Octavia took stock of the young woman. Her long brown hair cascaded well below her shoulders. Her Mediterranean features left Octavia remembering home. Anna seemed taller when she stepped out of her car to enter her home. Perhaps because she was closer now than at the lot. She was a striking young woman. If this Jaxon Burke were really immortal, he'd live long past those good looks. Octavia wondered if the love would remain.

She felt her cell phone vibrate and answered.

"Hey," she said.

"Where are you?" asked Kassidy on the other end.

"Hanging out in my car across the street from her home. She just got here."

"Got it. Listen, I got word from a Reaper who escorted a particularly ornery soul to the Void. His body was a mess, his mind apparently more so, but he murmured the name Burke a few times before heading off into the abyss."

"Seems our boy was busy," said Octavia.

"No doubt," said Kassidy. "Keiron is going to head back to Burke's place and sit on it while I head to the spot where the body was found. Let me know immediately if Burke shows up. I can be there the fastest."

"Okay. Will do. Be careful, Kass," said Octavia.

The phone went silent.

She wondered if there was still some bad blood between them, despite Kassidy's waving of the white flag and their heart to heart. Octavia walked on eggshells where Kassidy was concerned. Mostly out of guilt. Odds were good that had she not acted like a petulant child when she was younger, none of this would be happening now, and Kassidy would be Thanatos's granddaughter, not his daughter.

Changing the past was not in Octavia's toolbox. Working to make amends, however—that was a real thing. And something she'd been doing for a few thousand years.

A couple hours passed by with no sign of Burke, and Octavia was starting to wonder if this was the right move. She wanted to get out of the car and peek around, but if she were caught, she'd have no excuse to give for being there. A classics professor from a local community college getting caught in the bushes was not a good look.

Thankfully, the blood-curdling scream from Anna's home provided the perfect excuse.

Octavia left her car and bolted for the home like the skilled warrior she was. She lowered and braced herself, then ran shoulder first into the front door, sending it flying open to the surprise of those inside. Anna's head turned to the door.

So did the Wraith's.

Octavia reached behind and unsheathed two Celestial Onyx daggers and lunged forward. The Wraith quickly retracted its hand from Anna's chest and turned to face Octavia. The only things darker than the tattered cloak it wore were its eyes. In its current form, it would be difficult to battle. Octavia hoped it would transition to its human guise, but instead, it turned to Anna and spoke.

"Kassidy Simmons sends her regards."

The Wraith immediately dematerialized into vapor and exited the home.

Octavia was taken aback at the whole scene. The attack on Anna, the words, and the strange, abrupt departure left her perplexed. She sheathed her daggers and ran to Anna who was rocking back and forth on her couch in shock.

"Are you hurt?" asked Octavia.

Her question was met with silence.

"Can you hear me?" asked Octavia.

Several beats passed.

"Anna, talk to me."

A blank stare. Progress.

"Anna, I need to know if you're all right physically. Are you hurt anywhere?"

Anna shook her head.

"Good. That's real good. Listen, I want to get you out of here and take you some place safe. Would that be all right?"

Anna stared blankly.

Octavia was not of a mind to force someone to do anything, particularly after a traumatic experience like a Wraith attack. All signs pointed to this place being unsafe, though. If she couldn't get Anna out, she was going to have to stay. With only two daggers at her disposal, she'd simply have to do the best she could in the event of an attack.

Octavia grabbed a blanket from the arm of a recliner and wrapped it around Anna, who was likely to be incoherent for a while. Octavia went for her phone and realized she'd left it in the car.

Shit!

Looking around, she saw no landline. For the first time in a while, she longed for the eighties. She would have done anything for even a rotary phone. She found Anna's iPhone on the side table and grabbed it. It was password protected, but fortunately equipped with facial recognition. She held it up to Anna's face to unlock it and quickly called Kassidy, surprising herself that she could remember the number without looking it up.

Kassidy didn't answer, so she dialed again.

And again.

And again.

And again.

"Who the hell is this and how did you get this number?" demanded Kassidy.

"Kassidy, it's me."

"Octavia? What's wrong? Whose phone is this? Where are you?"

"I need you to get here right away. There was a Wraith attack," said Octavia.

Within seconds, Kassidy was shimmering into existence and bounding up the stairs into Anna's home.

"Are you all right?" asked Kassidy.

"I'm fine," began Octavia. "Anna, not so much."

"What happened?"

"I heard a scream, rushed in, and found a Wraith lurched over her trying to kill her. He—"

Octavia stopped mid-sentence as she fixated on a photograph on Anna's bookshelf. Her heart raced. In the distance, she heard Kassidy speaking, but the words were muffled. Her tunnel vision didn't register the chair or the end table in her way. She didn't feel the sharp pain from bumping into them. Standing directly in front of the bookcase, she grabbed the picture and stared. The woman was Anna, happy and smiling. But Octavia was focused on the man with his arms around her. His olive skin, short hair, and goatee sparked waves of memories. She heard her name echoing in the distance and finally felt an abrupt turn of her entire body.

"Octavia!" shouted Kassidy.

Octavia snaped back to the present and looked from the photo to Kassidy and back. She traced the man's features with her fingertips. She then looked to Anna, back to the photograph, then to Kassidy.

"Octavia, what the hell is going on?"

"The . . . the . . . man, in this picture . . ."

Kassidy stole a glance.

"Yeah. It's probably Jaxon. What's wrong with—"

"No. No. This . . . this . . . this is Ares," said Octavia.

Octavia shook.

Then cried softly.

CHAPTER FORTY-FOUR

AFTER SEEING ALL THE MOVEMENT DOWNSTAIRS, JAXON SCALED ANNA'S townhome and entered through an unlocked window. He moved slowly down the hall toward her bedroom and entered. He was surprised to find her in bed. He'd assumed the movement downstairs was her talking to friends, and he'd planned to text her once they were gone to let her know he was upstairs. Now, he was thoroughly confused.

He brushed her hair from her eyes and kissed her forehead. Her eyes flickered a few seconds before opening fully. There was shock in her eyes, and she immediately moved to the opposite side of the bed.

"Shh . . . Anna . . . it's me. It's Jax. Sweetheart . . ."

Jaxon was pleading in a low whisper. He stretched out his arm and repeated her name over and over, until she cautiously placed her hand in his. Once they touched, she moved back to him and buried her head in his chest. She was shaking, so he stroked her hair and spoke soothingly.

After several minutes, he laid her down, still holding her hand. She looked exhausted and frightened, yet somehow, she seemed present with him there.

"Can you tell me what happened?"

She shook her head.

"Please, babe. Tell me what happened so I can try and fix it."

She shook her head again.

"Did someone hurt you?"

She nodded.

"Was it those people downstairs?"

She shook her head.

Jaxon's anger was at the surface. Someone had hurt her, and he hadn't been there to protect her because he was too busy seeking revenge. He was relieved that she was being protected by people downstairs. But they shouldn't be needed.

"Can you tell me anything, babe? Can you tell me who did this?"

Jaxon felt her hand squeeze his. She pulled him closer and whispered words he'd not expected.

"Kassidy Simmons sends her regards."

CHAPTER FORTY-FIVE

JAXON SAT ON THE FLOOR OF HIS BEDROOM, CROSS-LEGGED, EYES CLOSED, attempting to meditate. A storm raged outside, but it paled in comparison to the storm that raged within him. He completed a thirty second countdown, took a deep breath, and silently mouthed his mantra. After a minute, his mouth stopped moving, and he spoke it in his mind, the rain offering a soothing soundtrack.

His meditation wasn't about control or clearing his mind, and it certainly wasn't about an absence of thought. It was his attempt to calm the rage that lived under the surface, that threatened to unleash itself upon the world if he were not careful.

When he had first realized it was there, he'd joined the army. What else could he have done? He had been alive, or awake—however one described the day he came into being—for four weeks and survived on kindness and thievery. When he'd snapped the wrist of the merchant who caught him stealing a loaf of bread, he surprised himself. To that point, Jaxon had no idea what he was capable of. The movement felt as fluid and as natural as breathing.

Then it happened a second time.

Then a third.

The pivotal moment was when he'd fought a soldier attempting to force himself on a young girl. It was not uncommon to see copulation in the dark recesses of the streets of Rome, especially when soldiers returned from some campaign. Normally, Jaxon would ignore them. That night, though, there was something different. The tearing of cloth and the muffled screams told a different story. Stepping closer, so too did the look on the young girl's face when then the soldier turned and tried to send him away.

Jaxon had moved like a panther.

He'd pulled the soldier away, thankful he had stopped him in time. After telling the girl to run, Jaxon set on his prey, each punch and kick a commentary on the soldier's actions. He'd broken the soldier's leg for the torn clothes. He'd broken his arm for the tears and fear he had instilled in the girl. He'd taken the sword that lay on the ground and removed the soldier's manhood to prevent him from producing another animal.

That is what he told himself anyway.

In truth, Jaxon did not know why he did it. It seemed right and felt good at the time. It satisfied some primal need to fight, to destroy, to win. What better place to satisfy that than on the battlefield with others? Besides, the army would be down a man. Seemed only right that he take his place.

Jaxon fought for years. And each time he did, he was shocked at his own prowess. It amazed him that he took to battle so naturally, needing virtually no training. He bested seasoned soldiers and his own trainers. He moved up the ranks quickly, leading men of his own. Throughout all of this, he was also shocked at how fast his wounds healed. He was not so good that he was never cut. It happened rarely, but it happened. And when it did, minor wounds were gone within minutes, larger cuts hours, and multiple cuts within a day.

He continued this life until his death.

His first death.

At least, the first to his knowledge.

He awoke in an infirmary, covered in a sheet. The disorientation was unforgettable. Except for this recent resurrection, none had felt so debilitating. Back then, running was his only option. He wanted to stay and fight. He wanted the glory, madness, and brutality of war. But coming back from the dead was too much to explain. He chose to flee lest he be branded a demon. So, flee he did. From the battlefield, from Rome, from the entire region. He travelled, he fought, he killed, and he learned. He learned about everything . . . except himself.

For seven hundred years, Jaxon Burke travelled, fought, killed, and learned, and in the end still knew nothing about who he was, where he had come from, or why he was the way he was. All the while, the deaths added up. They had only begun to bother him in recent months. He was plagued by the faces of those he had killed. Plagued with questions about who they were, whether they deserved it, and why they had to be the ones to satisfy his incurable blood lust.

Centuries of death.

Centuries of questions.

And now, he was exhausted.

When those flames first touched his skin the previous night, a part of him wondered why he had not tried this before. Had he known fire could consume him, he could have ended things long ago. But he had not known. He was, of course, very wrong.

The crack of thunder outside broke his mantra and compelled him to look at the time. He had completed twenty-two minutes. Two minutes too long, but that was okay. He gave himself some time to slowly recover. Another thirty second count, another few minutes to remain still and allow the sound of the rain to soothe him.

He stood and walked to the window. He stared out at the city. Chicago was indeed an interesting place, among his favorites. It was . . . real. Gritty, but elegant. Beautiful even when it was not. He would miss it. He would miss her. But he would take up Solomon Steele's offer. He would use his skills and help that strange and powerful creature achieve his goal. Was it a deal with the devil? He did not know. But he was certain of a few things. It was time for his tortured soul to find peace. It was time for him to pay for the crime that was his life.

It was time to find and kill the Mistress of Death.

CHAPTER FORTY-SIX

KEIRON ARRIVED AT THE ADDRESS KASSIDY GAVE HIM. BURKE HAD finally reached out through their mutual acquaintance, Alex Frost. Seemed fitting that Burke would want to meet in private, considering he was public enemy number one right now. Keiron wondered what would drive an otherwise private man, a master assassin, to commit such a public crime. Maybe he'd find out now.

Keiron entered the access code and bounded up the stairs. The building was modern, located in the South Loop. It came equipped with a gym, grocery store, and a post office. This stuff did not exist in St. John. Keiron was considering relocating. Maybe Chicago was the place to be.

Getting off the elevator on the fifteenth floor, Keiron took a right down the hall and prepared to knock on apartment fifteen thirty. He didn't have to, though, because the door was already opened slightly. Cautiously, Keiron entered, careful not to make a sound. Stepping into the living room, he felt the presence of something behind him. Whoever it was, he was sloppy. Keiron had trained warriors for centuries. Had he not had such a pacifist's heart, he might still be training. Few could catch Keiron off guard, and it certainly wasn't going to happen today.

As the man behind him came forward, Keiron ducked, stepped back and to the side of the attacker and delivered a shoulder check that sent him flying into the wall. The attacker turned to face Keiron and, for a split second, Keiron froze. Shock ran through him. The momentary lapse was enough to give the attacker a chance to plow into Keiron and send him into the bookcase. Disoriented, Keiron doubled over and took a knee to the face. When his attacker attempted to follow up with a kick, Keiron caught the foot lazily and pushed back.

Wobbly, Keiron stood, quickly regained his wits, and engaged. Keiron had not had a fight like this in centuries. In fact, he had not had a fight like this since the last time the two of them fought. Memories flooded in, but he stayed focused. The pair had broken lamps, framed photos, and a television. The authorities were likely already on their way.

"Listen, I'm a friend," said Keiron. "I'm here to help."

Keiron's plea was met with a punch, which he blocked.

"If we keep this up, the police will be here. They are not inclined to help you with what you need. But I am. Kassidy Simmons is. She sent me," said Keiron.

His words seemed to fall on deaf ears. The barrage of attacks continued, until finally Keiron decided it needed to end.

"I'm sorry," he said.

Keiron moved forward in a boxer's stance, jabbed twice, then punched, followed by three body blows and an uppercut. It was enough to disorient his attacker. Keiron quickly moved to get around him, then lock his arms around the man's neck. He struggled for a long while before finally succumbing to the sleeper hold.

"That's gonna suck when you wake up, old friend," said Keiron. He then retrieved his phone and called Kassidy as he heard sirens approach from the street below. With no time for pleasantries, he quickly told her what happened and what he needed. Within seconds she was there, and just as quickly, she shimmered out of the battle-riddled apartment with both men in tow.

CHAPTER FORTY-SEVEN

WHEN JAXON AWOKE, HIS HEAD WAS THROBBING. HE SHOT UP FROM THE floor only to lean back again, bracing himself with one hand.

"That wasn't a bright idea," he said to himself.

"You're gonna be a little lightheaded for a bit," said a voice behind him. "You might want to consider taking it easy."

Jaxon whirled quickly, moving to a defensive crouched position—only to fall over again. Strobe lights flashed; his vision blurred. Each blinding pulse of light matched the pounding in his temples.

"Easy, friend," said the voice.

"I'm not your friend. I don't know you," Jaxon managed to say through the pain.

Jaxon felt a hand on his shoulder, followed by another hooking under his arm.

"Let's get you up and over to this chair," said the stranger.

Jaxon rose slowly and began moving even slower. With each step, his head throbbed. He'd felt pain like this before, but he hadn't liked it any of those times either.

He felt himself lowered onto a cushioned chair. His arm brushed against a hard surface—a table. Reaching out, he placed his hand on it, palm down. It was cool to the touch, smooth, polished. He lowered his head to it and sighed softly as the cool sensation washed over him. He heard something being set on the table, then the slow movement of chair legs across the uncarpeted floor.

"You should drink that," said the stranger. "It'll help."

"I can't even see it," Jaxon said.

"It'll help that, too."

Jaxon reached out again, searching for the object he'd heard while trying to lift his head. The back of his hand hit it, and he almost knocked it over.

"Easy," said the stranger. "Let me give you a hand."

A hand grabbed Jaxon's and, seconds later, the chill of cold glass was against his palm. Grabbing it, he sat up straighter and brought the glass to his lips. The thought of drinking something unknown, given to him by someone equally unknown, raised an alarm or two. Several people were actively trying to kill him, and only one really gave him any concern.

Those black eyes.

As those thoughts swam in his brain, he realized that he honestly didn't care at this point. If, after seven hundred years on the planet, he was to die by poison at the hands of a stranger who'd been nice enough to help him up, sit him down, and hand him the drink he couldn't see, so be it.

He sniffed it first, anyway.

"What the hell is this? Scotch?"

"Yep."

"Scotch is your cure-all?"

"Drink it and prove me wrong."

Jaxon took a sip. A slow, drawn-out sip. Within seconds, he'd downed the whole glass.

"That wasn't Scotch," he said.

"No."

"But it smelled like—"

"It smells like whatever your mind needs it to smell like in order for you to drink it. Apparently, you needed it to smell like Scotch. You're like a good friend of mine in that way."

"Your friend gets blackout drunk on Scotch, too?" Jaxon asked.

"Bourbon, actually. She has been known to finish a bottle on her own, a time or two."

"I may need to meet her."

"I have a feeling your paths will cross soon," said the stranger.

Jaxon's vision went from a swirling blur to a fixed blur. Slowly, the edges of objects formed. Sloppy colors solidified, and the fog dissipated like a car vent working overtime on a windshield during the early December morning. As it cleared, he saw before him a man, dark skin contrasting with a beige turtleneck sweater. His eyes were a deep chocolate brown. They unnerved Jaxon because he was reminded of his own when looked at them.

"Where are we?" Jaxon asked, looking around the room.

"We're in a safe house of sorts. It belongs to a friend of a friend."

"I smell pizza."

"Yeah," the stranger began, "the safe house is above a pizzeria in Little Italy."

Jaxon inhaled deeply. Something about the smell made him feel more alive. No, it wasn't the smell, it was the drink. His vision was completely restored. He touched his temple at the realization that the pain was gone. A cut on the back of his hand was mending before his eyes.

"What was in that drink?" he asked.

"An old family recipe."

"You from a family of alchemists?"

"Not exclusively."

Jaxon chuckled, quietly curious why the man across from him wasn't chuckling, too. In Jaxon's time, he'd come across many people claiming to be alchemists, healers, or something supernatural or mystical. Some were real. Others, not so much. Either way, he'd had no need of them. His body healed on its own, he didn't age, and all in all, life was good.

Until recent years.

Worse in recent days.

"Who are you?" Jaxon asked, leaning forward, reflexively rubbing his temples.

"My name is Keiron."

"Keiron . . . ?"

"Just Keiron."

"All right, we'll work with that," Jaxon said. "I guess the other question is, why are you here? Why am I here?"

"Long story short—"

"No. No, no, no," Jaxon began, "I think I'm gonna need the whole damn thing. Add a prologue if you need to."

Jaxon stood and stretched. His limbs were tight, but his strength and awareness were returning. He walked around the darkened apartment. Like so many old Chicago apartments, especially those built above storefronts and restaurants, the space was small but functional. Large wooden beams decorated a ceiling that met brick walls on all sides. The few windows were single pane, single hung, with storm windows skillfully installed on the outside to battle the Windy City's harsh elements.

"You are Jaxon Burke, correct?"

"Yeah," said Jaxon, apprehensively.

"A few days ago, you came across a strange individual. Black eyes. Hands transform into weapons."

"Yeah," Jaxon responded, nodding slowly.

"That thing was a Wraith. They're constructs of the Angel of Death."

"Why would the Angel of Death be after me?"

"Well, he's not. He's not after anyone anymore. That bourbon-loving friend I mentioned earlier took care of that. The guy you met is after her, and we think he may try to use you in some way to get her."

"And she is . . . ?"

"Unimportant right now," Keiron said. "What is important is that this Wraith is bad news, and we need to work on a strategy to kill him."

"Ah, that old story."

Jaxon let Keiron's words settle in. He wasn't sure how much he should say at this point about what he knew. He needed this guy to lead him to Kassidy and didn't want to spook him. He was curious about the guy. There was something familiar about him.

"Why has this Wraith taken such a liking to me?"

"Because of who you are."

"That's funny. I don't even know who I am."

"I think I do," Keiron said.

"I doubt that," Jaxon said. "I'm much older than I look."

"As am I."

Jaxon watched as Keiron pulled up the sleeve of his sweater to reveal a mark on his arm. It was the same mark that Jaxon had on his chest. A red discoloration in the shape of a crescent. Jaxon tried to keep himself calm so as not to give anything away.

"Do you have one of these, by chance?"

Jaxon slowly nodded. All of sudden his desire to kill Kassidy was quelled by possible information about his past.

Then the voices came again.

The screams. Loud again. He heard the undeniable sound of horses galloping at high speeds and the clang of metal again as swords met. He heard maniacal laughter as soldiers were punched, impaled, and beheaded. Visons of battle filled his mind.

"Are you okay," asked Keiron.

"Um, yeah. Yeah, I'm fine. I get these . . . headaches sometimes."

When he caught Keiron's eye, he could tell that the man did not believe him. He needed to move the conversation along.

"How is it that you know me?" asked Jaxon. "How is it that we have similar marks?"

"This mark is common among those of similar bloodlines," said Keiron.

"Wait, are you telling me we're related? Like . . . brothers?"

"We are definitely not brothers, but related, yes."

"That's . . . not possible. It can't be. I'm . . . I'm alone in all this. For seven hundred years I've been alone."

"Seven hundred years?" asked Keiron.

"Yeah. So, you may want to rethink this whole notion of us being related."

"I would, but we are, so there's no getting around that. Why do you think you're so young?"

"Excuse me?" asked Jaxon.

"Why do you think you're only seven hundred years old?"

Jaxon eyes widened at the word *only*.

"I . . . I remember only the last seven hundred years of my life. I mean, I've always suspected I'm older, but I don't really know. I woke up in a field outside some small village about an hour's walk from Rome."

"And nothing before that? Not even the smallest image or memory?"

"Nothing. Well, until recently."

"And what do you remember now?" asked Keiron.

"They're just images. Bloody, violent images. And . . . and I hear screams. Yelling. There's a constant battle in my dreams and memories."

Jaxon walked back to the table and sat, not taking his eyes off the man. His gut stirred. Did this man, this stranger, have answers?

"Does it mean something?" Jaxon asked.

"It means everything," began Keiron. "It means the answers to your identity are right on the edge. You have to call to it."

"Call to it," said Jaxon with a frustrated laugh. "Why can't you just tell me? You seem to know. We're related, apparently. Tell me, damn you!"

Jaxon slammed his hands on the table, and his eyes turned blue. He saw Keiron take extra notice of his face.

"What?" asked Jaxon.

"You're closer to discovering your identity than you think. If I tell you before you're ready, it could be catastrophic . . . for a lot of people."

Jaxon stared, bewildered. He hadn't expected that response. He didn't know what he'd expected, though, if he were being honest.

"What? What people?"

He stood, walked to the window, and stared outside. If what Keiron was saying was true, if he was close to finding out who he was, maybe . . . maybe he didn't need to end his life. His struggles lately were the nightmares. There was blood on his hands from a life he'd never known, and he was adding more blood from the things he'd done in the life he'd created. He wanted death because he desperately needed peace.

He needed the monsters to go away.

Jaxon's walk back to the table was interrupted by the disintegration of the door. Ducking and shielding his face from flying pine splinters and chunks of particle board, Jaxon moved behind the table, quickly and efficiently flipped by Keiron to serve as a barrier from the threat in the hallway.

"I think the consequences of you throwing Charles Cartwright out a window have caught up with you," said Keiron.

"So it would seem. Any thoughts on how we might get out of this?" Jaxon asked.

"Possibly," Keiron said.

Gunshots replaced the sound of falling debris.

"This is a pretty shitty family reunion" Jaxon said.

"Trust me when I say, this is nothing," said Keiron.

Jaxon watched as Keiron typed out a message on his phone again. In the blink of an eye, a tall dark-haired woman in black appeared, her eyes shining bright blue. She ducked down, touched Jaxon and Keiron on the shoulder, and just like that, they were gone.

CHAPTER FORTY-EIGHT

"HMM, SO YOU'RE DEATH?" JAXON ASKED.

"First of all, you're welcome, you know, for saving your ass not once but twice tonight. And secondly, no, not exactly," said Kassidy. "I'm more of stand-in while he's . . . on sabbatical."

"Death is on vacation?"

"He's indisposed."

Can Death do that? Jaxon wasn't sure what to make of it. He wasn't sure what to make of any of this. In the span of a few hours, he'd gained a family member, avoided being shot up and thus forcing another regeneration, and traveled through some spectral plane of existence. So, Death being on vacation was par for the course.

Jaxon sat in the living room of Kassidy's family home. When they'd arrived, she'd mentioned that the place was being remodeled after some recent trouble. When he looked around, he got the sense that the trouble, as she put it, had been intense. His battle-hardened mind saw remnants of a fight. Strangely, it played out in his awareness as if he'd been there. This led him to think about his dreams, or memories, or whatever the hell they were. He wanted relief. He wanted to see an end to the torture. For that, he needed to kill this woman.

The woman who'd just saved him.

"I've been where you are. Recently, in fact," said Kassidy. "I understand that this is completely and utterly strange."

"After seven hundred years, you learn that there's a spectrum of strange."

Kassidy nodded and shrugged.

"So, are we related?" asked Jaxon.

"Honestly, who knows. Probably."

"Are you immortal?"

"Unknown. I haven't even reached my midlife crisis yet. Unless you count ascending to godhood a crisis."

"Sounds like a fairly decent life goal to achieve," said Jaxon.

"My only life goal was to get to a point where I felt normal. Everything about my life recently is the exact opposite of that."

"Fair enough," said Jaxon.

"Let's talk more about this Wraith," said Kassidy.

"Yeah, can you tell me a little more about them? Keiron gave me some background, but I'm still a little hazy."

"There are Reapers, beings charged with escorting souls to the afterlife—either the Beyond or the Void."

"I'm guessing the Beyond is the good place?" asked Jaxon.

"Bingo."

"So then, Wraiths?

"A Wraith is a Reaper on steroids. Like all Reapers, they were once human, they died, and upon death were recruited by the former Primus—"

"Primus?"

"Angel of Death."

"Of course," Jaxon said.

"Anyway, they were recruited, for whatever reason, to become Reapers so they could assist the Primus with ushering souls to the afterlife. At some point, the last Primus decided to use a portion of his power to create Wraiths. Their powers are augmented, but it takes a toll on what's left of their souls. They're the villains in this story, and the one who seems to be after you may be a bit more 'lost' than the others."

"Why?" Jaxon asked.

"Well, he's angry at me. This Wraith, Solomon Steele, was apparently the first of the order. He and Azra-El, the Primus, were apparently close—"

"How close?" asked Jaxon.

"Not sure. But there's a loyalty there that feels unmatched in anything I've ever seen in life. Azra-El had his sights set on ascension. He wanted to be the Death God. Maybe Solomon wanted to be rewarded for loyalty. I just don't know."

"And what happened to this Azra-El?"

"I cut his head off with a big knife that used to belong to Keiron's daddy a few weeks ago."

"Sounds badass."

"Definitely on my life's highlight reel," Kassidy said.

"This Wraith has tried to take my soul, but he couldn't. Instead, he's been siphoning off power. Why is that?" asked Jaxon.

"I'm still new at this, and honestly, I don't have an answer. I suspect your abilities and lineage make it difficult for him. What it does allow him to do, though, is act as Azra-El did. Just that fragment of your power is giving him the ability to absorb human souls and become stronger.

"Could he become a god?"

"I'm not sure. But I don't think it's a good idea for us to wait and find out," Kassidy said.

"So, what do we do next?"

"Research. I've got a professor full of knowledge on the way. She also happens to be my aunt."

"A god?"

"A human cursed with immortality after orchestrating the death of my half-brother by manipulating my mother's true love—who, in turn, tried to kill me."

"Sounds . . . complicated."

"Welcome to my life."

As they both shared a nervous laugh, Keiron burst into the living room. Jaxon moved into a defensive posture sensing tension in the man's demeanor. He noticed Kassidy stand quickly, only to drop to a knee as she grabbed at her abdomen. Had she been injured earlier? She'd seemed so focused. Had she been navigating through pain?

"Keiron, what's wrong?" she asked.

Keiron looked to Kassidy apologetically, then locked eyes with Jaxon. Confusion swirled in the immortal's brain. Had he been discovered? Did they know he was simply here to kill Kassidy?

"It's . . . it's Anna," said Keiron.

Jaxon dropped his guard and focused.

"Wait. What? Anna? My Anna?"

Keiron nodded.

"Octavia called. Solomon has taken her."

Raged filled Jaxon. His eyes immediately turned blue. Instinctively, he kicked Keiron, sending him back hard and fast against the wall, then he turned to face Kassidy.

"This is your fault!" he screamed.

Jaxon lunged forward.

As he did, he met an invisible wall keeping him from his prey. Kassidy's outstretched hand directed some type of barrier. In her other hand, a weapon appeared. This wasn't an extension of her body like the Wraith, though it seemed very much in tune with her. And it looked so familiar. As Jaxon tried to move through the barrier, Kassidy switched her stance and pointed the weapon at him. A pulse of energy propelled him backward. He felt a strange current run through him.

Current . . . and memories.

Centuries of memories flooded Jaxon's mind. The battles, the blood, the distrust from the Twelve. All his nightmares made sense. Hateful words from his father, his mother, and the emotional scars of loving someone who would never be his. Rage filled him. He propped himself up on his hands and knees and he screamed.

CENTURIES AGO

Thanatos stood over Ares, breathing heavily. His face was bloodied, his clothing torn, but compared to Ares, he was the picture of health.

Ares looked up at his foe, one eye open, the other swollen shut, his face bloodied and bruised. He attempted to get up, but with a broken arm and leg, that was impossible. It didn't help that Thanatos held the Scythe of Cronus at his neck.

"We had a deal, Ares! Tell me where they are!" demanded Thanatos.

Ares remained silent—as much out of desire to protect Octavia and her sister Allesandra as it was a challenge moving a partially fractured jaw. Ares had been in countless battles, and as a War God, had won most of them. The only time he'd been bested was by his sister, Athena, and his father, Zeus. Thanatos, like Zeus, was an Elder God, and as such possessed power that their offspring would likely never achieve. Ares and those of his generation were immortal and carried power, to be sure, but nothing like the original Twelve. Without the Scythe of Cronus, Thanatos was formidable. With it, he was unstoppable. No god dared cross him.

Until today.

"You had one task. You promised me, swore to me that you would do this. And now . . . you renege? For what? For her? For a mortal?"

Ares's breathing was labored. He knew he'd survive his injuries, but for now, the pain overwhelmed him. A part of him hurt so much that he wanted to die. He wanted Thanatos to end him with that damned blade. But even the Death God was bound by the covenant. He could not end the life of a god without the approval of the Twelve, and as hated as Ares was, even by his father, no one would sanction his death.

Overhead, thunder roared, and an unholy flash of lightning illuminated all around them. It was blinding. Thanatos even had to shield his eyes. Ares hated that sound. It was the harbinger of his arrival. A thunderbolt struck the ground nearby, and when the smoke cleared, Zeus stood there. He was the personification of power. Electricity crackled around him as his form further settled.

"Fa-fa-father . . ." said Ares.

"What is the meaning of this, Thanatos?" asked Zeus.

Despite his own power, Thanatos was reverential to Zeus, as all the gods were. Zeus commanded obedience. Even without the ultimate weapon, the weapon of Zeus's own father, the gods feared his power. Ares hoped that there would be some sort of concern over his welfare. He hoped that perhaps, this once, his father would take his side and offer some sort of comfort and protection.

"Lord Zeus," began Thanatos, "this is between me and Ares. I'd rather not trouble you with such things. Alas, we are at an impasse and—"

"And for that you fight and threaten him with the Scythe?" asked Zeus.

Ares looked between the two Elders and watched as Thanatos backed down. Thanatos was still embarrassed over his actions. The way in which he had responded to the death of his son, Tyran, the way in which he'd taken the mortal, Allesandra, only to lose her, had been most troublesome. Being locked away for a short time by unknowns, though? That had had been humiliating. The gods made fun of him. He hated that more than anything. If they found out he'd used Ares to track the woman down only to lose them again, he'd face even more ridicule. Pride and vanity were his greatest weaknesses. Thanatos was the Death God, but that did not mean he was a killer. He was passive in his duties. He was a psychopomp, charged with the peaceful transition of the soul. He considered himself the kindest and most fair of all the gods, removed from petty emotions like revenge, jealousy, and envy. But his actions over the death of his son had proven that he was no better than the others among the Twelve.

"I believe, Lord Zeus, that there's been a misunderstanding between Ares and myself. I was given false information about his intentions to steal the Scythe of Cronus. I reacted without providing him a fair chance. I beg your forgiveness and offer the War God sanctuary in my domain to heal."

"Is this true, Ares?" asked Zeus.

Ares looked from his father to Thanatos and back. Thanatos could not kill him, and he was unwilling to risk the rest of the Twelve discovering the truth of their deal. With that knowledge alone, he was safe from further altercation with the Death God. Though, with Thanatos, there were always loopholes. For now, keeping his secret seemed the best course of action.

"Well?" urged Zeus.

Ares responded with a slow nod.

"I am suspicious about this confusion you speak of Thanatos. Undoubtedly, whatever you were led to believe bears some truth where Ares is involved."

Ares felt his anger grow, tempered only by the pain he felt. As much as he hated to admit it, he longed for his father's love. At least he'd hoped for acceptance and respect. He received none. Ever.

"It is done now," said Thanatos. "We shall burden you no more with our squabble, and I shall take Ares to heal."

"Very well," said Zeus.

Ares caught a final look from his father before he vanished in a flash of light.

"You were wise to play along, War God," said Thanatos. "The truth could have started a war. Or, at the very least, further damaged my reputation and place among the Twelve. Though, given how much your father loathes you, telling him the truth may not have amounted to much. I cannot kill you. But I will not allow you to go unpunished for what you've done. And I will not allow you to expose my secret."

Ares watched as Thanatos used the Scythe of Cronus to cut a hole in space and time. While it was a formidable weapon, deadly to all, including the gods, it was also a valuable tool. It had been used to create the universe and carried with it the power to control the universe's elements. Anyone able to wield it could travel through time, accelerate life and healing, or create wondrous things.

Staring at the rip, Ares saw nothing but darkness on the other side.

The Void! He's sending me to the Void!

"You cannot stay here," said Thanatos.

As the Death God touched him with the blade, Ares felt his pain dissipate. His bones quickly mended, and his bruises healed. Thanatos kept the blade on him, though, and Ares felt something else. His thoughts were clouded. He could not sort through the present moment. It was as if understanding and comprehension had left him.

"I heal you, but take from you your memories, your very identity, and banish you to another time," said Thanatos.

Ares felt his body lift from the ground. Unable to fight off the pull, he found himself swept through the rip in time and space.

It was dark.

It was cold.

It was the end of who he once was.

CHAPTER FORTY-NINE

KASSIDY STARED AT THE LOST ASSASSIN.

"Dammit! What have I done?" she asked herself as she let the Scythe slip from her grasp.

It made sense. Releasing his memories, restoring what her father had stolen from him, made absolute sense. She had no idea the pain it would cause. There was physical pain, to be sure, but she suspected a man with his talent and seemingly high threshold for pain could tolerate that and brush it off as mere discomfort. But the emotional pain? Neither of them was prepared for that.

While she didn't feel it as directly, with their current proximity, everything he felt hit her hard. Shame, hatred, fear, rage, and an unquenchable bloodlust filled the area, and they were both locked in. As Jaxon agonized on the ground, Kassidy did her best to manage the influx of emotion wafting off him. She took a step back, then another, her fists clenched, and she pushed forward with her own power—the power of her father. It tempered things, but there was great internal struggle within.

Then the flash came.

All at once, Jaxon was on fire. Kassidy stared in horror, uncertain how it happened or even what to do.

"Oh my god! Jaxon!"

She watched the burning figure rise from his knees and stand. As the flames blew away, so too did the amalgam of emotion that tormented them both. All that remained was rage. Before her stood the source of that rage. With an outstretched hand he called to the weapon that carried the same blood and memories as he did—the Glade.

"Jaxon?" she asked.

"I know who I am," he replied.

"Ares."

It took half a beat before the War God rushed at Kassidy. It took half a beat for her to call upon her own power and summon the Scythe of Cronus back to her.

It was in her hands as the Glade came down.

CHAPTER FIFTY

KASSIDY BLOCKED THE GLADE WITH HER SCYTHE AND PUSHED JAXON off. She braced herself, squaring up for battle. She could taste the bitter bile of his rage on her tongue. He was consumed with it, and it threatened to overwhelm her. Continuing to call on her inner strength and that of the Scythe, she allowed her own power to fill her. The intensity of her eyes matched his, and she was ready for his onslaught.

"If you want out of this, say so now, little girl. My fight is with your father," said Jaxon.

"I told you, he's missing," replied Kassidy, with a grunt as she blocked a thrust from the Glade.

"Then maybe killing you will bring him out of hiding."

Jaxon's ferocity was surprising. She'd never met such primal determination, not even when she'd battled Azra-El. He moved like a wild beast, and yet there was purpose and gladiatorial elegance to it. Kassidy blocked each swing of the sword, but as skilled a fighter as she was, forgot that everything is a weapon in battle. She took an elbow to the face after she parried his swing. While dazed, Jaxon launched a side kick to her gut and followed with an uppercut as she was bent over that launched her into the air.

Kassidy landed hard, not far from Keiron, still knocked out from Jaxon's kick.

Her Scythe landed elsewhere.

Before she could move, Jaxon was on her. He picked her up by the throat with his left hand and pressed the tip of the Glade against her chest with his right. She struggled to break free. But the intensity of the fight and his emotions had broken through her calm and control.

"He took everything from me. My life! My memories! My love! And now, I'll take from him what he coveted the most."

"No!" screamed a voice from behind.

Kassidy knew the voice yet felt the sting of shock. It wasn't her own shock. It was his. Jaxon wasn't prepared for it. Kassidy took advantage by placing her feet on his chest and pushing forward to free herself from his grip. It worked. Landing on the ground, she quickly got up, called the Scythe to her hand, and went on the offensive with her attacks. She knocked the Glade from his grip and launched into a series of kicks and punches that had the War God on the ground in a matter of seconds.

She pressed the tip of the Scythe against his neck.

"You wanted to die, right?" she asked.

"Kassidy, please," said the earlier voice.

Again, the sting of surprise shot through Jaxon. It became stronger once Octavia came into view.

"Octavia?" asked Jaxon.

"Yes. It's me."

"How . . ."

"It's . . . a long story. One that I'm happy to tell. But the two of you must stop this. Please."

"I'm not the one who started this shit, Octavia. But I'm ready to fucking finish it," said Kassidy, pressing the tip on the Scythe further into Jaxon's neck.

"He's not your enemy," said Octavia, looking at Kassidy.

"Certainly doesn't seem to be the case."

"If not for him, you'd be very different. Remember, he helped to protect your mother. Helped her escape to the Nexus . . . where she gave birth to you."

"This . . . is the child of you sister?" Jaxon asked.

As Octavia nodded, Kassidy eased her pressure of the Scythe. Blood trickled from Jaxon's neck, and the sight of it caused her to back away completely.

Octavia helped Jaxon stand and, sensing a wave of confusion, Kassidy willed the Scythe of Cronus away. She no longer felt Jaxon's rage. In its place was compassion and . . . love.

"We should talk," said Octavia. "All of us."

CHAPTER FIFTY-ONE

KASSIDY'S ANXIETY WAS OFF THE CHARTS. WHEN SHE WAS FIGHTING, THAT was a good thing. She could direct those energies into the battle and, more often than not, she'd come out on top. Keiron said that it was her divine blood that gave her that edge. Kassidy said it was years of trauma from bullying, being physically assaulted and nearly raped, becoming a Reaper, and taking the lives of people before their time, all without the benefit of therapy. Keiron typically shut up after that. Her anxiety now resulted from fighting the War God, the second horseman to make an appearance to fulfill a prophecy. She felt his pain with such an intensity that she could actually experience some of his memories. She had no idea that power was within her.

So much she didn't know.

So much to learn.

Imposter!

The word lingered in the back of her mind as Octavia reconnected with Jaxon. She could see them in the kitchen. Keiron was with them, holding an ice pack on his head. When they all came back into the living room, surveying the mess that had been made, Kassidy could feel their tension almost as high as her anxiety.

"I had no idea who you were," said Jaxon.

"Well, how could you? My father stripped you of your

identity and hurled you through time. You lost—"

"Everything," finished Jaxon, as he looked at Octavia.

"I don't know what to do here," said Kassidy. "I don't know that there's anything I can do. It seems like everything that's happened, everything that's . . . gone wrong . . . is because of me."

"Stop that!" snapped Octavia. "We've talked about this before. All of this, everything we're experiencing was set in motion long before you were born. If anyone is to blame, it's me. I've been paying for my decisions all this time, trying to make amends, and instead of feeling sorry for myself, I've pushed forward."

Kassidy felt the sting of those words. She felt the weight of everything that had happened since her ascension. All she could see were the areas where she'd failed. The lives lost. The lives in danger, like Anna. The pain and shock Jaxon experienced because of her impulsive actions.

"And you have to do the same," continued Octavia. "You must push forward. Take what you've learned and do the best you can, each and every day."

"But . . . I'm not fit for this," said Kassidy. "I'm not fit to be a god. I wasn't meant to have this power. This responsibility is too great."

"If I may, Kassidy," said Jaxon. "Many of the gods are not fit either. Many of us are ill equipped to deal with the power we have. We are consumed by it, we squander it, we let it define us. You, and many demi-gods like you, are much better suited. You are the true blend of god and man. You carry within you the power to do almost anything, but the humility to understand that you can't just do whatever you want, because of the possible repercussions. There is a lot expected, but only because you put pressure on yourself to be something more than you need to be. All you need do . . . is your best."

The words Jaxon spoke, the sincerity in them, it was disarming. She didn't expect that from someone like him, someone with such ferocity inside. Perhaps seven hundred years of existence without being Ares taught him more than he could have learned by being among the Twelve. She looked over to Keiron, who simply inclined his head in agreement with Jaxon.

"I don't know that I can do that. I feel like something is missing," said Kassidy.

"Then your job is to find it," said Keiron. "But while doing that, you cannot give up."

Kassidy nodded.

She wanted a drink.

She wanted a pill.

She wanted peace.

"I know we're both scared right now," began Jaxon, "but we need to get to Solomon. We need to save Anna. She's innocent in all this."

Kassidy felt the concern in his voice combined with hurt from Octavia. Finding the love of her life after all these centuries, only to realize his love for another was paramount in his mind, was bound to hurt. To her credit, she didn't show it, but the briefest eye contact they'd made spoke in her stead.

"You're right. He's caused enough damage. We need to put him down and keep her safe," said Octavia.

"You're the master strategist, right?" Kassidy asked Jaxon.

"I'm more of a blunt instrument," said Jaxon.

"I don't know about that," said Kassidy. "Word on the street is you're the best shooter in the business. You don't get that way by being a blunt instrument. You want me to believe in myself? I'm gonna need you to do the same."

There was shared confusion and pain in the air. Kassidy did

her best to absorb the feelings and not be controlled by them. She'd not dealt with the emotions of a god before, though. It was something quite different.

"Very well," said Jaxon. "Keiron, I could use your help in strategizing. You've trained some of the best."

"Let's get to it, then," said Keiron.

"So, what do we know?" asked Jaxon.

"We know he's got a raging hard-on for me," said Kassidy. "Wants me dead in the worst way."

"And he's willing to do anything to make that happen," added Keiron.

"Then, let's give it to him," said Jaxon.

"Pardon? I'm not sure I heard you right," said Octavia.

"If we want to lure him out, we need to give him what he wants, which is Kassidy," said Jaxon.

"Then?" asked Kassidy.

"Then we take him down."

Kassidy folded her arms and listened as Jaxon laid out his plan for luring Solomon in. Keiron made some suggested alterations based on the location. It wasn't the best plan, but then, not many were. It always came down to execution. The group executing this plan consisted of a newly restored War God, an immortal bookstore owner with deadly skills, a broken-hearted warrior and college professor, and an anxiety-riddled, insecure Death God.

What could go wrong?

CHAPTER FIFTY-TWO

SOLOMON MATERIALIZED FROM THE DARK CLOUD THAT TOUCHED DOWN ahead of Jaxon and Kassidy. Anna DeBartolo was at his side. To his delight, Kassidy appeared worn, weathered, and broken. That delight was augmented by the sight of Jaxon holding the Scythe of Cronus in his hands.

"He did it," he whispered to himself.

Pride filled him realization that his plan had worked set in. He still didn't know what Jaxon Burke was, but he had the pretender on her knees and the Scythe in front of him. In mere moments, he'd have the weapon in one hand and the bitch's head in the other.

After that, he could easily dispatch Burke and go about the business of restoring order in the Reaper ranks the way Azra-El . . . no, the way *he* wanted.

"You've done well, Jaxon," said Solomon. "I dare say, you've exceeded my expectations."

"You wanted her, you got her. Our deal stands, right?"

"You mean, me taking you out with that beautiful piece of weaponry you're holding?"

Jaxon nodded.

"I wish you'd reconsider. You're a valuable asset. Besides, I'm sure this young lady here would be sad if you died," said Solomon, gesturing toward Anna. "But if you feel it's your time, then I feel obligated to help you with that. I know what it's like to be tortured and immortal."

"Then why do you go on?" asked Jaxon.

"Well, I also know what it's like to be tortured and *mortal*," said Solomon. "I much prefer it this way."

"Anna, are you okay?" asked Jaxon.

His question was met with a blank stare. She seemed to still be in shock from everything.

As he stepped closer to the pair, Solomon felt his anger growing. His disdain for Kassidy was all-consuming. He couldn't understand why Azra-El had chosen her decades ago, but he understood that she was a means to an end. Now, knowing her lineage, he was fully aware of her value. A part of him wondered if he'd incur any wrath by killing her. Then he realized it wouldn't matter. He'd have the Scythe of Cronus. No one would dare cross him. And if they tried, they'd meet the same fate she was about to.

"How did you manage to bind her?" asked Solomon.

"Wizard," said Jaxon.

"That Frost guy? I thought he was an exorcist?"

"Magical jack of all trades."

Solomon smiled. He'd have to connect with Frost on his own once this was all over. If he could bind a Death God—

"Oh, the possibilities," he whispered.

Standing before the so-called Death God, Solomon studied her. On one hand, it was a shame he'd have to kill her. Someone with her talents could be as useful as that wizard could potentially be. But she had to go. Not for her power, but for what she'd done to him. For what she'd *taken* from him.

Squatting in front of her now, he brushed hair from her face—and she spat in his. Wiping it away, he sneered, then smacked her with the back of his hand.

"A long time ago, I made a vow to never hurt a woman. You weren't around then, but it was important to me to hold true to that. You see, I promised my Dominique that I would look out for all women. Not just those in her line . . . in *our* line . . . but all of them. Then came you."

Solomon stood and began pacing.

"Please tell me this isn't the part where the bad guy rambles on and on," said Kassidy.

Solomon stopped, turned, and grinned. Her smart mouth was one of the things he'd hated about her. She rarely showed respect to Azra-El. And certainly never showed respect to—

"You killed her!" screamed Solomon as he rushed her, grabbed her by the neck and hoisted her in the air.

"K-k-killed . . . who?" she struggled to ask.

"The only link to my love. The only link to my family. You killed Senaya!"

He threw Kassidy to the ground, walked to Jaxon, and snatched the Scythe of Cronus from his hands. The sound of Kassidy coughing and gasping for air filled the silence. He watched her eyes widen as realization that he had her weapon set in.

"What in the fuck are you talking about? What does that bitch have to do with any of this?"

"She was my granddaughter!"

◆ ◆ ◆

Kassidy recoiled at the shock. As if she needed more of them tonight. She didn't even know how to process what she'd heard. When he spoke the name, when he said *Senaya*, Kassidy felt a ripple of love, compassion, guilt, and loss all bundled together. There was definitely something there. Whether it was real or not, he believed it to be so. And that was a most powerful thing.

"How . . . how is that possible?" Kassidy asked.

"We all used to be something else," said Solomon. "I was a slave, a slave and a husband, then a slave, husband, and father. I was all those things before I died. Azra-El found me when I was still human and offered me salvation. He gave it to me when it was my time, then came my time for a reckoning."

"You got vengeance?" asked Kassidy.

"Against them all!" yelled Solomon. "And once the masters were slaughtered, I made certain my wife got out. She gave birth, raised a daughter, and that daughter did the same. Senaya was the last of my line, and you took her."

Kassidy felt his pain. It was on his skin for the world to see. She saw him in a different light for the briefest of moments. In the distance, she also saw Anna, another victim of his obsession and machinations. Her sympathy was quickly tempered. She saw Octavia near Anna, about to get her out of the area. So far, Jaxon's plan was working. They were going to need to keep him talking a little longer to allow Octavia and Anna's escape.

"I . . . I didn't know. I didn't even know about you," said Kassidy.

"It's not your place to know. It was your place to follow, and you failed at that. Just like you're failing as a god. But we can fix that."

Solomon raised the Scythe of Cronus above his head and prepared to bring it down on Kassidy. Kassidy caught sight of Octavia, and the fear leapt across the field.

Oh shit. No Octavia, stick to the plan.

"No!" screamed Octavia.

A distracted Solomon turned, saw the other two women, then dematerialized and reappeared in front of them, his weapon raised. Kassidy quickly shimmered, shedding her ropes, then reappearing on her feet. Jaxon was running toward the action and stopped in mid-stride as he saw Anna fall, the Scythe through her heart. He shouted, then ran to her as Solomon and Octavia engaged in battle. Octavia held her own. She'd taken out Wraiths before, but Solomon was older and still carrying some of Jaxon's essence. Kassidy ran to her to save her, to protect her. Stretching out with her powers, she commanded the Scythe to appear in her hand. She continued, now armed, ready to take him down.

Kassidy caught Solomon's eye and saw the smile spread across his face. As she neared, he quickly pivoted. She raised the Scythe, preparing to strike, and at the last moment, Solomon grabbed Octavia and shoved her forward.

Kassidy cried out in horror.

CHAPTER FIFTY-THREE

OCTAVIA FELT THE TIP OF KASSIDY'S BLADE PIERCE HER SKIN. IN THE background she heard Jaxon and Solomon now engaged in battle. Everything seemed to happen in slow motion, and a small part of her wondered if that were a trick of the Scythe of Cronus. Slowing time amid one's death? What could possibly be more torturous. At first, it felt like nothing more than a pinprick. A tiny incision in her body that expanded painstakingly slowly. She could feel the rip of her skin as more of the blade entered. The tip touched, pierced, and sliced through muscle and organs; each connection sent a jolt of electricity to her brain registering the excruciating agony. If this were happening in real time, it would be quick, easy, and final. But it lasted a lifetime. The only thing more painful was the look in Kassidy's eyes as she realized what had happening.

Octavia was not sure if Kassidy was experiencing this in the same delayed time. It did not matter, because the horror, hurt, and sorrow was there and would remain in any speed or reality. Octavia felt a rip in her stomach and the slow rush of blood. Time was so slow, things were so silent, that she could almost hear her own inner workings in distress. There would be no recovery from this. This wound was caused by the Scythe of Cronus. Even though she was immortal, death loomed.

Time returned to normal as the blade exited Octavia's body.

Kassidy's attempt to quickly remove it to minimize any deadly damage, no doubt. It was too late, though. They likely both knew. Octavia certainly did.

"Oh no. No, no, no, no, nooooooooo!" screamed Kassidy.

Octavia fell to her knees first, pulling Kassidy down with her. The Scythe fell to the ground, and Kassidy gathered her aunt into her arms.

"No. No. No. I'm so sorry. Please, no. Please . . . don't go. I'm so sorry."

Octavia found herself cradled in her niece's arms and immediately flashed back to the day Kassidy was born. The newborn had not cried. There had been this almost preternatural awareness that both Octavia and Allesandra sensed the moment Kassidy had arrived. Octavia remembered holding Kassidy and feeling this overwhelming sense of love, acceptance, and wonder. As a baby, Kassidy had reached out to caress Octavia's face, and it was not until now that she wondered if it was the newborn's way of forgiving her, of absolving her for the guilt she felt because it was her actions that set everything involving Thanatos in motion.

Now, it was her turn.

Octavia reached out to caress Kassidy's face. She wiped away tears, and had hoped to wipe away guilt and responsibility.

"It's okay, my dear. It truly is," said Octavia, her breath short. "My time has come."

"No. No. No, it hasn't. I just found you. I can . . . I can . . . I can bring you back. I can use the Scythe to bring you back. I can do that. I'm the Death God now. It's in my power to . . ."

"No. You mustn't. You have to let me go."

"No, no, no, no, no. Not now. Not like this. Please . . ."

"I set all this in motion with my jealousy. This is my

penance . . . and I'm okay with that. I've lived a long life. I've paid for my mistakes"—Octavia shuddered and coughed—"and most of all, I kept my promise to my sister." A line of blood trickled from the corner of her mouth. "You have become a beautiful, talented, and gifted woman . . . worthy of being a god."

In the space of a blink, Octavia saw a younger version of Kassidy.

"I need you to go and fight," said Octavia. "You are the key, my sweet, sweet girl. Save him. Save them all."

Octavia's mind drifted briefly to Jaxon as Ares. Tall, majestic, fierce, cunning, and loving. Her anger toward him had long since dissipated. She felt happy that he would be here to help Kassidy, and she felt confident that her niece could save him from himself.

"I love you," said Octavia.

"I . . . I . . . I love you, too."

CHAPTER FIFTY-FOUR

KASSIDY LOOKED UP AT JAXON ENGAGED IN BATTLE WITH SOLOMON. Jaxon was wild with rage and unarmed, the Glade resting on the ground, a distance away from the fight. Every move was sloppy and filled with hate. His memories had returned, his skills further augmented, but he was in no place to battle someone as cunning as Steele.

Kassidy withdrew into herself, paralyzed with uncertainty. Octavia was dead. So was Anna. The world was practically ablaze with hate and war. The prophecy was coming. Somehow, some way, no matter how hard she fought against it, she knew she'd be responsible for bringing about the apocalypse.

"It doesn't have to be like this," said a voice from behind.

Kassidy turned and saw her doppelgänger stepping forward.

"How . . . how are you here? What are you?" Kassidy asked.

"I'm just like you. I am you."

"No. No you're not. You're nothing like me."

The doppelgänger dropped her hand and let it transform into a sickle. After quickly reforming her hand, she extended her arm and called the Scythe of Cronus to her. She stalked toward Kassidy with the weapon, her eyes shining bright, and gently set it down as she knelt.

"So, what? I have a twin?" asked Kassidy.

"No. I'm not a twin. I am a part of you. A part of you left behind in the Nexus."

"How?"

"I've been there since you left all those years ago. After your first battle with Azra-El. The trauma, the heartache, the pain of everything you experienced caused a split. You wanted to walk away from that world, away from the Reaper life, and when you did, you left me behind."

"I . . . I don't remember that," said Kassidy.

"Of course. It wasn't conscious. It was instinct, a spiritual instinct from a powerful demi-god."

Kassidy sat with this revelation. Could it be possible? Could this be the reason she'd never felt whole? Was this why she felt most complete in the Nexus?

"What am I supposed to do?" asked Kassidy.

"You're supposed to do the best you can. There are no guarantees save one."

"What's that?"

"If you don't fight, we're all dead."

Kassidy absorbed the weight of that. She looked down at Octavia again. Her life aura was red. Someone should be escorting her soul. She wanted to run to the Nexus to do it herself, but she knew she couldn't. She had responsibilities here, in this world.

Kassidy and her doppelgänger stood. Extending her arm, Kassidy called to the Scythe of Cronus, and it appeared in her hand. She looked at her doppelgänger, then looked beyond her. She saw one Reaper, then two, then three. Within minutes, there were a dozen. She turned and saw there were more. All around her now.

All at once, they took a knee, and lowered their heads in deference.

"We are here. We are with you," said the doppelgänger.

Kassidy took a deep breath, closed her eyes, and stretched out with her senses. There was so much happening in the immediate area, and so much beyond. Kassidy allowed it all to fill her, and she controlled it. It did not consume her. Instead, all the emotions, for the first time ever, lived with her. She opened her eyes again. They shone bright. She looked to her doppelgänger again and watched as she stepped forward, phased, and integrated with her.

Kassidy was whole.

Kassidy was accepted by her Reapers.

No longer an imposter.

She was Death, and there was a reckoning ahead.

◆ ◆ ◆

Jaxon took a punch from Solomon that sent him to the ground. He didn't understand how this being was standing toe to toe with him. The Wraith was beneath him, an abomination. A demonic construct of a disgruntled supernatural with plans for domination. Jaxon could not fathom how this battle was not over.

"Seems you've lost your will, Mr. Burke," said Solomon. "Yield now, and I'll make your death quick."

Jaxon felt conflicting emotions. He'd longed for death for so long. Even though he had Anna, he'd longed for it. Now that she was gone, there truly was no reason to go on. He'd lost her, found and lost Octavia, all in the same night. He was fighting to release rage and to die, not to win. Jaxon let the realization wash over him. He got to his knees and stared at Solomon.

"Do you worst, Wraith," said Jaxon.

"As you wi—"

Solomon's words were cut off by the appearance of a sword in his abdomen. Not just any sword. The Glade, sword of Ares . . . his sword. Tracking its trajectory, Jaxon followed its path to Kassidy's outstretched hand.

"If you want to die, that's fine. I'll be happy to do it myself. But not until you help me take this son of bitch down," said Kassidy.

Jaxon grabbed the pommel of his sword and retracted it. He rose from his knees, spun, and brought his blade around for another blow. Solomon blocked it with his sickles, but he was in pain. Jaxon escalated his attack. His sword was a blur, his ferocity unmatched. Solomon, unable to maintain the pace, fell to his knees. Jaxon prepared his strike. As the Glade came down, Solomon raised his arms to block the blow with both sickles crossed.

"Now!" yelled Jaxon.

Kassidy shimmered into view behind Solomon and plunged her hand into his back. It phased through harmlessly, and when she retracted it, Jaxon saw a glowing orb in her hand. She placed the orb in her mouth, swallowed, then nodded to Jaxon.

Jaxon spun and drove his sword backward, impaling the former Wraith in the chest, piercing his cold dark heart. He did not turn to watch Steele turn to ash, but he heard the soft whispers of ash floating on the wind. Satisfied, he walked forward, toward Anna, and knelt by her side.

He felt Kassidy's hand on his shoulder.

"So much death. I've caused so much death," Jaxon said.

"It's not your burden to bear," said Kassidy.

"Isn't it? It's why I was so hated by the Twelve, by my own father. It's why Thanatos sought me out. It's why Octavia is . . ."

Jaxon couldn't finish. He wanted to cry, but he was too

numb. He wanted everything to feel better. But he did not have that in him. His power was rooted in death and destruction. He was war. No more, no less.

"There is more coming," said Kassidy. "The world needs balance. The world needs you, Ares. All you can do is your best, right?"

Jaxon looked up at Kassidy. He noticed a difference in her. There was confidence, a regal air about her. Certainly more than there'd ever been with her father. It was strange, and at the same time, inspiring.

"I don't know if I can," said Jaxon.

"Maybe not now. But soon, you'll be able to. You'll feel the pull, and you'll rise."

Jaxon looked down on Anna again. He stroked her hair and whispered a silent prayer.

"Can you bring her back?" Jaxon asked.

"No. I can't bend the natural order. You know that. That's not how things work."

"Gods also aren't supposed to be stripped of their identity and thrust into the future with nothing but instinct and will," said Jaxon through gritted teeth.

He looked back at Kassidy who seemed unphased by his declaration.

"Please," he said. "Death owes me a debt."

Jaxon stared deeply into Kassidy's eyes and watched as they changed to a bright metallic blue. There was an ethereal glow emanating around the Scythe of Cronus. Jaxon heard a low rumble and felt electricity in the air around him.

Then the world went black.

EPILOGUE

ONE

"I thought you didn't do funerals?"

"I don't. But since I've caused enough of them, seems only right that I finally see what one is like," said Jaxon.

"This wasn't your fault," said Kassidy.

"Wasn't it? I made the deal with your father. I dragged her into my mess—"

"She fell in love with you. You didn't drag her. She went willingly."

"And if she hadn't, if I'd avoided her . . . I used her to get what I wanted," said Jaxon.

"And yet she loved you anyway. In the end, you tried to make it right," said Kassidy.

"Too little, too late."

Kassidy said nothing. Now that he was fully returned as Ares, she couldn't feel his emotions anymore. But she didn't need to feel them to know what he was experiencing. His guilt was palpable. In some ways, she was glad. He should feel that. Had he not set out to use Octavia in his bargain with Thanatos, Octavia would not have been cursed with immortality, and perhaps Kassidy's mother would not have needed to flee to the Nexus. Through all of this, though, Kassidy had learned a great deal about fate and decisions, and simply playing the cards you're dealt.

"Being a god may imply omnipotence, but it does not entitle you to being less human."

Kassidy turned to face Jaxon, his raised eyebrow a sign that she'd caught his attention.

"You and the other gods taunted my father for reacting like a human when my mother ran away from him. Your father throws a temper tantrum when he's pissed, and the world shakes. Your mother gets mad, and she tries to kill babies—"

"That's a bit exaggerated . . ."

"Nevertheless, whether the legends are real or imagined, being a god does not absolve you from feeling, reacting, and making shitty decisions. Especially when love is involved. It makes you—"

"Us?"

Kassidy sighed.

"Fine. It makes *us* as human as the rest of the world. You fucked up, you tried to fix it, you did your best, and in the end, you got played. What's important now is how you choose to deal with it. You gonna continue to beg me to take your head and end your existence? Or are you gonna man up, deal with your shit, and persevere?"

It didn't matter much to Kassidy that she was talking to a War God. He was a bruised and battered warrior with an insatiable bloodlust who'd likely enjoy a good fight and would take any excuse to start one. This conversation could be such a catalyst, and probably would have been . . . at one time. She hadn't known him before. She didn't really know him now. But Kassidy got the sense that he was exhausted from allowing his nature to dictate his actions.

"You have your mother in you," said Jaxon.

"So, I've heard."

"Perhaps dying is not the way to go. Maybe . . . there's work for me to do here."

"Atonement?"

"Balance."

Kassidy considered the implications of that, particularly coming from the War God. But looking into his eyes, she saw that his idea of balance might not be that bloody and destructive.

"We still have this prophecy to sort out," said Kassidy.

"We? Oh no, Lady Death. That's all you," said Jaxon.

"You're literally the War Horseman."

"Then sort it out so I don't have to be."

"And if I can't? Can I count on you to help?"

The silence was a symphony of uncertainty.

"I'd be in your—"

"Don't you fucking dare," said Jaxon.

The two gods looked at each other and grinned.

"Thank you for everything, Kassidy Simmons. If you need me, I'll be back. For now, I need to figure some things out," said Jaxon.

He gave a slight nod, took one last look at Octavia's casket, then turned and walked away.

"How will I find you?" asked Kassidy.

"I'm a War God. Start some shit, I'll come running."

TWO

Looking at Anna through the window as she read reminded him of the first time they'd met. Jaxon had followed a target to a bookstore and saw her at the checkout counter. Apparently, she'd come in looking for a rare leatherbound copy of *Great Expectations* for her father. She wanted something that "looked weathered and worn yet strong enough to still provide joy and comfort, like my dad." It sounded odd, but there was a love in that request that Jaxon had not heard in centuries.

He knew he needed to leave. He didn't want to, but it was necessary. To figure things out? Maybe. To keep her safe? Definitely.

He knew she'd be home. Her sister was getting married and was coming over to go over wedding plans. Jaxon told her he'd be back. But he hadn't kept that promise. And he wasn't going to. Deep down, he hoped she would be too preoccupied with her sister to think about it too much.

He peered through the window of her townhome and watched as Anna sat in her brown, oversized loveseat with her legs curled underneath her. Her long, dark hair fell around her shoulders providing a start contrast to the white V-neck t-shirt she wore. She wore no makeup, but then, she rarely ever did. Her olive skin was flawless. Even the beauty mark on her cheek was perfectly placed. As he looked at her now, the emptiness in his stomach vanished. His thoughts slowed, and he was able to focus on the here and now.

Even though the here and now meant that he needed to walk away from her—maybe forever.

Jaxon put his hand to the glass as Anna brushed hers through her hair. It made his heart skip when she did that. It was her tell. She only did that when something made her nervous or anxious. Despite that feeling, it was almost always followed by a smile. Like the one she had on her face now, telling herself to relax, to calm down—a silent reminder that everything was going to be okay. Anna brought light to the darkness inside. She gave him hope and kept the boogeymen away. He knew that he loved her like no other, even Octavia.

With one final look, Jaxon said goodbye. He turned to leave her only to be met with the sting of a dart. He fell to his knees as he simultaneously reached for his neck. Jaxon pulled the dart from his skin and examined it, but to no avail. His vision was already blurred, and his body was weakened.

He saw a dark figure walking toward him as he slumped over to all fours in a desperate attempt to stay upright. He felt as if he were floating in a pool. His body felt heavy, yet somehow supported by something other than his own muscles.

"Time to try something else, Jaxon," said the voice above him.

He couldn't respond.

Jaxon Burke fell to the ground and, once again, darkness overtook him.

THREE

"The girl is remarkably resourceful, isn't she?"

"She's got spirit," said Jacen.

"And she's learning. Becoming more comfortable with herself and her abilities."

"Also true."

"That's good. That's real good."

Jacen let those words linger in his mind for a while. Was it good? In the end, did the world need that? There were bad things on the horizon, and making a pit stop to watch Kassidy's ascension and the possible fulfillment of an ancient prophecy was a small pothole compared to the minefield ahead. He'd come this far, against better judgment, and possibly even better advice. If it came down to it, he could stop this.

At least he thought he could.

"Are you sure we need to continue with this?" he asked.

"Oh, my dear boy, yes. Yes, we do," said the Diva. "The Four are the key to everything."

"And if they're not?"

Jacen suddenly found himself flying through the air and pressed against the window, an invisible vice around his throat. The Diva glared at him, arm outstretched, fist tightening.

"You're not losing faith, are you, Jacen?"

He gasped, desperate to find air, clawing at the nothingness restricting his airway.

"After everything we've been through, I'd hate to think I was losing my favorite ally," said the Diva.

Jacen managed to shake his head.

"Good. Because what we're doing is important. And . . . well, I can't do it without you. But I will if I have to," she said, tightening her fist further.

Jacen felt his mind wander. Spots formed behind his eyes. As he felt his arms fall, so too did the rest of his body. He struggled for air in between a bout of coughing as he propped himself up on his hands and knees. Even those with great power succumb to those with greater power.

"I . . . I . . . I'm with you," he managed to get out.

Jacen looked up to find the Diva squatting before him. Her eyes aglow in metallic blue. She was magnificent in so many ways, but her mind teetered on the brink of madness. It was that madness, the possibility of her going completely over the edge that kept him around. It was why he assisted Kassidy and her companions from the shadows.

"I knew you would be. Sometimes, you just need a little

reminder. I get that. When you've been around as long as we have, we can forget the little things, right?"

"Right," said Jacen.

The Diva kissed him on the forehead, rose, and walked away.

"Where are you going?"

"I'm off to Atlanta. The CDC to be exact. I need to see how things are progressing."

As the Diva shimmered out of view, Jacen allowed himself to collapse onto the floor. Rolling onto his back, he stared up, still recovering.

"Oh no. Kassidy, I'm so sorry," he said.

FOUR

"Your time is running out."

"I know, Mom. I know," said Traci.

"I told you. I warned you. But you wouldn't listen to me. You just had to find her, you had to know her, and for what?"

"She saved me, Mom. She . . . she . . ."

Traci couldn't finish. She'd tried to explain it to her mother so many times, but no matter how she pieced the words together, there was no acceptance. As far as her mother was concerned, Traci had sold her soul for the chance to be with someone she was never meant to know beyond one fateful encounter. Traci had derailed her own destiny . . . for love.

"I know what you're going to say. I've heard it before. Yes, she saved your life. Yes, she made you see the importance of accepting your own gifts. But you went too far."

"And so you want to spend my last days throwing that in my face?" asked Traci.

Her question was valid, and it caused her mother to pause. She wasn't angry, and Traci new that. Well, she was, but not at the situation—more so, at the helplessness of the situation. Traci had embarked on a path that she'd never be able to return from, and her mother felt helpless, as any mother would. Traci moved closer to her, held her arms out, and breathed an internal sigh of relief as her mother embraced her.

"I just . . . I . . . I don't want to lose you."

"I know, Mom. And believe me, I don't want to leave. But I did this, and I have to live up to my end of the bargain."

They separated, and Traci closed her eyes as her mother reached out to tuck her hair behind her ear. She'd done that her whole life, and it took Traci back to her childhood. She loved her mother dearly. It had been only the two of them for so long. And now . . . now her mother would be alone.

"Are you going to tell her?"

"I don't know, Mom. I don't know what she'd do if she knew. She just lost someone, and she took that hard. She blames herself."

"But this isn't her fault."

"Really, Mom?"

Traci inclined her head. Her mother probably hadn't meant it as a jab, but being extra sensitive, it was easy to take it that way.

"I didn't mean anything by that. Just . . . she shouldn't take it hard because there's nothing that can be done."

"But she would take it hard, and she'd probably find a way to take it personally. She'd think she was cursed or something because of all the people dying around her."

"Oh my," began Mary. "How many people have died?"

"Let's say it's been a rough couple of months for her."

"Then, all the more reason for you to tell her. She needs to be prepared. She needs to accept this."

"I've got thirty days, Mom. I don't want to waste them on her worrying about me. There's so much more happening in the world and in her life. I'm going to enjoy the time I have left and let the chips fall where they may."

"Oh . . . baby . . ."

"It's going to be okay. It was worth it. She was worth it. And these next thirty days will be amazing."

Traci fell into her mother's embrace again. She may not have believed the words she spoke, but she certainly believed the love she felt in her mother's hug. And for now . . . that was enough.

ACKNOWLEDGEMENTS

The journey to published author began long ago for me with great uncertainty coupled with great ignorance. I knew little about the art of writing and, by extension, had virtually no understanding of the business of publishing. Throughout my journey there were a few authors who were instrumental in providing lessons that helped me stay motivated.

First up, Tessa Dawn, author of the Blood Curse Series. She is a generous author who gives back and thoroughly engages with her readers. That, in and of itself, was an important lesson to learn. She was also kind enough to give me feedback on a short story sample early on in my writing career. The fact that a successful and incredibly busy author took the time to read the words of a novice and offer tips, blew me away. Tessa, I appreciate you for your great stories, and ultimately, for all you did to encourage me to keep writing. Thank you!

Next, Jonathan Maberry. Thanks to a discounted "First in Series" promo on Audible, I was introduced to your work and, of course, the voice that is Ray Porter. You are the reason why many writers I know in the San Diego area continue to write. You inspire, and most importantly, you teach. The knowledge you've shared about the business of publishing has been invaluable, as has everything you've shared about the craft of writing. I, like so many others I know, get better with each attempt thanks to you. Cheers, brother.

Shout out to Keith Strunk, Jon McGoran, Gregory Frost, and Merry Jones, hosts of the Liars Club Oddcast for having me as a guest. Thank you for making my first podcast so memorable. Many thanks to Michael Steven Gregory and the staff of the Southern California Writer's Conference for inviting me to share my journey as one of your keynote speakers this past spring. Thank you to Kathleen Hanke, Melanie Thurber, and the organizers and supporters of the Fox Cities Book Festival. I cannot tell you how much I appreciated the opportunity to be a part of that event. Thank you, Dr. Janina Scarlett for inviting me to be a part of your Comic-Con 2021 Virtual Panel. As a lover of Comic-Con, that was a true bucket list item for me. I hope to have the opportunity to join in on another with you.

I absolutely have to thank my Acorn family. I don't have the words to express my gratitude to Holly Kammier and Jessica Therrien for continuing to take a chance on me and Kassidy. Your support and encouragement mean the world to me. To my fellow Acorn authors, you continue to inspire me with your hard work and dedication to the written word. It's an honor to be counted among you and I wish nothing but continued success for us all.

For those of you thinking of writing, I am a proponent of building a support network. If you've ever said, "I have a story in me and I need to get it out", I cannot stress enough the importance of reaching out to writers and building a community that can lift you up when you're not feeling so "wordsy". My network has grown tremendously over the last two years. I'd likely need a few pages to name them all, and like every Oscar acceptance speech, I'd forget to add a name or get played off the stage. Instead, I'll simply give thanks and love, because I can honestly say that your success has been inspiring, and it challenges me each day to consider paths that I may not have normally tried.

Let's face it, this acknowledgement page would not be happening if not for you, my readers. You read, connected with, and loved Kassidy Simmons, and you dared to come back for more. The support for *Death's Legacy* and the encouragement to complete this book was tremendous, and so needed. I hope you've enjoyed *Death's Debt* enough to want to stay tuned for the next adventure.

Because there's definitely more to come.

ABOUT THE AUTHOR

Dennis K. Crosby grew up in Oak Park, IL and completed his undergraduate work at the University of Illinois in Chicago. With a degree in Criminal Justice, he spent six years working as a Private Investigator and during that time developed an affinity for writing poetry. While working on a master's degree in Forensic Psychology, Dennis *transitioned* to social service where he worked with men and women experiencing challenges with mental health and addiction. He currently serves as Director of Apprenticeship Programs for a non-profit agency that provides culinary arts training to adults seeking new opportunities.

With a lifelong passion for writing, Dennis wrote dozens of short stories, tapping into his creative side, but did not pursue the finer points of the craft until later in life. After leaving Chicago and moving to San Diego, Dennis had the opportunity to get more involved in the writing community where he strengthened his skills. To further augment his writing skills, Dennis completed an MFA program at National University.

Death's Debt is the follow up to his bestselling and award winning debut novel, *Death's Legacy*. Dennis still lives and writes in San Diego, CA.

Made in the USA
Middletown, DE
19 June 2022

67299953R00177